KU-038-069

# CONTENTS

# FOREWORD

## ALEXANDER McCALL SMITH

ONE of the questions I am asked most frequently at literary events is this: why have you chosen to write about women? This question, I suspect, is a familiar one for male authors who choose to have female protagonists in their books, and no doubt the answers they give are varied. My own answer focuses on the nature of the conversation that my female detectives have. If that small office in Gaborone were to be home to two male detectives rather than two female sleuths, I imagine that the conversation would be much less interesting. This is not to say that men – and male detectives – do not talk about things that matter; it is just that they would be less likely to make the same observations that Mma Ramotswe and Mma Makutsi make. Their conversation, in effect, would be less personal, less subjective – and less emotionally engaging. Of course any generalizations about the behaviour of men and women will give rise to accusations of gender stereotyping, but why deny that, for one reason or another, there are differences in the perspective that men and women have on the world? Certainly it would be an unobservant detective who failed to notice these.

Why do we so enjoy reading about female detectives? Part of the enjoyment, I suspect, lies in the satisfaction that we derive from seeing women, who have suffered so much from male arrogance and condescension, either outwitting men or demonstrating that they are just as capable as men of doing something that may have been seen as a male preserve. We live today in a society in which gender equality has been, to a very large extent, realised. At the time at which *The Female Detective* was written, of course, things were very different. The relegation of women to a subservient position within society – a position in which they were outsiders to the world of work and affairs that was dominated by men – meant that it was a novel thing for women to be involved in the investigation of crime. Today one might expect that novelty to have faded, as women do all the jobs previously monopolised by men. Yet the idea of the female detective as being special or unusual still persists in literary and cinematic treatments of criminal investigation. Why do we still think that female detectives are in some way special and make, for that reason, good reading?

The explanation probably has to do with gender stereotypes. At the time of *The Female Detective*, these stereotypes would have had the force of established truth. Middle-class women did not engage in what were seen as 'unladylike activities'. They were protected from the harsh realities of life; they were thought to be in regular need of smelling salts; they were assumed to have no interest in sex; there were many jobs that a woman simply could not be expected to do because they were viewed as unsuitable for finer female sensibilities. The idea of a woman being involved in the murkiness of criminal detection must have seemed a radical and adventurous one in Victorian times: women simply did not do that sort of thing. That, of course, has changed. Women are expected now to do everything that men do, including taking on the role of submariners, infantry soldiers, and, of course, forensic pathologists. Yet even as they are cast in these roles, there may be a residual feeling, shared, perhaps, by women as much as by men, that there is something in certain functions – including fighting crime – that is at odds with the more gentle nature of women. Nonsense say the proponents of equality: men and women are the same when it comes to the vices and the virtues. That may well be true, but it is also true that there is a residual belief that women are inherently more endowed than men are with qualities of sympathy and care. A concomitant of this, then, would be that the woman sleuth is somehow slumming when she ventures into a criminal world that is dominated by crude, unsympathetic and cruel men.

Of course there are those who argue that such a view of woman's nature is old-fashioned and sexist. That may be so in certain expressions of it, but then feminist philosophers themselves have been at pains to stress what they call the 'ethics of care', suggesting that woman do have a greater ability to show care in their dealings with others than do men.

There are other factors, though, that I suspect lie behind the popularity of the female detective. One is that the woman sleuth is often portrayed as the outsider in the male world of policing and criminal investigation. This operates in two ways: one where the woman is a member of a police force, and one where she is the freelance who operates either at the request of the official investigators or as a well-meaning bystander. In the case of the female detective who is part of a police team, the outsider status results from the fact that women police detectives frequently operate in a male-dominated force. They are frequently portrayed as having to deal with sceptical and sexist superiors who are only too eager to detect weakness and when we see them defeat these overbearing men we feel the satisfaction that usually accompanies the victory of the underdog.

Another source of pleasure is the way in which the female detective uses the apparent marginality of her position to good effect. Once again we are in the territory of stereotype. Men are to be distrusted but women are assumed not to be interested in whatever it is that is being concealed. Then we suddenly realise that it is the woman who has seen and understood what is happening without ever being suspected of being a threat to anybody. Of course the world is not like that. If one is in the position of having to distrust others, then one would be well advised to distrust everybody regardless of gender.

This book has a claim to be the beginning of a rich and continuing tradition in crime literature of the female detective. That tradition shows no signs of abating, even if the factors that distinguish the respective roles of men and women in society are becoming increasingly irrelevant. Society may be becoming more androgynous, but the niche occupied by the female detective will continue to be a rich source of literary pleasure. The world of the narrator in *The Female Detective* is far removed from our own, but just as we recognise hers then she would probably recognise ours. Human nature and the struggle between good and bad – that essential kernel of the detective novel, as Auden famously declared – has not changed much in the years that separate us from Victorian England. Crime and deception still flourish, but so too do the curiosity and intuition that we see so charmingly portrayed in these pages. Ultimately there may be a woman to set things right, which prompts the Freudian conclusion that the female detective, when all is said and done, is mother.

# INTRODUCTION

## MIKE ASHLEY

THE detective you will meet in the following stories is usually regarded as the first female professional detective to appear in fiction. She is a mysterious and somewhat shadowy figure. We learn little about her – even her name is not revealed. At times she calls herself Mrs Gladden, though admits that this is 'the name I assume most frequently in my business'. Even the police don't seem to know her real name, referring to her simply as 'G'. She often works undercover and only introduces herself as a detective when the need arises and her investigations come to a close.

All this obfuscation makes sense when you realise that when *The Female Detective* was first published in May 1864 there were no women detectives in Britain – in fact there were no women police officers either, and would not be, officially, for another fifty years. Indeed, the Metropolitan Police Force, the first organised police agency in Britain, had only been established since 1829, and its plain-clothes detective branch, the first Scotland Yard, was not created until 1842. The word 'detective' did not pass into common usage until 1843.

In the United States the Scottish-born Alan Pinkerton, whose renowned private-detective agency had been established in 1850, employed Kate Warne as a detective from 1856. She was aged only twenty-three at the time and was the first professional woman detective in America. It was not until 1908 that America employed its first official policewoman, Lola Baldwin, who assumed her duties in Portland, Oregon in April of that year.

In Britain, the Women Police Volunteers was formed in 1914 chiefly to patrol the streets and parks to keep an eye on the activities of young women. Eventually, in 1918, the London Metropolitan Police established its own Women's Police Patrols.

All this shows that *The Female Detective* was years ahead of its time. Little wonder that 'Miss Gladden' operated undercover and regarded herself as one of the 'secret' police. And the nation seemed more than prepared to accept the idea. Only months after *The Female Detective* appeared, *Revelations of a Lady Detective* was published anonymously but usually attributed to William Stephens Hayward. Both volumes were an attempt to chart new territory in the 'police procedural' novel or 'casebook' which had become popular following the publication of *The Recollections of a Policeman* by the pseudonymous 'Waters' in 1852.

Both these books, though, are something of a false dawn. Further stories or novels featuring women detectives did not appear for some years and did not start to become popular until the turn of the century. In Britain, Catherine L. Pirkis introduced her resourceful amateur detective in *The Experiences of Loveday Brooke, Lady Detective* in 1894. Baroness Orczy, best known as the creator of the Scarlet Pimpernel, created her police detective, Molly Robertson-Kirk, in *Lady Molly of Scotland Yard* (1910). Often credited as featuring the first professional female detectives, these books appeared over thirty years after *The Female Detective*, serving to emphasise the book's significance.

Women had appeared as amateur detectives, not always willing ones, in many stories and novels prior to 1864, notably in 'Das Fräulein von Scuderi' by E. T. A. Hoffmann, published in 1819, where the eponymous fräulein helps establish the innocence of a man accused of murder. In *The Adventures of Susan Hopley* (1841) by Catherine Crowe, Hopley finds herself in the role of an amateur detective in trying to right many wrongs which her family have suffered. Wilkie Collins's heroine in the short story 'The Diary of Anne Rodway' (1856) shows exceptional detective skills in her pursuit of a murderer.

These works, though, involved women who, by circumstance, were forced to investigate matters. The idea of a woman actually being paid as a detective was something else entirely. Despite her secrecy, it becomes evident in *The Female Detective* that the mysterious 'G' is not employed directly by the police force. Rather she is a form of enquiry agent who works independently but on behalf of the police. The police officers certainly know her, but not all would necessarily be aware of the cases in which she is involved, some of which, such as 'Tenant for Life' which opens the collection and is illustrated on the cover, are ones that she herself initiates. She therefore acts independently but also in collusion with the police. It is also evident that by the time these stories are told she has retired as a detective and is now able to reveal all.

By all accounts the police did employ such female agents, their identities usually hidden, but their work occasionally reported when cases came to court. The benefits of their role were not overlooked. Reflecting upon her own work, 'G' acknowledges that women can get into places that men cannot, as they are not seen as a threat, and also that other women will frequently talk openly to them when they would not speak to men. Such opportunities come to the fore in the following stories which may well be based on true events, for all that the activities of female agents were usually unreported and unpublicized.

If so, how did the author create such cases, and who was the author? When the book was first published it was credited to Andrew Forrester, Jr. Forrester's name had appeared on two earlier collections, both of the police casebook variety: *The Revelations of a Private Detective*, published in July 1863, and *Secret Service, or Recollections of a City Detective*, which followed in January 1864. A later volume was *The Private Detective* (1868). Written in the first person, these stories purported to be true, though the first volume had barely been on the shelves a fortnight when two retired London police officers, the brothers John and Daniel Forrester, wrote to *The Times* disclaiming that any of the accounts related to their own work and that 'no such person as Andrew Forrester' was known to them.

The Forrester brothers, former Bow Street Runners, were well known in their day. The editor Edmund Yates recalled how alike they looked, as he often saw them standing outside the Mansion House in the City of London. George Augustus Sala passed their offices in Whitechapel, noting that they were already at work early in the day. They were regarded as 'bounty hunters' by some and enquiry agents by others. Their activities became especially well known in 1858 due to their involvement in the high-profile case of the Royal British Bank where the bank's directors were charged with conspiring to defraud their shareholders and customers. The

Forresters were the leading City detectives for forty years. Even if the stories by 'Andrew Forrester' were not drawn directly from their cases, theirs was a notable name to adopt.

The true identity of Andrew Forrester remained something of a mystery, though it should not have done. *The Female Detective* contains a story 'A Child Found Dead: Murder or No Murder' which had first appeared as a separate pamphlet in 1862 under the title *The Road Murder* by J. Ware. Apart from the two versions of the story having a slightly different form of opening words, they are basically the same. It was a reworking of the notorious murder of the infant Francis Saville Kent at Road House in Wiltshire in 1860, a case that Forrester specifically refers to in a footnote at the start of 'A Child Found Dead'.

The Road Murder became one of the most infamous murders of the decade and has more recently been resurrected for a new generation of readers by Kate Summerscale in *The Suspicions of Mr. Whicher* (2008). In her endnotes to this thoroughly researched book, Summerscale draws attention to the connection between Ware and Forrester, a link that had otherwise been overlooked or forgotten for over 140 years.

J. Ware was James Redding Ware (1832–1909), a writer and editor who turned his hand to all kinds of subjects, producing books on such diverse matters as the Isle of Wight, card and board games, dreams, famous centenarians and English slang. It is unlikely that he earned much money from his writings because in 1877 he reported (in *The Times*) that his lodgings in Lincoln's Inn Fields in London were in a dilapidated state of repair but that he lived there because it was cheap. He even had to suffer another resident playing a chamber organ in the rooms below and went so far as to bring an injunction against the organist to stop the nuisance, though his action failed.

The fact that 'A Child Found Dead' had first appeared in 1862 might suggest that the character of the 'Female Detective' had been created two years before the appearance of the book, but in fact she does not appear in the 1862 version. In the 1864 version 'G' is simply recounting a case that she says had been given to her in manuscript form and thus the investigation is not her own. The same applies to 'The Mystery', the final story in the collection. This is also presented as a story told by another, and had first appeared without an introduction by 'G' in the issue of the weekly magazine *Grave and Gay* for 14 June 1862 under the title 'The Mystery of Harley Street'. This tells us that Ware did not create the character 'G' until he came to write *The Female Detective* in 1864.

*Grave and Gay* may well have been edited by Ware. It ran much of his material under both his own name and as Forrester, as well as anonymously (at least one example later appeared in a collection of stories credited to Ware). This included an historical novel set in medieval France, *Rolande: A Tale of the Great Massacre* which does not appear to have been collected in book-form. Another story, 'What Happened at a Morning Concert' in the issue for 26 July 1862, later appeared in *The Private Detective* as 'The Troubles and the Escape of a "Perfect Young Lady"'. Perhaps most remarkable of all, and worth a brief aside, is that *Grave and Gay* began, in its short life, the first English serialization of Victor Hugo's *Les Misérables*, which was not available in a book edition in England for another three months. The English translation was undertaken by Lascelles Wraxelles, but the abbreviated serialization in *Grave and Gay* is uncredited and one cannot help but wonder if it was abridged by Ware himself.

In *The Female Detective*, especially in the longer stories 'Tenant for Life', 'The Unraveled Mystery' and 'The Unknown Weapon', Ware developed a strong, three-dimensional character, with ingenious skills of deduction and logic. 'G' is not a woman who undertakes her investigations lightly or simply for the thrill of adventure. She has a conscience that, though it does not interfere with her following her investigations to their natural conclusion, does often present her with a dilemma and a feeling that seeking a legal right is not necessarily the same as finding true justice.

Although these cases are written by a man, they depict a woman's outlook, and one of determination and conviction. It is quite probable that, inspired by his investigations into the Road Murder, James Ware became fascinated by other police cases which resulted not only in his Forrester books but also a later collection, *Before the Bench: Sketches of Police Court Life* (1880), and in the process he might have encountered some cases involving women enquiry agents. Whether inspired by real events or entirely fictional it is clear that the mysterious 'G' is first and foremost the pioneering female detective.

# THE FEMALE DETECTIVE.

## INTRODUCTION.

WHO am I?

It can matter little who I am.

It may be that I took to the trade, sufficiently comprehended in the title of this work without a word of it being read, because I had no other means of making a living; or it may be that for the work of detection I had a longing which I could not overcome.

It may be that I am a widow working for my children—or I may be an unmarried woman, whose only care is herself.

But whether I work willingly or unwillingly, for myself or for others—whether I am married or single, old or young, I would have my readers at once accept my declaration that whatever may be the results of the practice of my profession in others, in me that profession has not led me towards hardheartedness.

For what reason do I write this book?

I have a chief reason, and as I can have no desire to hide it from the reader, for if I were secretively inclined I should not be compiling these memoirs, I may as well at once say I write in order to show, in a small way, that the profession to which I belong is so useful that it should not be despised.

I know well that my trade is despised. I have all along known this fact so well that I have hidden my trade from those about me. Whether these are relations or friends, or merely acquaintances, I have no need here to tell.

My friends suppose I am a dressmaker, who goes out by the day or week—my enemies, what I have, are in a great measure convinced that my life is a very questionable one.

In my heart of hearts I am at a loss to decide at which side I laugh most—at my friends, who suppose me so very innocent, or at my enemies, who believe me to be not far removed from guilty.

My trade is a necessary one, but the world holds aloof my order. Nor do I blame the world over much for its determination. I am quite aware that there is something peculiarly objectionable in the spy, but nevertheless it will be admitted that the spy is as peculiarly necessary as he or she is peculiarly objectionable.

The world would very soon discover the loss of the detective system, and yet if such a loss were to take place, if the certain bad results which would be sure to follow its abolition were made most evident, the world would still avoid the detective as a social companion, from the next moment he or she resumed office.

I have said I do not complain of this treatment, for

as I have remarked, I am quite aware that society looks upon the companionship of a spy as repulsive ; but, nevertheless, we detectives are necessary, as scavengers are called for, and I therefore write this book to help to show, by my experience, that the detective has some demand upon the gratitude of society.

I am aware that the female detective may be regarded with even more aversion than her brother in profession. But still it cannot be disproved that if there is a demand for men detectives there must also be one for female detective police spies. Criminals are both masculine and feminine—indeed, my experience tells me that when a woman becomes a criminal she is far worse than the average of her male companions, and therefore it follows that the necessary detectives should be of both sexes.

Let it suffice, once for all, that I know my trade is a despised one, but that being a necessary calling I am not ashamed of it. I know I have done good during my career, I have yet to learn that I have achieved much harm, and I therefore think that the balance of the work of my life is in my favour.

In putting the following narratives on paper, I shall take great care to avoid mentioning myself as much as possible. I determine upon this rule, not from any personal modesty, though I would remark in passing that your detective can be a modest man or woman, but simply to avoid the use of the great I, which, to my thinking, disfigures so many books. To gain this end, the avoidance of the use of this letter, I shall, as much as possible, tell the tales in what I believe is called the third person, and in what I will call the plainest fashion.

I may also point out, while engaged upon these opening lines, that in a very great many cases women detectives are those who can only be used to arrive at certain discoveries. The nature of these discoveries I need here only hint at, many of them being of too marked a character to admit of their being referred to in detail in a work of this character, and in a book published in the present age. But without going into particulars, the reader will comprehend that the woman detective has far greater opportunities than a man of intimate watching, and of keeping her eyes upon matters near, which a man could not conveniently play the eavesdropper.

I am aware that the idea of family spies must be an unpleasant subject for contemplation; that to reflect that a female detective may be in one's own family is a disagreeable operation. But, on the other hand, it may be urged that only the man who has secrets to hide need fear a watcher, the inference standing that he who fears may justifiably be watched.

Be all this as it may, it is certain that man and woman detectives are necessities of daily English life, that I am a female detective, and that I think fit to make some of my experiences known to the world.

What will their value be?

I cannot guess—I will not say—I do not care to learn. But I hope these narratives of mine will show that granted much crime passes undetected, much of the most obscure and well-planned evil-doing is brought to the light, and easily, by the operation of the detective. Furthermore, I hope it will be ascertained that there is much of good to be found, even amongst criminals, and that it does not follow because a man breaks the law that he is therefore heartless.

Now—to my work.

# TENANT FOR LIFE.

It often happens to us detectives—and when I say us detectives, of course, I mean both men and women operatives—that we are the first movers in matters of great ultimate importance to individuals in particular, and the public at large.*

For instance, a case in point only came under my notice a few weeks since.

A lady of somewhat solitary and reserved life, residing alone, but for a housekeeper, died suddenly. Strangely enough, her son arrived at the house two hours before the lady breathed her last. The house in which the death took place being far from a town, and it being necessary that the son should almost immediately return to London, the house was left for some time in the care, or it were more consistent to say under the control, of the housekeeper already mentioned—a woman who bore a far from spotless character in the neighbourhood of her late mistress's dwelling.

---

* It is perhaps as well here to remark that the MS. of this work has been revised by an ordinary literary editor. It does not appear as actually written by the compiler. This supervision may be injurious to the *vraisemblance* of the work, but by its exercise some clearness of style has been attained.

To curtail that portion of this instance of the but poorly comprehended efficacy of the detective police which does not immediately bear upon the argument under consideration, it may be said in a few words that in the time which elapsed between the departure and arrival of the son, the house was very effectively stripped.

The son, of course, was put almost immediately in possession of the suspicions of several neighbours as to the felony which they felt sure had been committed, and this gentleman was very quickly in a position to convince himself that a robbery had been effected.

The housekeeper was spoken to, told of her crime, which insolently she denied, and was at once dismissed, she foolishly threatening law proceedings, on the score of defamation of character.

The son of the deceased lady refused to take any action in the matter of the robbery, urging that he could not have his mother's name and death mixed up with police-court proceedings, and he allowed the affair, as he supposed, to blow over, though it should be here observed that he suffered very considerable inconvenience by the absence of certain papers which were associated with the death of his mother.

Four months pass, and now the police appear upon the scene, and with an efficiency which is an instance of the value of the detective force. The police had, of course, in the ordinary way of business, heard of the robbery referred to, but could not move in it while no prosecutor gave them the word to move. But if the police had not moved in the case, they had not forgotten it.

A robbery takes place in the neighbourhood, and a search-warrant is granted. A search is prosecuted, and in a shed beyond a small house, belonging to a couple whom the housekeeper already mentioned knew, and who had been up at the house while the housekeeper was left in sole charge of it, was found a japanned cash-box.

The detective who made this discovery almost immediately identified the box with the robbery at the house of the late lady, and upon finding, after a close examination, the initial of her surname scratched upon the lid, he became so convinced his conjecture was right, that, upon his own responsibility, he took the tenant of the house in question into custody.

The case went clear against the unhappy man. The police, by a wonderful series of fortunate guesses and industrious inquiries, found out the son, and this latter was enabled to produce a key, one of a household bunch belonging to his late mother, that opened the cash-box in question, which had been forced in such a manner that the cash-box had not been broken.

This gentleman, however, refused to prosecute, and the prisoner got off with the fright of his arrest and an examination.

Which of the two, the gentleman or the detective, did his duty to society, is a question I leave to be answered by my readers. My aim in quoting this instance of the operation of the detective system is to show how valuable it may become, even where should-be prosecutors make the mistake of supposing that leniency and patience form a much better course of conduct than one of justice and fair retribution.

The detective police frequently start cases and discover prosecutors in people who have had no idea of filling any such position.

Many cases of this character, several of them really important, have come under my own direction. Perhaps the most important is that which I am about to relate, and to which I have given the title of "Tenant for Life."

This case, as it frequently happens, came upon me when I was least expecting business, and when, indeed, I had "put the shutters up for the day," as an old detective companion of mine—a fellow long since dead (he was killed by a most gentlemanly banker who had left town for good, and who, after flooring John Hemmings, left England for good also)—would say.

It was on a Sunday when I got the first inkling of one of the most extraordinary cases which has come under my observation. It is on Sundays that I always put the shutters up. Even when I am engaged hot in a case, I am afraid I relax on a Sunday. I will not work if I can help it on a Sunday. I swim through the week, so to speak, for Sunday, and then I have twenty-four hours' rest before I plunge into my sea of detections once more.

I am what is called a talking companion, and I am bound to admit that women are in the habit of talking scandal, with me for a hearer, within three hours of my making their acquaintance.

Amongst others that I knew some years ago was a Mrs. Flemps. I think I first made her acquaintance because her name struck me as out of the common—it was out of the common, for I had not known her twenty-four hours before I learnt that she was married to a cabman, who on his father's side was a Dutchman who had been in the eel trade at Billingsgate market.

It was this acquaintance, it was the mere notice of the name of Flemps, which led to the extraordinary chain of events which I shall now place before the reader exactly as I linked them together—premising only that I shall sink my part in the narrative as fully as I shall be able.

As I have said above, I make Sunday a holiday, and coming to know the Flempses, and ascertaining that the cabman—perhaps with some knowledge of that cheerful way of spending the Sunday which I have heard distinguishes foreigners—was in the habit of using his cab as a private vehicle on a Sunday, and driving his wife out, I found my seventh days even more cheerful than I had yet discovered them to be. In plain English, during the summer through which I knew the Flempses, I frequently drove out of London with them a few miles into the country.

Flemps used to drive, of course, and I and his wife were inside, with all the windows down, in order that we might get as much of the country air as possible.

I find, by reference to the diary I have kept since I

entered the service, and at which I work equally for pleasure, and to relieve my mind of particulars which would overweight it, for I may add that in this diary, which would be intolerable printed, I fix down every word of a case I hear, as closely as I can remember it, and every particular as near as I can shape it—I say I find, by reference to my diary, that it was the fourth Sunday I rode out with the Flempses, and the sixth week of my acquaintance with those people, whom upon the whole I found very respectable, that I got the first inkling of one of the best, even if one of the most dissatisfactory, cases in which I was ever engaged.

The conversation which called up my curiosity I am enabled to reproduce almost as it was spoken, for by the time the ride was over I had got so good a thread of the case in my head, that I thought it necessary to book what I had already learnt.

Mrs. Flemps was a worthy woman, who loved to hear herself talk, a failing it is said with her sex. From the hour in which I made her familiar with me, I ceased to talk much to the good woman; I listened only, and rarely opened my mouth except to ask a question.

By the way, I should add here that I in no way spunged upon the Flempses; I always contributed more than one-third to the eatables and drinkables we took with us in the cab, and thereby I think I paid my share of the cab, which would have taken them whether I had been in London or Jericho.

The first words used by the couple in reference to the case attracted my attention.

We had got into the cab, she and I, and he was
looking in at the window as he smoothened his old
hat round and round.

" Jemmy," he said, her name being Jemima, " where
shall us drive to-day ?"

" Well, Jan," said she—he had been christened after
his Dutch father—"we aint been Little Fourpenny
Number Two way this blessed summer."

" *That's* it," said Jan, with a triumphant, crowing
tone.   " Little Fourpenny Number Two."

And mounting his box, he drove out of the yard so
briskly that for a moment, as we went over the kerb-
stone, I thought the only road we were about to take
was that of destruction.

The extraordinary highway we were about to take
naturally led me to make some inquiries; for it can
readily be understood by the public that if there is
one thing a detective—whether female or male—is
less able to endure than another, it is a mystery.

" That's a queer road we're going, Mrs. Flemps,"
said I; and speaking after the manner of her class—
for I may say that half the success of a detective depends upon his or her sympathy with the people from
whom either is endeavouring to pick up information.

" Yes," said Mrs. Flemps; and as she sighed I knew
that there was more in the remark than would have
appeared to an ordinary listener.   I do not use the
words " ordinary listener" at all in a vain sense, but
simply with a business meaning.

" Is it a secret ?"

" What, Little Fourpenny ?" she called out, as we bumped over the London stones.

" Number Two," I added, with a smile.

She shook her head.

" There was no number two," she replied, " though there ought to have been."

Now this answer was puzzling. Both husband and wife felt mutual sympathy in the affair of " Little Fourpenny Number Two ;" and yet it appeared no Little Fourpenny Number Two had ever existed.

" Tell me all about it, Mrs. Flemps," said I, " if it's no secret."

She answered in these words—" Which I will, my dear, when we reach the gardings, but can't a jolting over the stones."

We drove six miles out of London, and got on the level country road. There is no need to say whither we went, because *places* are of no value in this narrative.

It is enough to say it was six miles out of London, and on a level country.

As we made a turn in the road Mrs. Flemps became somewhat excited; and almost immediately afterwards the cabman turned round, and looking at his wife, he said—

" We're a coming to the werry spot."

The cab was drawn about two hundred yards further on, and then Jan Flemps pulled rein, and got off his box.

" There's the werry milestone," he said, pointing to one at the side of the road ; " and the werry identical where I lost Little Fourpenny Number Two."

And it was at this point that Mrs. F. remarked—

" Cuss the thutty pound."

" Never mind, old woman, we wanted it bad enough
then, Lord knows ; and but for it this cab might never
ha' been druv by me, so put an han'some mug on it,
old woman."

The reader will concede that this conversation was
sufficiently appetizing to attract any one—to a detective it spoke volumes.

I said nothing till the cab was once more in motion,
and I could tell how heartily the cabman appreciated
the spot by the slow pace at which we left it behind
us, and by the several times he looked back linger-
ingly at the milestone.

Meanwhile Mrs. Flemps, within the cab, was shaking
her head dolefully ; and I could see, by the wistful,
far-away appearance of her eyes, that in thought she
was a long way beyond me and the cab.

When she woke up, which she did in a short time
with an exclamation, and such a rough, cutting sentence as I have noticed the rougher sort of folk are in
the habit of making the termination of any show of
sentiment, I reminded her that she had promised to
tell me the history of Little Fourpenny.

" Wait, my dear, till we get to the gardings, and Jan
himself will oblige.   He tells the tale better nor I do."

Therefore I said no more till we had ended our plain
dinner at the tea-gardens, which were our destination.
The meal done, and Jan at his pipe, I reminded Mrs. F.
once more of her promise ; and she mentioning the
matter to the cabman, it appeared to me that he was

not at all disinclined to refresh himself with a recital of the history.

It is necessary that I should give it, in order that the reader may appreciate how a detective can work out a case.

"I were a going home in my cab one night, more nor a little time ago——"

"It were in 'forty-eight, when the French were a fighting Louy Philippe," said the cabman's wife.

"I was a goin' home, not in the best o' humours, when a comin' across 'amstead 'eath I overtook a woman a staggerin' under what I thought were a bundle."

"It were a child," said Mrs. Flemps.

"Yes, it were," the cabman continued; "and it had on'y been in this precious world a fortnight. I pulled up, seein' her staggerin'; and to cut it short hereabouts, I told her she might come up on the box along o' me, for it were not likely I could let a tramp in on the cushions. She were werry weak, and the infant were the poorest lookin' kid I ever seed—yet purty to look at as I sor by the gass."

"As he sord by the gass!" responded Jemima.

"Well, arter some conversation with that young woman, I pulled up at a public, and treated her and your obedient; and which whether it were the rum put me up to it, or it were in me before and I knowed it not, no sooner had I swallowed that rum than the idea was plain and wisible afore me. 'What are you a goin' to do with it?' I said, pointing to the young un. 'I don't know,' says she, a lookin' out towards

London. 'Father?' says I. 'No,' says she. I then
looks out, and points towards London, which she
thereupon shook her head; but she didn't turn on the
water, being, I think, too far gone for that. 'Which,'
said I, 'if you can do nothin' for her (knowin' as she'd
told me it was a girl) somebody else may—my old
woman and me, you see, never havin' had no family.' "

"Never having had no family—more's the pity,"
responded Mrs. Flemps.

" 'Why,' says she, continued the cabman, 'who'd be
troubled with another woman's child?—women have
enough trouble with their own.' 'I would,' says I,
'my old woman never having had any, and not likely
to mend matters.' 'Will you?' says she, and such a
hawful light came upon that young woman's face as I
never wish to see on another. 'Yes,' says I, 'and it
shall be all fair and above board, and I'll give you my
old woman's address, and what money I've got for her'
—which it came about she got called Little Fourpenny, being that sum I had in my pocket after payin'
for the rum, after a whole day out and only a shillin'
fare. Well, the longs and the shorts of it are that
that there wretched young woman gave me up the
baby, and I gived her the fourpence, and she got down
off the cab and went down a turning, and blest if ever
she looked back once, and blest if ever she called at
our place once—p'r'aps she lost the address though,
and if she did, why she were not so bad after all, and
p'r'aps she died—anyhow, that's how we came by Little
Fourpenny."

"That's how we came by Little Fourpenny," responded Mrs. F., adding, as a kind of Amen, "blesser little 'art."

"Yes," said I, "but what of Little Fourpenny Number Two?"

"Ha, that's on'y five year ago. My Jemmy—meanin' Jemima, wasn't best pleased when I brought that poor Little Fourpenny home, and I think she thought I knew'd more of it than I did till she growed so uncommon unlike me—but let my wife have thought as she might, I'm sure no mother was ever sorrier than her were when Little Fourpenny was took and changed for the better."

"Much for the better!" said Mrs. F., with two or three tears in her eyes, as I detected.

"Lord, I see her now a comin' with my dinner, bein' not so much nor ten year old, and *all* the rank with a word for Little Fourpenny. All the fellers o' the rank wanted to stand when Little Fourpenny went off the road, which it was but nat'ral. Yes, we missed her when she died at nine."

"At nine," responded Mrs. F., adding, "five years ago."

"And it was but nat'ral we should think as our Fourpennurth was a good one, and as we was alone and might find another, which was the reason, as p'r'aps I began lookin' after Little Fourpenny Number Two, and bless you, my dear, cabmen, and I dersay policemen, don't have to look far any night o' the week without finding a wand'rin' woman as 'as got a little un she don't know what on earth to do with."

"Little Fourpenny hadn't been off the rank three

months afore, sittin' on that very milestone as I pointed out, and one evenin' in this very month o' July, there I saw her. My 'art was in my mouth, for it was as though all them years had never been, and jest as though Little Fourpenny's mother was jest afore my hoss's head agin. *It* was another on 'em. She was a woman with a little un as she didn't know what on earth to do with. Which I spoke to her, and havin' that experience of our gal, I soon made 'er understand me, though I do assure yer my 'art was in my mouth as I thought o' the other. She didn't understand me a' fust, but she did at last, and I thought she were orf 'er 'ed abit by the way she went on, sayin' as Providence 'ad interfered, when it were on'y *me*. And she took the address greedy-like, but when I offered her the five shillin's, doin' it pleasant like and callin' her mate, she shrinks back she does, and calls out to Heaven if she can sell her child. Which then promisin' to call and see my old woman, and kissin' the child till it got into my throat agin', she run orf with her arms wide out, and goin' from side to side like a jibber—which *she* never come to see the old woman!"

"Which she never come!" responded Mrs. F.; adding, "which if she had what could I 'a said, and which if she'd tore my eyes out I could not ha' complained."

"*For* you see," continued the cabman, "that there child and that there old woman o' mine never met."

"Never met!" responded Mrs. Flemps.

"*For* you must know," continued the cabman, "*I* sold that there child o' that there woman afore I'd left that there milestone a mile behind."

"A mile behind!" adds Mrs. Flemps, shaking her head.

"Lord lead us *not* into temptation, but I could not rersist that there thutty poun', bein' at that identkle time werry hard up, owin' to havin' to pay damages for runnin' down a hold man which was more frightened nor hurt, but the obstinest old party ever a man druv, and had to pay 'im that identkle sum o' thutty poun's, which it seemed to me a kind o' providence when the woman offered that identkle sum, since it seemed to me as I was taken pity on acos of runnin' down that obstnit hold gent while hard a thinkin' o' lost Little Fourpenny."

Now by this time my curiosity had been thoroughly roused. It was impossible to avoid comprehending that the child that the wretched mother had given up to the cabman had been literally sold by him within twenty minutes of the time when he came into the possession of her.

And perhaps it is necessary that I should remark that I was not struck with the idea that it was at all unlikely that this cabman should have met a second woman in his life ready to part with her child. I am, detective as I live, almost as much ashamed as pained to admit that there is not a night passes in this large city of London during which you are unable to find wretched mothers ready to part with their children. Perhaps I should add that my experience leads me to believe that these poor women are mothers for the first time—mothers of but a very short duration, and that therefore, while they have not been with their little ones long enough to be unable to separate from them, they are still under the influence of that horror of their position, and consequent fear or dread of the child, which is the result of their memory of a time when they were free and respected. These young women are mostly seduced servant and work girls. Poor things!—we detectives, especially us women detectives, know quite enough of such matters.

Said I to the cabman—

" Who was the woman who took the child ?"

" Why, 'ow should *I* know ? I was a joggin' on, with the little un on the floor o' the cab, atween the two cushions to prevent co-lisons, when she calls ' Cab !' to me. ' 'Gaged,' says I. ' I'll pay you anythink, says she. ' Well,' thinks I, ' anyhow you're a queer customer.' She were about thirty—a wild looking party as ever I saw by the gas-lamp, under which she was standin', but she were a real lady, and had dark eyes. ' Can't do it,' says I. Then she says, ' Have you come far down the road ?' ' About three miles,' says I. ' Ha,' says she, ' 'ave you seen a woman with a child ?' which, continued the cabman, you might ha' knocked me orf my box when she made that there remark —' a poor woman,' says she, ' with a very young child ?' And then as luck would have it—or *ill* luck—which sometimes I think it were one, and at other times I'm sure it were the other ; as some luck would 'ave it, at this identkle moment, the child sets up a howlin' fine. ' What's that ?—oh, what's that ?' she asks, a flyin' at the cab-windy, and I can tell you I was nearly a tumblin' orf my box, I was so took

aback. 'Heaven 'ave sent it !' says she, lookin' in the
cab, and I s'pose seein' on'y the child there at the
bottom o' the cab, ' which,' says I, ' it's that identkle
young woman's you was speakin' of !' Then she
screals out she does ; an' if there'd been a p'leaceman
about *I* should ha' been in Queer Street, savin' your
presence, my dear, a talkin' about the p'leace on a
Sunday. Then I ups and tells her that me and my
missus have lost our Little Fourpenny, and how I've
got the kid ; and then she calls out again that Heaven
is at the bottom of it, and she says—' My good man,'
says she, ' here's thutty poun's,' which there was, all
in gold, ' and take it, and give me the child ;' and
then she says how that I can have no love for the
child—not havin' ever seen it afore, and 'ow by doin'
as she wished, I might do great good, and, to cut it
short—after a time—I gived 'er the child, and I took
the thutty poun's ; and that's how it was my old
woman never, never saw the little un, and how it was,
as I hoped that there poor mother ud never call at
our house. She never did ; so p'r'aps them poor
mothers are all alike, and don't care to look them in
the face as they once deserted, and can't reasonubly
ask back again, and that's how it was that my old
woman never saw Little Fourpenny Number Two."

"Never saw Little Fourpenny Number Two !" responded Mrs. Flemps.

Now I may say at once that this tale, told in
common English, by an ordinary man, smoking his
common clay pipe in a plain tea-gardens in the suburbs
of London—this tale called forth all the acumen and

wits with which nature has endowed me. The detective was all alive as that extraordinary recital, told with no intention for effect, was slowly unfolded to me, with many stops and waves of the pipe, and repetitions with which I have not favoured the reader.

It was a most remarkable history, that of the woman who had obtained the child, from beginning to end.

The series of facts, accepting the cabman's statements as honest, and as he had no purpose to serve in deceiving me, I was at once inclined to suppose he spoke the truth—as he did; the series of facts was wonderful from the beginning of the chapter to the end.

The extraordinary list of unusual facts began with a woman, evidently belonging to a good class, being out late at night and hailing a cab. Then followed her inquiry concerning a woman with a very young child. To this succeeds the discovery of the child in the cab, and the ejaculation that Heaven has been good to her; and finally had to be considered the fact of her having thirty pounds in gold with her, and which she offers at once to the cabman for the child.

Accustomed to weigh facts, and trace out clear meanings, something after the manner of lawyers, a habit common to all detectives, before I began in a loose, half-curious way to question Flemps upon the history he had betrayed to me, I had made out a tolerable case against the lady.

As she knew that the woman had passed that way it appeared evident to me that she had seen her, guessing her to be a beggar, at some earlier period of the evening than that at which she addressed the cabman. And as after the cabman refused her for a fare she expressed great joy at hearing the crying of the infant, the inference stood that her despair at the cabman's refusal was in some way connected with the child itself.

Continuing out this reasoning—and custom was so ready within me that the process was finished before the cabman had—I came to the conclusion, after duly balancing the fact of her having with her thirty pounds in gold, and her bribing the cabman with it, that for some reason unknown she had pressing need for a child. I felt certain that she had seen the woman in an earlier part of the evening, that she had set out to overtake the woman, to purchase the child of her, if possible, and that meeting the cab, the driver of which could have no knowledge of her, she had hailed him in the hope of more speedily overtaking the woman and child.

The questions, as a detective, I wished answered were these :—

Who was she ?

Why did she act as she did ?

Where was she ?

At once I apprehended I should have little difficulty in ascertaining where she was, provided she still lived in the district, and provided the cabman could give me some clue by which to identify her.

For I may tell you at once that I saw crime in the whole of this business. Children are not bought in the dark in the midst of fear and trembling, if all is clear and honest sailing.

So pretending to be really interested in the story, which I was, I began putting questions.

" Did you ever learn anything more ?"

" Nothink," said he.

And his wife, of course, responded and repeated.

" You never saw the woman again ?"

" Never."

Echoed by Mrs. F. I will leave her repeats out from this time forth.

" How long ago did it happen ?—you interest me so much !"

" Five years this blessed July."

" Then it was in the July of 1858." I knew that by the date of Little Fourpenny's death.

" It was."

[I should here point out to the reader that though I put this singular case, " Tenant for Life," as the leading narrative in my book, it is one of the later of my more remarkable cases.]

" You are quite sure about the milestone ?" I said.

" Quite," he replied.

" What kind of a woman was she ?"

" Which," the cabman continued, " I could no more say nor I could fly—save she was wildish-looking, and had large black eyes, and was an out-and-out lady."

" Did she—pardon my being so curious—did she have any peculiarity which you remarked ?"

" Any pecooliarity ? No, not as I am aweer on."

"No mark—no way with her which was uncommon?"

"None sumdever," said the cabman. "Ha! I year 'er now. '*Firty* poun's,' says she, which I could hardly unnerstand 'er at fust; '*firty* poun's for that child,' says she, 'firty poun's.' But what 'ave you started for, my dear?" he asked me.

"Which," here his wife added, "well she may start, pore dear, with you a tellin' about Little Fourpenny in a way to child 'er blood."

Now, the fact is, I had started because I thought I saw the end of a good clew. We detectives have quite a handbook of the science of our trade, and we know every line by heart. One of the chief chapters in that unwritten book is the one devoted to identification. The uninitiated would be surprised to learn how many ways we have of identification by certain marks, certain ways, certain personal peculiarities—but above all, by the unnumbered modes of speaking, the form of speaking, the subjects spoken of, and above all the impediments or peculiarities of speech. For instance, if we are told a party we are after always misplaces the "w" and "v," we are inclined to let a suspected person pass who answers in all other ways to the description, except in this case of the "v" and "w." We know that no cunning, no dexterity would enable the man we are seeking to prevent the exhibition of this imperfection, even if he were on his guard, which he never is. He may change dress, voice, look, appearance, but never his mode of speaking—never his pronunciation.

Now, amongst our list of speech-imperfections is one

where there is an impossibility to pronounce the troublesome " th," and where this difficult sound is replaced by an " f," or a " d," or sometimes by one or the other, according to the construction of the word.

This imperfection I hoped I had discovered to be distinguishable as belonging to the woman who had purchased the child.

" Do you mean, Mr. Flemps," I said,—" do you mean to say that the woman said *firty* instead of *thirty?* How odd."

"' *Firty,*' says she, and that were the reason why I could not comperend 'er at fust. ' *Firty,*' says she ; an' it was on'y when the gold chinked as I knowed what she meant."

" And you have never seen nor heard from her any more?"

" It wasn't likely as she would, if you'd a seen her go off as she did."

" And which way did she go?"

" Why a co'rse as I *met* her, my dear, and as she was coming from somewhere to foller the young woman with the kid, she backed to'ards London, and I 'ad to pass 'er afore I left her behind, an' she never so much as looked at me."

I did not ask any more questions.

I suppose I grew silent; and especially so when we got in the cab and were driving once more home.

Indeed, Mrs. Flemps said she had no doubt that *he* had quite upset me with their tale of Little Fourpenny.

When we reached the milestone, however, Mrs. F.

was as full of the subject as ever ; and I need not say that—though perhaps I said little—I was very hard at work putting this and that together.

After we had passed the milestone, every house on each side of the way had a strange fascination for me. I hungred after every house as it was left behind me, fancying each might be the one which sheltered the infant.

That I would work it out I determined.

So far I had these facts :—

1. The woman must have lived near the road, or she would not have seen the beggar and her child, provided these latter had been on the high road when seen by the former.

2. The time which had elapsed between seeing the woman and meeting the cabman could not have been very great, or she never would have hoped to find the mother and child.

3. The occurrence had only taken place five years previously, and therefore the woman might not have moved out of the neighbourhood.

4. The purchase of the child in such a manner suggested it was to be used for the purpose of deception—in all probability to replace another.

5. Therefore, deception being practised somebody was injured—in all probability an heir.

6. The woman was not needy, or she could not have offered thirty pounds in gold to a stranger, and evidently at a very short notice, for it was clear there could have been no demand for the child when she saw it with the mother.

7. Whoever she was, she had the far from ordinary failure of speech which consists of an inability to utter the sound of " th."

8. Finally, and most importantly, *I had dates.*"

Poor Flemps and his wife—they little thought what a serpent of detection they had been nourishing in their cab. I believe they thought I was a person living on my small property, and helping my income out by a little light millinery.

With the information I had already obtained, I determined to try and sift the matter to the bottom; and I may as well state that, not having anything on my hands at that time, I set to work on the Monday morning, telling Mrs. Flemps that I had some business to look after, and being wished luck from the very bottom of her heart by that cajoled woman.

I took a lodging in the first place as near that mile-stone as I could find one—it was a sweet little country room, with honeysuckle round each window.

I may at once say that the first part of my work was very easy.

Within two days of my arrival at my little lodging at the honeysuckle cottage, I had found out enough to justify me in continuing the search.

As I have said, I could have no reason to doubt the cabman, because he could have nó object in deceiving me. But evidence is what detectives live upon.

The first thing I did was to find traces, if possible, of the mother.

It will be remembered that the mother showed great sorrow at losing the child, and that yet she never knocked at the cabman's door. The inference I took was this, that as she had shown love for the child, and as she had never sought to see it after parting with it, that she had been prevented by one of two catastrophes—either she had gone mad, or she had died.

Where was I to make inquiries?

Clearly of the first relieving officer who lived past the milestone, at which she had parted with the child, and in the opposite direction to that which the cab had taken—for I know much of these poor mothers—they always flee from their children when they have parted from them, whether this parting be by the road of murder, or by desertion, or by the coming of some good Samaritan (like the cabman) who, having no children of his own, is willing to accept a child who to its maternal mother is a burden.

I went past the milestone, made inquiries, and in time found the relieving officer's house. I was answered in double quick time. I think the man supposed I was a relation, and that perhaps I would gain him some credit by reimbursing the parish, through his activity, its miserable outlay in burying the poor woman.

For she was dead.

Circumstances pointed so absolutely to her as the woman who had parted with her child, that I had no reasonable doubt about my conclusion.

In that month of July, on the night of the 15th, a woman was brought in a cart to the officer's door. The man who drove stated that he found the woman lying in the road, and that had not his horse known

she was there before he did, she must have been run
over.

The woman was taken to the union infirmary, and
that place she only left for the grave.

She never recovered her senses while at the union
hospital. She was found, upon her regaining half
consciousness, to be suffering from fever, and as she
had but very recently become a mother (not more
than a fortnight) the loss of her child made the attempt
to overcome that fever quite futile.

She died on the tenth day it appeared, and she had
not spoken at her death for three.

[I should perhaps here remark that I am condensing
in this page the statements of the relieving officer and
a pauper woman who was nurse in the workhouse
hospital.]

I was at no loss to understand that this speechless-
ness was due to opium, which my experience had
already taught me is given in all cases where a fever-
patient has no chance of life, and in order to still
those ravings which would only make the death more
terrible.

But during the preceding week she had said enough
to convince me, upon hearing it reported, that she was
the mother of the child. She had called out for her
baby, pressing her poor breasts as she did so, and
frequently she had shrieked that she heard the cab
far, far away in the distance.

I returned to my little cottage lodging not over and
above pleased. If there is one thing which foils us
detectives more certainly than another, it is death,

Here we have no power. Distance is to us nothing—but we cannot get to the other side of the tomb. Time we care little for, seeing that during life memory more or less holds good. Secresy we laugh at in all shapes but that of the grave.

It is death which foils us and frequently stops a case when it is so nearly complete as to induce the inexperienced to suppose that it is perfect.

I saw at once that I had lost my chief witness—the mother.

Now came the question—was the child itself alive?

If dead, there was an end of my inquiry.

However detectives never give up cases; it is the cases which give up the detectives.

It now became necessary to ascertain what children were born in the milestone district in the month of July, 1858, for I have already shown that the purchaser of the child must have come from somewhere in the neighbourhood of her purchase, and I have hinted that a child purchased under such circumstances as those set about the sale of the child in question, presupposes that the infant is to be used in a surreptitious manner, and in a mode therefore, *primâ facie*, as the lawyers say, which is in all probability, illegal, by acting detrimentally upon some one who benefits by the child's death.

To ascertain what children had been born in the district during that month of July, was as easy a task as to convince myself that the child in question had been registered as a new birth by the woman who had purchased him of the cabman.

The reader has in all probability made out such a suppositive case as I did, and to the following effect :—

The woman-purchaser saw the mother and child an hour or more before she met the cabman, and had some conversation with her.

This supposition was confirmed by the knowledge I obtained that this woman, found in the road, had a couple of half-crowns in the pocket of her dress. It will be remembered that she refused Flemps's money.

Between the time of seeing the woman and bargaining with the cabman, it may readily be supposed that a pressing demand for a newly born child had become manifest, when the woman recalled to her mind the beggar and child she had seen, hoped the poor creature's poverty would be her temptress's opportunity, and so set out to find her ; when a chain of circumstances, which the ordinary reader would call romantic, but which I, as a detective, am enabled to say is equalled daily in any one of many shapes, led to her possession of the infant.

I searched two registers, and made such inquiries as I thought would be useful. Happily in both cases I had to deal not with the registrar, but with his deputy, who is, as a rule, the more manageable man. We detectives have much to do with registrars in all of their three capacities.

I knew that in all probability I had to deal with, what we call in my profession, *family* people. It was no tradesman's wife or sister I had to deal with. The cabman had said she was a *real* lady, (your cabman is one who by his daily experience has a good eye at guessing the condition of a fare), and the immediate command of thirty pounds told me that money was easy with her.

My readers know that the profession or trade of the father is always mentioned in the registration of birth; and therein I had a clue to the father or alleged father.

The probability stood that he would be represented as " gentleman."

There were three births I found, after both registers were examined, in that month, in the registration of which the father was set out as " gentleman."

The addresses in each case I copied—giving, I need not say, some very plausible excuse for so doing; my acts being of course illustrated with several silver portraits of her majesty the Queen.

And here I would urge upon the reader that he need feel no tittle of respect for my work so far. To this point it had been the plainest and simplest operation in which a detective could be employed. Registers were invented for the use of detectives. They are a medicine in the prosecution of our cures of social disorder.

Indeed it may be said the value of the detective lies not so much in discovering facts, as in putting them together, and finding out what they mean.

Before the day was out I dropped two of my extracts from the registers as valueless. The third I kept, feeling pretty sure it related to the right business, because of two facts with which I made myself acquainted before the day was over. The first of these lay in the discovery that the house at which the birth in question had been alleged to take place was within nine hundred yards of the milestone, where this business had commenced; the second, that the mother of the child had died in giving it birth.

I felt pretty certain that I was on the right road at last, but before I consulted my lawyer (most detectives of any standing necessarily have their attorneys, who of course are very useful to men and women of my calling), I determined to be quite certain I was not wasting my time, and to be well assured I was not about to waste my money; for it often happens that a detective, like any other trader, has to lay out money before he can see more.

Learning that the household consisted of the infant —an heiress, then five years of age—the father, and his sister, I fixed my suspicions immediately upon the latter, as the woman who had purchased the child.

If she were the woman, I knew I had the power of convicting her, in my own mind, by hearing her speak; for it will be remembered that I have said that imperfection of speech is one of the surest means of detection open to the use of a high-class detective.

Of course I easily gained access to the house. It is the peculiar advantage of women detectives, and one which in many cases gives them an immeasurable value beyond that of their male friends, that they can get into houses outside which the ordinary men-detectives could barely stand without being suspected.

Thoroughly do I remember my first excuse—we

detectives have many—such as the character of a servant, an inquiry after some supposed mutual friend, or after needle-work, a reference from some poor person in the neighbourhood, a respectful inquiry concerning the neighbourhood to which the detective represents herself as a stranger. I introduced myself as a milliner and dressmaker who had just come to the neighbourhood, and, with the help of an effective card, which I always carry, and which is as good as a skeleton-key in opening big doors, soon I reached the lady's presence.

Before she spoke I recognised her by the large black eyes which the cabman had noted, even in the night-time.

She had not spoken half-a-dozen words before she betrayed herself; she used the letter "f" or "v" where the sound "th" should properly have been pronounced as "Ve day is fine," for "The day, &c."

This mal-pronunciation may read very marked in print, but in conversation it may be used for a long time without its being remarked. The hearer may feel that there is something wrong with the language he is hearing, but he will have to watch very attentively before he discovers where the fault lies, unless he has been previously put upon his guard.

I had.

I went away; and I remember as I left the room I was invited to return and make another visit.

I did.

Thus far all was clear.

I had, I felt sure, found the house—the purchaser of

the child—and the child herself, for the infant was a girl.

What I had now to find out was the reason the child had been appropriated, and who if anybody had suffered by that appropriation.

It was now time to consult with my attorney. Who he is and what name he goes by are matters of no consequence to the reader. Those who know him will recognise that gentleman-at-law by one bit of description—he has the smallest, softest, and whitest hand in his profession.

I put the full case before him in a confidential way of business—names, dates, places, suspicions, conclusions, all set out in fair order.

"I think I see it," said he, "but I wont give an opinion to-day. Call in a week."

"Oh, dear me, no!" said I, "my dear M——, I can't wait a week. I'll call in three days."

I called on the third day—early in the morning.

The attorney gave me a nod, said he was very busy, couldn't wait a moment, and then chatted with me for twenty minutes. I should say rather he held forth, for I could barely get a word in edgeways; but what he says is generally worth listening to.

He wanted further information; he desired to know the maiden name of the wife and the place of her marriage to Mr. Shedleigh—which I will suppose the name of the family concerned in his affair.

I was to let him know these further particulars, and come again in three more days.

At first sight this was a little difficult. Singularly

enough, the road to this information I found to be very simple, for as a preliminary step, ascertaining from the turnpike-man in that neighbourhood where Mrs. Shedleigh had been buried, I visited her tomb, in the hope perhaps that her family name and place of settlement might appear on the stone, which often happens amongst the wives of gentry.

In this lady's case no mention was made either of her family name or place of residence, but nevertheless I did not leave the cemetery without the power of furnishing my lawyer with information quite as good as he required.

The lady had been buried in a private vault at the commencement of the catacombs, and the coffin was to be seen through the gratings of a gateway, upon which was fixed a coat of arms in engraved brass.

Of course as a detective, who has to be informed on a good many points, I knew that the arms must refer to the deceased, and therefore I surprised the catacomb keeper considerably when, later in the day, I spoke once more with him, and told him I wanted to take a rubbing of the brass plate in question.

The request being unusual, the usual difficulties of suspicion and prejudice were thrown in my way. But it is surprising how much suspicion and prejudice can be bought for five shillings, and to curtail this portion of my narrative I may at once say I took away with me an exact copy of the late lady's coat-of-arms. I need not say how this was done. Any one knows how to take a fac-simile of an engraved surface by putting a sheet of paper on it, and rubbing a morsel of charcoal, or black chalk over the paper. The experiment can be tried on the next embossed cover, with a sheet of note-paper and a trifle of lead pencil.

This rubbing I took to the lawyer, and then I waited three days.

He had enough to tell me by the end of the second.

In the simplest and most natural way in the world, he had discovered a reason for the appropriation of the child, and not only had that information been obtained, but the name of the man injured by the act, and his interest in the whole business was at the command of the attorney.

We neither of us complimented the other on his discoveries, each being aware that the other had but put in force the principles and ordinary rules of his business.

I had gained my knowledge by reference to registers, he his by first consulting a book of the landed gentry and their arms, and secondly by the outlay of a shilling and an inspection of a will in the keeping of the authorities at Doctors' Commons.

The lawyer had found the arms as copied by me from the tomb-gate in a book of landed gentry, had learnt an estate passed from the possession of Sir John Shirley in 1856, by death, and into the ownership of his daughter, an heiress, and wife of Newton Shedleigh, Esq. The entry further showed that the lady, Shirley Shedleigh, had died in 1857, and that by her marriage settlement the property descended upon her children. A child of this lady, named after her Shirley Shedleigh, was then the possessor of the estates, which were large, while the father, Newton Shedleigh, as sole surviving trustee, controlled the property.

So the matter stood.

"I can see it all," said the lawyer, who, I am bound to say, passed over my industry in the business as though it had never existed. "I can see it all. The defendant, Newton Shedleigh, marries an heiress, who, by her marriage settlement, maintains possession of her estate through trustees. As in ordinary cases, these estates devolve upon her children, supposing her to have any, and that they *outlive her.* But here comes the nicety of the question. If she have children, and they all die before her—granted that her husband outlives her, he, by right of the birth of his and her children, becomes a tenant for life in her possessions, though by the settlement, in event of the wife dying without children to inherit her property, it passes to her father's brother."

"Well?" said I.

"The motive for a supposititious heir is evident. The lady dies in childbed, as the dates of her death and of the birth of her assumed child testify—in all probability her infant is born dead, and therefore the mother dying without having given the father a just claim to the tenantage for life—by the conditions of the settlement the property would *at once,* upon the death of the wife, pass to her uncle, her father's brother. To avoid this, the beggar-woman's child has been made to take the place of the dead infant. The case is about as clear as any I have put together."

"But——" Here I stopped.

"Well ?"

" Your argument suggests accomplices."

" Yes."

" Four—the father, his sister, the doctor, and the nurse."

" Four, at least," said the lawyer.

" Do you know, or have you heard of the true owner of the estates ?"

The reader will observe that I and the lawyer had already given in a verdict in the case.

" I do not know him—I have made two or three inquiries. He is Sir Nathaniel Shirley. From what I can hear he does not bear a very good name, though it is quite impossible, I hear, to bring any charge against him."

" This will cost money," I said.

" It will cost money," echoed the lawyer.

I have always noticed that when a lawyer has anything not too agreeable to say, generally he echoes what you yourself observe.

" Is he rich ?"

" Who ?" asks the lawyer, with that love of precision which irritates any woman, even when she is a detective.

" Sir Nathaniel Shirley."

" I hear not."

" Who, then, is to pay expenses ?"

" Who is to pay expenses ?" says the lawyer, repeating my words. And then, after a pause, as though to show he made a difference between my own words and his, he adds—" Expenses there certainly will be."

" Shall we speak to Sir Nathaniel at once ?"

"*You* can speak to Sir Nathaniel at once. As for me, I shall wait till the baronet speaks to me."

"Oh !" said I.

"Yes," replied my attorney, softly turning over a heavy stick of sealing wax, such as, in all my detective experience, I never saw equalled out of a law-office.

It stood clear that the case was to be left in my hands till it was plain sailing, and then the lawyer would take the helm. I have noticed that the law gentlemen with whom I have had to do are much given to this cautious mode of doing business.

We detectives, who know how much depends upon risk and audacity, are perhaps inclined to look rather meanly upon this cautiousness, knowing as we do that if we were as fearful of taking steps we should never gain a crust.

"I'll see you again, Mr. M——, in a few days."

"Well," said he, looking a little alarmed I thought, "whatever you do don't drop it; turn the matter over in your mind, and let me see you again in three days."

"Thank you," said I ; "I'll come when I want you."

I think I noticed a little mixture of surprise and satisfaction on the lawyer's countenance—surprise that I showed some independence, satisfaction by virtue of the intimation my words conveyed that I did not mean to abandon the case.

Abandon the case !

Good as many of the cases in which I had been engaged might have been, I knew that not one had been so near my fame, and, in a small way, my fortune,

as this; for I may tell you we detectives are like
actors, or singers, or playwrights, who are always
hoping for some distinction which shall carry them to
the top of their particular tree.

I had saved some money, for I am not extravagant;
and though my necessary expenses were large, I had
for some years earned good money, and had laid by a
trifle, and so I determined myself to find the money
which was required to begin and carry on this inquiry.

So far I had got together only facts.  Now I had to
prove them.

To do this, it was necessary that I should gain an
entry into the house.

I had, as the reader knows, planted my first attempt
by calling at the house and presenting at the outset
a small written card, setting out that I was Miss
Gladden, a milliner and dressmaker, who went out by
the day or week.

This *ruse*, practised with success upon Mrs. Flemps,
and resulting in two caps and a bonnet for that lady, I
had always exercised; indeed, I may say, that I took
lessons as an improver in both those trades, in order
the better to carry on my actual business, which, I
will repeat here once again, is a necessary occupation,
however much it may be despised.

If this world lost all its detectives it would very
soon complainingly find out their absence, and wish
them, or some of them, back again.

But I could not wait till Miss Shedleigh sent for
me, even supposing that she remembered me and my
application.  Even this supposition was questionable.

It therefore became necessary to tout that lady once again. I sent up to the house a specimen of my work, and with it a letter to the effect that my funds were running low and I was becoming uneasy.

The answer returned was that I could come up to the house on the following day at nine in the morning.

I was there to time.

The house was very splendid—magnificently appointed ; and the number of servants told of very considerable wealth.

The lady of the house, this Miss Catherine Shedleigh, was one of the pleasantest and most delightful of women—calm, amiable, serene, and possessing that ability to make people at home about her which is a most rare quality, and which we detectives know sufficiently well how to appreciate.

I was located in the housekeeper's room, and I was soon surrounded with work.

I had not been in the mansion two hours before I saw the little girl upon whose birth so much had depended.

She was a very pleasant child—nothing very remarkable ; and her age, as given by the housekeeper, tallied exactly with the cabman's story.

The arrival of the child, who, to look upon, was comely without being pretty, gave me that opportunity for which I was waiting. I had felt pretty sure I should soon see the heiress ; knowing that if children are not desirous of seeing new faces in a house, their younger nurses always are.

"The little missy has lost her mother, hasn't she ?"

I asked the housekeeper, an open-faced and a candid spoken woman. Somehow we close-mouthed detectives have a great respect for open, candid-speaking people.

"Yes," said the housekeeper. "Miss Shedleigh never knew her mamma."

"Indeed! how was that? Will you kindly pass me the white wax?——Thank you."

"Mrs. Shedleigh died in childbed."

"Dear me, poor lady!" said I. Then, after a pause, I asked, "Did you know her, ma'am?"

The housekeeper looked up for the moment, a little offended. She soon regained her ordinary amiability, and replied—

"Yes, I was housekeeper to her mother, and afterwards to her father, up to the time of her marriage, and we both came to this house together."

"Ha! then you were present at her death, poor lady?"

"Pardon me, my dear," the old lady continued. "I do not think there is any need to pity my lady—as I always called her after her mother's, Lady Shirley's death—she was sufficiently good not to fear death over much."

"Did she die peaceably, may I ask, Mrs. Dumarty?"

"I was assured she did."

"Oh, you were not present, Mrs. Dumarty?"

"No, my dear, I was not; and I shall never forgive myself for having been away at the time. But the fact is, that we did not expect any addition to the family for fully two months from the time when the poor dear lady suffered; and I—I shall never forgive

myself—had gone down home into the country to see
our relations—I mean mine and my lady's, we both
coming from one part."

" Oh !" I said, balked ; for it was clear, as far as she
herself was concerned, Mrs. Dumarty was valueless as
one of my witnesses.

" There never was such an unfortunate business as
that ; and dear me, my dear, talking about it has so
confused me that I think I must have made a wrong
seam ! . Yes, I have—it's two different lengths !"

" But the lady was not alone ?" said I.

" No, not alone," replied the housekeeper ; and then
she broke off from the tone of voice she was using, and
said, in a higher key, " But you do seem strangely interested in the family ?"

" O dear, no," said I ; " but it is a way of mine
when I am working for a family.   I beg your pardon,
and will not offend again."

The old lady nodded her head seriously as she pursed
up her lips and began to unrip the seam she had
foundered on ; but she was not silent for long.   Soon
she began to speak again ; and as a kind of apology
for having been a little severe, she became more com-
municative than she had hitherto shown herself.

" My lady was not alone," she said, " though more
might have been about her.   For instance, Mr. Shedleigh was away from home, though to be sure his sister
was in the way."

" What ! was he not in the house when his wife
died ?"

" No, poor dear ; and I'm told that when he learnt

the catastrophe—by electric telegraph—he was near
broken-hearted, and mayhap he would have been had
it not been for the little daughter. It upset him so he
could not travel for two days. *I* learnt the news by
electric telegraph, and I shall never forgive myself that
I was away."

Here was information!

It was clear, if the housekeeper was to be believed,
and she could have no aim in deceiving me, that the
father was as ignorant as Sir Nathaniel Shirley of the
real state of the case.

" Do you think," said I, leading up to another line
in the case—" Do you think the doctor who attended
the lady was a clever man ?"

" Bless you, my dear," said the housekeeper ; and I
began to notice that she was becoming gratified rather
than angry at the interest I was taking in the family,
" Dr. Ellkins was the cleverest of medical men."

" *Was ?*" I said, interrogatively.

" Dead," the housekeeper replied, in a kind of fatal-
istic voice. " He was never a very strong man, I
should say, and he ought never to have tried the
journey. He went to Madeiry, my dear, and in Madeiry he died."

So here was another of the four witnesses upon whom
I relied beyond detection.

" Perhaps the nurse neglected the poor lady," I said,
turning to another branch of my case.

" Ah me !" said the old housekeeper, " that could
not be, for it was all so sudden and unexpected, and
the death followed the birth so soon that she was not

sent for till hours after my poor lady lay dead. The only one she had to help her in her trouble was her dear sister, Miss Shedleigh, who saw her through all her trouble. Miss Shedleigh herself narrowly escaped with her life, and she has been like a mother to our little darling ever since."

So, of those four supposed witnesses to the birth, one only existed who could be of use to me in unravelling the secret ; that one was she who had been entirely guilty of the fraud—the sister-in-law of the late lady, and sister of the self-supposing father, whom I now looked upon to be in all probability as certainly deceived as Sir Nathaniel Shirley himself. He had not reached home till two days after the death of the lady, and therefore two days, at least, after the supposed birth of the child which now stood as the heiress to the property, which was very large.

The father was not in the house at the time of the birth or death.

The nurse had not been sent for.

The doctor was dead.

The sister-in-law alone remained. How could I approach her ? It was she whose interest it was chiefly to be silent. She would be on her guard, and I could hope for nothing from her.

I began to see my chances of success getting narrower and narrower.

But I did not despair.

That same evening, after I had left the mansion for the night, I went down to the house in which Dr. Ellkins had lived, having learnt the address of the housekeeper, and I found that it was still in the occupation of a medical man, who, to be here short, was he who had purchased Dr. Ellkins's business of that gentleman, when he decided upon leaving England.

To inquire if Dr. Ellkins had had an assistant, and, if so, where he could be found, was child's play.

No ; Dr. Ellkins had had no assistant.

I had thanked the doctor's housekeeper for her information, and was turning away, when I blushed for myself at the omission I had made when she remarked—

" The doctor had a 'prentice."

" And where is he ?" I asked.

" Dear me, mum, how ever should I know ! At one o' the 'spitals up in London I suppose, leastways, I know he said he was a going to a 'spital, and likewise to be a Guy."

This statement gave me courage, for I had had some experience of medical students. Having had a case in which one ultimately became my prisoner, I knew that when this young man had said he was going to be a Guy he meant he was about to become a student at Guy's Hospital over London Bridge.

" What was his name ?" I asked.

" Dear me, mum ! I do hope he's got in no trouble —his chief fault, while he was with us, being dancing —which were his fascination."

" No ; no trouble. I want to ask him a question."

" Blessed be !" said the old lady ; " his name was George Geffins—a young man with the reddest hair, which he were ever trying to change, and it coming out the brighter for what he did to that same."

Saying I would call again (I never did), I left the old housekeeper.

That same night I sent up word to the housekeeper at Shirley House, as Mr. Shedleigh's mansion was called, that I should not be able to be with her on the following day, and when the next sun rose it found me in London.

I was soon at Guy's Hospital, and within a quarter of an hour of seeing the building I had learnt that a Mr. George Geffins was a student at that place, and the porter, with a grin, had given me his private address.

It was then half-past nine o'clock, and upon reaching the house and getting into the passage I guessed that Mr. Geffins was at breakfast by the clicking of a spoon against a cup or saucer which I heard distinctly.

When the landlady said a lady wanted to see him, the clicking of the spoon ended.

Accustomed to hear with more than ordinary acuteness—for I have the belief that the senses may be sharpened up to any extent—I heard Mr. Geffins say—

"Why the devil didn't you say I was out?"

Then he bawled—"Is that you, Matilda?"

"No," said I; "it's not Matilda."

"Ho!" said he; (it struck me he spoke in a relieved tone)—"Ho!" coming to the door; "then who the devil *are* you, ma'am?"

It further struck me, and I am willing to admit it, that when he saw me, the gentleman in question betrayed no extraordinary inclination to become better acquainted.

The disinclination was the more marked when I said I had come upon business.

He was a dissipated looking young man, and it appeared to me lived about three years in one twelve-month.

However, he asked me into his parlour—the most forlorn and furniture-damaged apartment which I ever entered—and then awkwardly he asked me, his land-lady having quitted the room with a disturbed air, " What I wanted." He put " the" and a strong word between " what" and " I," but I refrain from quoting it.

" You were a pupil of Dr. Ellkins?"

" Oh, yes," he said, with a relieved air.

" You were so in 1858?"

" In 1858."

By this time, having got over his evident dread of me, he was beginning to suspect me, I saw.

" I only want to know whether you remember the birth of a child at Shirley House in the July of that year?"

" What, Mrs. Shedleigh's child? Oh, yes, _I_ remember specially. What on earth are you asking me this for?"

" Simply because I want to find out the date of some business which relates personally to me, and which I can tell if once I know the date of the birth of Mr. Shedleigh's daughter."

" Well, I _can_ tell you," said Mr. Geffins, " by as odd a chance as ever you heard. Sit down, ma'am, and excuse me going on with my breakfast; I've got to get to lecture by ten."

I sat down. It is the first lesson of a detective to oblige a victim; his second is to accept that victim's hospitality if he offers it. Nothing opens a man's or woman's mouth so readily as allowing him or her to fill yours.

"Will you take a cup of tea?" he asked.

I did immediately.

"Bless my soul," said he, "I remember the day only too well—the 15th of July it was—for well I remember seeing it on the summons paper—'That on the said fifteenth of July, 1858, you did wilfully and of malice aforethought, &c., &c.' You see the fact stood, it was our guv's old housekeeper's birthday, and I had promised her a surprise, and she got it in the shape of a whole bundle of crackers, all set alight at once just under her window. And the constable passing at that time, why I got summoned, and had to pay five shillings fine and thirteen shillings costs— well I remember the date. I have got the summons now. I remember it was the governor going up to Shirley House which gave me the chance of firing 'em. But by Jove," he continued, taking a great bite out of his dry toast, "I must be quick, or I shall never be in time for lecture."

"Excuse me, sir," I continued, "but I want to hear every particular about times. At what hour did Dr. Ellkins come home from Shirley House?"

"I think it was about ten—and at eleven he was rung up and had to go back to the house again!"

"Ha, exactly!" I said. "Now comes the point which especially interests me. I know he returned to the house, or I never could have wanted to know anything about this matter. May I ask why he returned to the house, or what excuse he made to you when he left his house? Did *he* say he was going back to Shirley House?"

"Oh yes! and I am quite sure he did go there, because it was the groom who came down for him."

"Is it possible? I wish you would tell me all about it!" I said in an eager tone, "seeing as you must I am indeed most interested in the details."

"Well now, look you here," and I must confess the lad improved upon acquaintance exactly as an ugly dog frequently will; "I'll tell you all about it. Ellkins was not expected to be up at the big house on that job for a good two months, and therefore you may guess he was rather surprised when he was sent for at ten p.m., on the 15th of July. He came back before eleven, and I remember I asked him if it was all right, and I remember he said no, and it never was likely to be all right."

"What did he mean by that?" I asked.

"Well, you are not easily shocked, are you?"

"No," I said, looking the young man plainly in the face.

I cannot reproduce the statement he made, but it ran plainly to the effect that Mrs. Shedleigh had not given birth to a living child, and that it was highly improbable that such could ever be the case.

Now this was the very information I wanted, but it would not have done to show this was the case, so I said, in as impatient a tone as I could assume—

"But, now, I want to know what was the time when the doctor again went to the house—if ever he went at all, which I doubt.".

I must have completely thrown the young man off his guard as to my real attempt, for he set his cup down, and speaking in a far more gentlemanly tone han any he had yet used, he said—

"Oh, but I assure you that he did go to the house, and returned in about three hours. He looked amazingly upset, I assure you, and when I asked him if anything was amiss he replied Mrs. Shedleigh was dead. He said no more, and went into his room without wishing me good-night, which for him was a very extraordinary thing to do—he being rather a civil man. Well, you may judge of my surprise the next morning when old Mother Smack—I beg your pardon, when the doctor's housekeeper said to me, 'So there's an heiress up at the great house. I suppose we shall have rare doings?' Well, it was so ; and when I asked the doctor he told me to hold my tongue, and added another birth had taken place. Then he begged I would say nothing about the affair, nor have I until now. But it matters little now, for I might talk about it, and damage the poor old doctor's reputation ever so, and he would not feel it, for he has left the faculty and gone up above ; let's hope for his diploma. You see, *he* had made a mistake, and I was afraid to say anything about it, for perhaps he helped the poor lady into her coffin—doctors *do* do that sort of thing sometimes, and it can't be helped ; but really I hope, ma'am, you've got no more questions to ask me, and I hope I have been of service to you. If I stop any longer I shall be too late for lecture, and there'll be no end of a row."

Well, no, I replied, he had not been of much use to me, but I thanked him all the same, and would he allow me to call upon him again?

His jaw dropped. Well, he said, he did not care much to have women about his room, for that sort of thing got about and did a fellow no good, but I might come again, and—for *he* did not want to know my name—and would I kindly send in the name of Walker? I would remember the name— "Walker, you know." But really he *must* be off.

And so saying he bolted, leaving me in the parlour and actually alone with his landlady's silver spoons.

I had learnt far more than he supposed, more than even he, doctor as he was, had ever suspected, and I had no need to call upon him again, although at the time I suspected I should have to surprise him by appearing in my true character, and being instrumental in sub-pœning him as a witness.

What had I learnt in addition to what I already knew of the case?

More, far more than I can openly tell my readers, and yet they must be put in possession of my discovery in some more or less circumloutory manner.

Know then that nature can bear such evidence of the inability of certain women to become mothers of living children, that long after death, even hundreds of years after death, if the skeleton be perfect, medical men could swear that such an incapacity had existed.

With the knowledge I gained I knew that I had the proof of Miss Shedleigh's guilt in my own hands. An examination of the remains of the late body would set the question at rest, and the cabman, if he could identify her, as I had no doubt he could, would bring home the guilt to her if she denied it.

. What should I do ?

My actual duty was at once to inform the legal heir, Sir Nathaniel Shirley, of my discovery. But where was he ?

This I could most readily find out, in all probability, by returning to Shirley House and making further inquiries.

Upon reaching the mansion early on the following morning I could not help looking upon it with a kind of awe, the knowledge being strong within me that only a short previous time it had been to me only as other houses.

The housekeeper welcomed me with a cheerfulness which went to my heart, but I told myself I was to remember that I had to deal with justice not pity. The end of the detective's work is justice, and if he knows his place he must not look beyond that end.

What I was thoroughly to understand in this business of a "tenant for life" was this—that by a fraud people were enjoying property to which they had no claim. This was a state of things which I, as a detective, had a right to set right, and this was the work I intended to complete.

I little thought how sincerely I was to wish I had never moved in this business—that I had never questioned the cabman's wife, and never followed up these inquiries.

It appeared I had given great satisfaction by the work I had completed, and Miss Shedleigh had pleasantly said to the housekeeper that I was a "needle and thread treasure."

I presume it was this success which paved the way to the housekeeper's familiarity. Let that be as it may, it is certain this morning she answered most of my questions—questions which resulted so absolutely out of her own remarks that she could have no suspicion I was cross-examining her, poor dear old lady.

I learnt very much during that long day's work as I sat in the housekeeper's room.

To begin with the master of the house—the housekeeper said he was a most "welcome" master, but "crotchetty, my dear;" and a question or so put me in possession of his crotchettiness, which took no other shape than the endeavour to reap double as much wheat to the acre as had ever been raised by the most advanced farmers.

"Miss Shedleigh says," continued the housekeeper, "that her devoted brother hopes if he succeeds to annihilate starvation—which our miss very truly says must be the case if he doubles the quantity of wheat in the land; seeing that then it will be so plentiful that people will not want bread, as they do now."

I own that this statement touched me; for though I may be a detective, I am still a woman. It struck me as good and beautiful that a man should work all his life for the benefit of his fellow-men; and this the master of Shirley House certainly did, if the house-keeper's statement were truthful. I saw no reason to doubt her words.

Every day throughout the year, I learnt, he was hard at work making experiments either on the land or in a kind of chemist's shop which it appeared he had in the mansion.

He took no pleasure, dressed plainly, ate sparingly, and slept little.

Was he happy? I asked.

"How can he be off being happy," said the old housekeeper, wise in her simple experience, "when all his life is spent in trying to help in the happiness of others?"

I changed the subject. Was he fond of his daughter? I asked.

It appeared he was devoted to his daughter in a plain, simple way; but that he had given her up almost wholly to the care of his sister.

Had he loved his wife very much? I asked.

For a moment the old housekeeper looked as about to assert her dignity again, but apparently she thought better of it, for she smiled and said—

"Yes, my dear; but she was fonder of him."

"Indeed!" I said.

"Yes; though he was almost old enough to be her father. She was but twenty when she died, my dear; and very beautiful she looked, I do assure you, and like a woman who had done her duty. She loved him, my dear, because he was trying to do good to the world; and though she was so much younger than her

husband, it made not the least difference, my dear—it
made not the least difference, I assure you. And when
my lady was dead, she looked like a woman who had
done her duty."

"Did her family approve of the match, ma'am?" I
said, "if I may make so bold as to ask the question?"

"My lady had only her father to consult, my dear;
for the only other relation to the family was Sir
Thomas's brother, now Sir Nathaniel, who was far
away at the time, and who was no welcome visitor
down in Rutlandshire, where we come from   Mr.
Shedleigh lives near London to attend the societies,
and to be amongst gentlemen of science."

"Do you ever see Sir Nathaniel, now?" I asked,
going on with my stitching.

"Oh, no, we never see him; Mr. Shedleigh and he
are not getting on well together, though it's my impression our gentleman allows him an income, and a larger
one than Sir Thomas paid him."

"But—though perhaps you will think I am impu-
dent in asking questions?"

"Not at all," the housekeeper said; "by no means.
You have done that last piece beautifully."

"Then I was going to ask, how is it that Sir
Nathaniel did not get the estates with the title, for
I thought estates and titles generally went toge-
ther?"

Said the housekeeper, "So they do, my dear, but in
*our* case it was different.   Sir Thomas did not inherit
the estates from his father, but made the money which
purchased them by banking, for he was a banker, and

the greater part of the money he began with he had
from a first wife, for they were poor as a family, the sixth
baronet having spent everything he could spend, and
that is the reason Sir Thomas left all the estates to his
daughter, for which I know Sir Nathaniel never for-
gave him—never."

"Where is Sir Nathaniel?" I asked.

"He lives, my dear, though I must say you are very
curious about him, for the best part at Brighton; for
he has been a terrible man, and his health is not what
it ought to be—but for all that he looks a gentleman,
and to speak to, he is one."

"What has he done amiss?" I asked.

But here the housekeeper failed in her reply. She
could only adduce very vague and faint rumours, all
of which tended to prejudice me in favour of the man
to whom I knew it was my duty to submit a history
of my discoveries.

"That there must be something bad about Sir
Nathaniel is certain," said the housekeeper, " or surely
he would be welcome here; and he is not welcome
here, though from here, I am pretty well sure, he gets
what enables him to live as he does—the life of a
gentleman."

There was then a pause. I broke it by saying—

"Was Mr. Shedleigh rich when he married your
young lady?"

" As compared with my lady, my dear—no, but as
not compared with her he was well to do—very well
to do. People down in our parts, of course, said my
young lady, a heiress, and beautiful, had thrown her-

self away; but that was nonsense, my dear, for never was woman happier."

And so the morning wore away. Each moment I picked up some new little fact that might be useful to me; but this is certain, that by the time the house-keeper's dinner arrived, my opinion of the brother and sister Shedleigh was much softened, and I began to look with some doubt in the direction of Sir Nathaniel; for there never was a truer remark than the observation that every grain of scandal helps to weigh down a character.

I may say at once that I remained working more than a week at Shirley House, and by the seventh day my opinion of the Shedleighs was very much altered for the better.

For you must note that we police officers see so much of the worst side of humanity, that, instead of following out a Christian principle, and believing all men to be honest till we find them out to be thieves, we believe all men to be thieves till we are certain they are honest people. Hence, when I dropped upon what I call my great changeling case, I supposed, quite as a matter of course, that I had to do with a crime—as undoubtedly I had; but it should be added at once that I found the crime tinged with a character of almost nobleness. It was crime, nevertheless.

However much I might find my opinion of the Shedleighs improved, I never once wavered in my determination of ultimately informing Sir Nathaniel of the means by which he had been defrauded. This was but justice, and justice, I have already said, is the true end of the detective's work.

For a week I worked in that house, and during that time I had ample opportunities of convincing myself of the characters of the people in it, and of obtaining all particulars which might be useful to me, and about which the housekeeper was able to yield me any information.

It will perhaps be well to condense at this point the work of that week.

In the first place, I think I have said that Sir Nathaniel only inherited the title; the property left by Sir Thomas Shirley to his daughter being made by himself in his capacity of banker. That property consisted of no less than four large landed estates, the income from which was accumulating at what may be called compound interest.

And it was during this week that, by a suggestion from my attorney, the case appeared in another light from that in which it had previously stood. The existence of the little girl and heiress kept the father from the enjoyment of the full income yielded by his late wife's property, which he would have possessed had the child died. It was, therefore, clear that in substituting a living child for the dead infant, and caring for that child, something more was meant than fraud. It was clear that if the desire to obtain the life-possession of the property, and this desire alone, had been the motive for fraud, a person or persons who could commit such an act would not be very delicate in removing the substituted child, or, at all events, in turning her to the best possible advantage. Yet this latter benefit had not been taken, for the

supposed father actually made no claim upon his supposed daughter's estate, but left the whole of the
yearly income to accumulate.    (This fact we learnt
with some difficulty.)

This discovery, into the particulars of which I need
not go, as they are not necessary to the elucidation of
my case nor very creditable to myself, tended still
more to stagger me in my first conviction that the
motive for the substitution of the living for the dead
child arose in the desire to keep possession of the
property.

During that week, I saw Miss Shedleigh twice.
Each time I was working at some kind of needlework.

"Good morning," she said.    (She was going out.)
"Does not working so many hours make your head
ache?"

"No, thank you," I replied.

"The garden is quite open to you when you wish
to walk," she said.

And this was how I came to see Mr. Shedleigh;
for taking advantage of that permission to use the
garden, and grounds (detectives must take all the advantages offered them and all they can otherwise obtain),
I came upon him examining several patches of
wheat of various kinds, and with which produce it
appeared to me the garden was half filled.

He was a wonderfully pleasant, open-faced man,
with dark, deep eyes, and an extraordinarily sweet,
loving expression of countenance—something like that
of a very young and high-class Jewess.

As detectives are always asking questions about

everything which they see and cannot understand, it may be readily guessed that I asked what was meant by growing wheat in a garden.

The answer I obtained made me still more desirous of clearing away that first conviction of mine, to the effect that the substitution of the one child for the other was a crime of greed.

It was from my general informant, the housekeeper, then, I learnt Mr. Shedleigh passed his whole time (in winter in the laboratory, in spring, summer, and autumn in his garden and various trial-fields on the various estates) in making experiments with wheat and other cereals, with a view to increasing the average yield of wheat per acre.—I see I have here indulged in a repetition.

It is not often that criminals try to be so good to their fellow-men—if they did, or could, they would be happier—and, therefore, the probability of Mr. Shedleigh being a criminal became still more faint as I learnt this good trait of his character. My experience is this, that a man or woman who tries to benefit society is rarely bad at bottom—if either were, he or she would not think of any other than him or herself.

Mr. Shedleigh spoke very pleasantly to me, asking me what I thought of this and that, and taking his garden-glove off in order to pull me some strawberries.

I think I went back to the house a little ashamed of myself, and possibly had I come upon an unexpected looking-glass, I might have blushed for Miss Gladden and for her work.

But I never wavered for one minute in my determination to deal out justice, to see Sir Nathaniel and let him know all. I should not have been fitted to my trade had I allowed myself at any time to be turned from my duty by pity, or any argument based on expediency.

The second time I saw Miss Shedleigh I was going home to my small lodging for the night. Said she,—" There is a person living near you—a Mrs. Blenham, I think she is called—who, I believe, is in very poor circumstances, but who hides her poverty out of respect for the better days she has passed through. I wish you would find out the true state of her case. You could perhaps manage it much better than myself."

I did manage it, and I had the pleasure and the pain of seeing Miss Shedleigh doing that best of woman's work, an act of necessary charity.

I had previously learnt from the housekeeper that Miss Shedleigh passed almost all her time in looking after the wants and the children of the parish.

To be plain—these Shedleighs appeared to be about as good folk as any I had ever come across.

And it was I who was to throw down the house!

I was sick of my work by the end of the week, and perhaps, without being sentimental, I may admit that I had made up my mind that I would make no money by it. My legitimate expenses, a return of what I had laid out, and no more. This was my determination with reference to money matters, and one in which I meant to be resolute when dealing with Sir

Nathaniel. For I assure you we detectives are able to have consciences, and to deal in points of honour.

At the end of that week I had my plans set out, and I left Shirley House with some downheartedness, thoroughly well knowing that the next time I entered the place it would be in my true character.

Within six hours from saying "good evening" to Miss Shedleigh I was at Brighton, and in presence of Sir Nathaniel Shirley.

I had sent up word that a person of the name of Gladden (that is the name I assume most frequently while in my business) wanted to see him, and I am bound to say that the answer I heard him send down was anything but complimentary.

I was not baffled of course.

I sent up a card on which I had written "Shirley House business."

"Tell her to come up," I heard him say.

And up "she" went.

From the moment I saw him I didn't like him. In outward appearance a gentleman beyond any doubt. But he belonged to a class of men, I could see at a glance, who never say a rude thing to your face, and never think a kind one either before your countenance or behind your back.

Self!—you could see that in every feature. Gentlemanly selfishness, no doubt; yet nevertheless perfect greed notwithstanding. With some people it calls for far less an effort to be civil than brutal, as conversely many a harsh speaking man has a heart as tender as that of a good woman.

"What do you want?" he said, in a civil tone, as I entered the room, but not looking towards me.

"To see you," I said, in as civil a tone as I could adopt, and shutting the door as I spoke.

He looked at me quickly. He had those shifting eyes which can look at no one or thing for five seconds together. I have often wondered if such people can even look steadily at their own reflections from a glass.

"Who are you, pray?"

"I am a detective," said I.

I saw him visibly shrink in his chair. Woman as I was, I suppose he thought I was a man in that disguise.

He recovered himself in a moment, but I noticed that the skin about his lips went black, and that the lips themselves became of a muddy white.

"Indeed," he said; and by the time he spoke he was, as to his words, quite collected.

Have I said he was about fifty? He was near that age. His hair was thin, and turning grey, but he brought it over his forehead nattily, and curled it effectively. He dressed very young, and in the latest fashion.

"I have come," I said, "to give you some information."

"Go on."

"When Mrs. Shedleigh died, she left a daughter."

"Go on."

I knew by the tone of the words, though they were said with great good breeding, that he was already bored.

"At least," I continued, "it was supposed she died, leaving a daughter."

He was about to start, but he thought a great deal better of it, and remained quiet. I saw, however, that the darkness about his lips increased.

"In fact," I continued, "she did not leave a daughter."

By this time he had quite conquered his agitation, and I am prepared to declare that till the remainder of our interview he never betrayed the least emotion. Whether this callousness was the result of disease or determination I have never been able to decide.

"What did she leave?" he asked.

"No children whatever."

"Ho!—then you mean to say that the Shirley property is mine?"

"Yes."

He turned in his chair, and looked hard at me. I saw he was used to such battles as had experienced him in gaining victories.

"And you know all about it?"

"All about it."

"Why do you come to me?"

"Because you are the proper person to come to."

"Why haven't you gone to them?"

"Who do you mean?" I asked.

"The Shedleighs," he replied.

"I have just left Shirley House," was my answer.

"I thought so," he added, dropping back in his chair; and harsh as this answer may appear, I can assure the reader it was uttered in the softest tones.

"Why," I urged, "how could I have learnt the particulars of this business without going to the house?"

"How much?" he asked, speaking as civilly as ever.

"How much?"

"Yes," he continued, "how much? I suppose, my dear creature—for I accept what you say, and agree that you really are a detective—I suppose you will make your market between me and those Shedleigh people. You have been to them, and now you come to me. How much? I dare say we can manage it. I suppose you will want it in writing?"

"You mean, Sir Nathaniel, what reward do I expect for the information?"

"That's it, my dear creature—how, much? and let me know at once. I suppose I should have to pay more than the Shedleighs if your news is true."

"I beg your pardon," I replied; "but the Shedleighs know nothing at all about the discovery I have made, and I have come to you at once—I have only known the truth of this matter less than a couple of weeks."

This was strictly the truth.

"Ha! I see; you are going to them after leaving me. I don't blame you—rather admire you, in fact. Decided clever woman, if you can carry the affair through. Come, whatever they offer to you to keep the discovery dark I'll pay you double to make it as clear as you can against them—what do you say to that?"

"Excuse me," I said, and I am bound to admit I

already felt as though I should like to get out into the fresh sea air once more; " but I do not care to make money for this work."

He turned and looked at me without any excitement, but with an expression on his face which clearly meant —" Is she a fool, or is she fooling me?"

" All I should require," said I, " would be the return of the money I have laid out, and payment for my time at the ordinary pay I receive from the Government."

" Ha!—exactly," he replied—the expression of his face had changed the moment I began to speak of my reimbursements—" you must have the money you have laid out returned to you, with interest. But first, my dear creature, prove to me that you are really speaking reasonably."

" I shall have to go into long particulars," I said.

He looked calmly at me; then he said—

" You will not perhaps mind much if I smoke, will you?"

" No," I replied, wishing myself, still more heartily, in the fresh air; for I remember it struck me that I was speaking to a being neither alive nor dead, to a kind of man who was neither fit for the grave nor the world. I think I never approached such a passionless human being.

However, it was my business to tell him of his good fortune, if indeed all kinds of fortune were not the same to him.

I began the case exactly as it occurred to me, commencing with the cabman, Flemps, and so working to the culminating point in the evidence of the medical student, George Geffins.

The only interruption he made was to ask the addresses of the cabman and the student. After writing down each, he said, " Yes !" and again became perfectly motionless.

" You know now as much as I do," I said, at last.

And I am willing to admit that I was heartily sick of my man. I apprehend I felt that kind of disappointment and ashamed anger which a man would experience who found that the answer to his offer of marriage was a blank stare.

" I suppose I can do nothing till Monday ?"

" What ?" I asked.

It will be remembered it was late on Saturday night.

" Nothing till Monday ?"

" May I ask, Sir Nathaniel," said I, " what you intend to do on Monday ?"

" Why I suppose, give them into custody."

" CUSTODY ?" I asked.

" Of course ; what else is there to do ? They have been robbing me for five years, and these people deserve to be punished. What else can I do than give them into custody ?"

For a moment, it need hardly be said, it was a difficulty for me to find any reply. At last I said—

" No, Sir Nathaniel, the Shedleighs will not have robbed you, because you will recall that I have told you Mr. Shedleigh has not touched any of the income arising from the Shirley estates."

" But I am not to know that. Much better give

them into custody, detective, and see what comes of it."

I confess I never had anticipated any conduct approaching such cool, business-like mercilessness as this. I had designed a dozen ways of setting to work in this matter during the week, each more considerate than the previous mode as those seven days came to a termination — not one of them approached the idea of giving Mr. and Miss Shedleigh into custody.

"I do not think I would, Sir Nathaniel; much better think it over," I replied.

"Can't see what there is to think over," said the baronet. "They've robbed me, and therefore the only thing to do is—give them into custody."

"You had better sleep on it, sir," said I. "I'll see you on Monday morning, if you please."

"Why not to-morrow?" he asked; "why not go up to-morrow and give them both into custody? I certainly shall."

"Thank you, Sir Nathaniel," said I, and I fancy I spoke a little resentfully; "I do not care to do anything but rest to-morrow, and I am quite sure that the business is not very pressing."

"Not pressing, when they have been robbing me? What nonsense you are talking, my dear creature. Well, if you like, Monday," he said, after he had gone to the window and looked out at the night. "It will be fine to-morrow, and I may as well have the day here as not. Good night, detective."

"Good night."

" Here, ma'am, though, you have not given me your address."

I gave him a card, but not one word. I believe in my own mind I was beginning to quarrel with him.

" This is your right card, I suppose, ma'am ?"

" Of course it is !"

" And you're not fooling me, my dear creature !"

" No ; what could I gain by fooling you ?"

This answer appeared to satisfy him.

" Where are you stopping in Brighton, detective ?"

I gave him the name of a little public-house in the town at which I had rested on several occasions.

" Good night," I said, going towards the door.

Something I suppose in the tone struck even his dull senses.

" If you want any money, or that sort of thing," said he, " I can let you have some." The most positive expression I had yet seen on his face I had now the power of remarking. " I'm not a rich man, you can pull along till to-morrow with——"

And here, with some exertion of a slow will, he took half-a-sovereign out of his porte-monnaie.

I had brought him news which was to put some thousands a year in his pocket.

" No, thank you," I said, hurriedly, and thereupon I left the room.

I did not directly go to the little house I have mentioned.

I crossed the parade, and began traversing the cliff walk.

To those who have walked on a summer moonlight

night high up on the Brighton cliff, with the light
wind whispering as it courses by, the soft sea kissing
the rattling shingle beneath, I have no need to tell how
all those natural, gentle sounds increased, and at the
same time saddened, the mental pain I was suffering.

He had not uttered a word of thanks—he had not
shown a spark of gratitude for his good fortune.
Mind, I was not wounded in my vanity by the
omission of any expression of gratitude to me, but I
was pained that he showed no gratitude whatever.
His good fortune came, and he took it as a right.
I know that I could not avoid associating him with a
certain monkey I had seen at the Zoological Gardens.
This animal—and I watched him for an hour during
that holiday of mine—stood still, holding out his hand
without appearing to think of what he was doing, and
when anything was put in his palm, he closed his
fingers upon it, shoved the goody in his mouth, and
without looking at the donor, or without testifying
any knowledge of the gift, again he dropped his hand
out between the bars of his cage. He took what came
—what more could be wanted of him ?

I had done my duty as an honest detective, and I
was, as I do not mind confessing, since I am out of the
business, sorry I had completed it.

Let me add here, at once, since I have said I have
retired from the practice of detection, that I did not
effect that retirement on the money I made in that
profession. I had a small income left me, which of
course now I enjoy. Detectives rarely make fortunes.

When I reached the little inn to which I have

already twice referred, I made inquiries touching Sir Nathaniel Shirley, and I need not say I heard no good of him. I do not assert that I discovered any positive harm concerning him, but people spoke of him with a kind of reserve, as though their sense of justice and their prejudices were pulling different ways. What, however, I did ascertain certainly agreed with the man. He had a good income, yet he was rarely out of debt. I could understand that. He never could refuse himself what that personage desired to possess; and, though he spent all his income, no one could say who was the better for it. He always had his worth for his money, and the impression appeared to be that he rarely lost in the game of life. Unquestionably, from what I heard, he was frequently made to pay very dear where he had to pay beforehand for his pleasure—but he had it. No one could give him a good word, yet at the same time not a witness was to be found who could pronounce upon him a downright bad verdict.

I am accustomed to fall asleep the moment I get to bed, being healthy, and, as the world goes, honest and clear in my conscience. But that night I could not fall off.

The idea of Sir Nathaniel going up to town and arresting the brother and sister, just after the manner of a machine, kept me hopelessly awake. I felt it was no use appealing to his mercy—I might just as well have harangued the steam hammer in Woolwich Dockyard.

It was a nightmare of itself to imagine Mr. Shedleigh taken away from his good work of trying to make the abundant earth more fruitful—to conceive of Miss Shedleigh divorced from her poor, from her lady-life, and locked up in a prison cell.

What was to be done?

And I fell asleep only when I had quite decided what was to be done. I determined to go up in the morning by the first train, hurry to Shirley House, warn and save them. Such an act was no breach of duty. My work was to obtain Sir Nathaniel his heritage, not to punish Mr. and Miss Shedleigh.

I was awake betimes, though I had slept but for a short period, and getting up with a new sense of imprisonment and weight upon me, I made for the station, and before eleven I was in London.

Taking a cab, I reached the neighbourhood of Shirley House, and there for the first time I faced fairly the enormous difficulty I had to encounter.

I saw her as she was leaving the church. She had a very plain black prayer-book in her hand, and as she came out into the porch, a smile spread upon her face as she addressed first me and then another of those she saw.

She was one of the simplest and most unaffected ladies I ever knew.

She saw me, and nodded.

As she did so, a lady came up and touched her on the arm.

But it was absolutely necessary that I should warn her; so I went up to her and said—

"Miss Shedleigh, may I speak with you?"

"Certainly," she replied, with extreme frankness.

" I mean up at the house."

" Oh, call when you like."

" Can I come now ?"

She looked at me a little eagerly I marked, and then she said smilingly—" Will not to-morrow do ?"

"No," I replied; and it is evident I must have spoken wistfully, for she turned slightly pale.

" Come up at three," she said. " I shall be quite disengaged."

I bowed, and was falling behind her, when she turned quickly, and said, with some little asperity that I marked—

" Is anything the matter ?"

"Nothing but what can be repaired," I said, smiling, for I saw it would not do to alarm her.

But between that time and three o'clock I had discovered new cause for alarm. I saw by reference to my " Bradshaw" (a book with which the library of a detective is never unprovided) that an express train left Brighton directly after church-time. What if Sir Nathaniel should send for me at the Brighton address I had given ?—and what if, finding me gone, he should take that express train and hurry on to Shirley House, with a policeman as his companion ?

He was quite capable of such an act I felt sure, but I hoped, on the other hand, that his natural laziness, and his cynical belief that I had more to gain than lose by him, would together prompt him to refrain from making inquiries about me.

If he, however, did take the 1 P.M. train, it was perfectly competent for him to be at Shirley House by three, the after-lunch hour appointed by Miss Shedleigh for my interview with her. And I desire here to remark that this lady must have been one of most unusual kindness and consideration to give way to my request—I who was almost a stranger to her, and to agree to see me on that day which those ladies most devoted to their poor look upon as private, and to be passed without interference.

The time between one and three was not past very pleasantly.

At three I stood on the door-steps of Shirley House.

I confess I was ashamed of the work I had in hand.

When I came to the room in which I knew I should find her, I declare I was afraid to follow the man, and when being in the chamber, the servant had left it, and she had said, "And pray, my dear, what is it that is so important that it cannot wait till to-morrow?" I had for a few moments no power to answer.

"I am afraid," said I, "you will not feel very great pleasure in what I have to say."

"Let me hear it," she replied, with a fine, delicate smile.

"I learnt a secret of your life quite by chance two weeks since."

"A secret of my life!" she said, after a pause, during which she hesitated, and evidently tried to reassure herself, though she turned paler at the moment.

"Poor thing," thought I, "it is clear she has but one great secret, which indeed is one no longer."

"Yes," I replied, "and I must speak to you about it."

Here there came a little feeling of pride to her support, and she said, though very softly and coolly—

"Must ?"

"Must," I echoed.

"Pray," she continued, speaking a little highly, "to whom am I addressing myself, that I hear such a word as—*must ?*"

"I am a detective," said I, using the phrase which I have so frequently uttered when secrecy has been no longer needful.

"A detective ?" she said, evidently not knowing what such an officer was, and yet too unerringly guessing.

"Yes," I continued, "one of the secret police."

She started, and muttered something to herself. She uttered no cry, no exclamation of fear; indeed my long experience assures me that in the majority of cases where a sudden and terrible surprise comes upon people, the shock is so great that they generally receive the news with but little expression of their feelings. It appears as though shock rather stupifies than excites.

In a very few moments she became comparatively calm.

"What do you want ?" she said.

"Indeed," I answered, "to save you."

"From what ?"

"From the consequences of my duty."

She looked at me intently, and at last she smiled.

"True," she said, "you have your duty to perform as well as others. What does this conversation mean ?"

"It means, Miss Shedleigh," I said, "that I know

the little girl who is in this house is not Mr. Shedleigh's child."

She thought she had prepared herself for the worst, but she had not.

She trembled, and uttered a short, sharp cry, which touched one's very heart.

"There can be no doubt about it," I said, desirous of preventing her from the attempt to fence with me and my information. "The cabman from whom you obtained the little girl pointed out the very spot where he placed the child in your arms. Pray do not fancy the case could not be proved. The doctor, Dr. Ellkins, may be dead, but he said enough to an apprentice he had, and whom I have seen, to show that the late lady could not have been the mother of the little girl who goes by her name. Avoid any proceedings which might be terrible. I do not know, if you denied everything, but that Mrs. Shedleigh's remains might be brought in evidence against you."

These words, as partially I intended they should, shocked her inexpressibly.

"Surely they could not so outrage my poor sister's grave?"

"Indeed you are mistaken," I said; "the law knows no pity while the truth is doubtful."

"But—but what would you have me do?"

"Confess all to Sir Nathaniel Shirley."

"Sir Nathaniel—do you know him?"

She was now truly alarmed. But she did not betray any wild excitement, such as I believe most people would suppose she would have shown.

" I left him only last night !"

A blank, deadly expression, or rather want of expression, stole over her face.

"Then all is indeed lost," said she.

" No ; not yet," I replied.

" Woman, you come from him ?" she said, in a tone of weeping defiance, if that term can be comprehended.

" No, indeed," I replied, " I have come of my own will to warn you against Sir Nathaniel."

" And yet you have come so recently from him." Then catching, as the drowning man at the shadow of himself on the surface of the water, she said—" Perhaps *he* does not know all ?"

" He does," I said, wofully ; " all, even to the addresses of the people necessary to prove his case."

" And you furnished him with this power ?"

" I did.   I grieve to say I was forced to do so."

" Ch, woman, woman ! if you did but know what you have done."

" I have done what it was but justice to do."

" You have done a wretched thing," she said.   " Sir Nathaniel will have no mercy upon *me*, and I must suffer—I alone must suffer."

" Mr. Shedleigh," said I ; " had not he better know——"

" Know ?   Know what ?"

" Why, that the—the fraud has been discovered."

" Woman, he thinks the child his."

" What ! he has heard nothing of the truth ?"

" Nothing ; the deception was practised on him

in pity, and now you come, after four years' peace, and may perhaps kill him."

"But," said I, apologetically, "remember you have deprived Sir Nathaniel Shirley of his property."

"Sir Nathaniel—Sir Nathaniel," she repeated; "it were well for him that he should never be rich, and well for him that what was done was well done."

I shook my head. I knew that right was right, and that the property was by law the baronet's.

"Sir Nathaniel," she cried, beating her right foot upon the ground—by this time all fear for herself was past—"Sir Nathaniel, had he obtained the property, would have been a beggar by this time, whereas he would never have been unprovided for had you not learnt my secret. Now he will take the estates, though, if the wish of the late owner, my sister-in-law, could be consulted, I know she would keep every poor acre from her uncle. Oh, woman, woman, if you could but judge of the injury you have done!"

"I shall have a quiet conscience, Miss Shedleigh, whatever happens," I said; "but it will be quieter if you will but let me, who have been the means of bringing destruction near you—if you will but let me save you. I am afraid of Sir Nathaniel, he seems so merciless."

"First hear me," she said. "Before you speak again you shall hear my excuse for my conduct—hear me, nor speak till I have finished. I know not by what terrible chance it has happened that you should learn a secret which I thought lay hidden in my sister's grave and my heart. How you have pieced your information together I am unable to imagine, but since you know so much I would have you know the rest, and in learning it, believe that I am to be as much pitied as to be blamed."

I bowed, feeling rather that I was the poor lady's prisoner than she in a measure mine.

"You know my brother's wife brought a dead child into the world; you know that that child, being dead when born, in event of my sister-in-law's death her property could not be enjoyed by her husband for life, simply because the child had not breathed. It was she who put it into my head first. My sister's distress came upon us very suddenly, weeks before we expected, and no preparations had been made. When she learnt that she could not be a mother, news which she inferred rather than learnt, I believe the humiliation felt by her was so great that it led to her death, as certainly as that before she died she prayed Heaven to send her a child to comfort her husband after she was gone, for from the moment the doctor left her she never believed she would rise from her bed again. It was when she cried out that many a poor woman would be glad to find a home for her puny child, that the idea came upon me of the woman and infant I had seen pass the house about nine, as I came in at the south gate, and to whom I had spoken. I gave that poor woman some silver, pitying her much when she told me her child was barely a fortnight old.

"Perhaps I had no right to speak of this mother and child to my sister, for she was not quite herself at any moment from the time the doctor left to the moment of her death—perhaps I should not have excited her already excited brain. But no sooner did she comprehend what I said than she cried that heaven had heard her prayer, and bade me go and seek the woman. I refused at first, but she looked so powerful that it seemed to me as though she was inspired, and so I said yes, I would go, and I went quickly from the house and down the road, in the direction which the poor woman had taken.

"And when I heard the child crying from within that miserable common cab, I also thought that Heaven had had pity on us. I know now how guilty I was— how very guilty I was.

"I had not left the house twenty minutes when I was returning with the child, and when I came into her room, carrying the infant, I found her still alone, though I had taken no precautions to keep her by herself. She cried out, saying Heaven had been kind, and declaring how a good angel had brought it to me.

"There was no one in the house to see my act. It was the free-school *fête* day, and the servants, with the exception of one, were at Velvet Dell, three miles away—the only girl that had remained at home had gone down to the surgery with the doctor.

"Before a quarter past ten, at which time the servants came trooping home—they had been given to ten, and there had been nobody to send for them during that terrible hour-and-a-half—before a quarter past ten she was dying in the presence of Dr. Ellkins, who looked much confused and puzzled.

"Even then I felt the enormity of the crime in which I had engaged—I did indeed. Even then I felt that had I opposed my sister's wild idea instead of having fostered it, she herself would never have laid such injunctions upon me as she did.

"It was before the doctor arrived for the second time—and the moment the lady's maid returned with the medicine, I sent her back for the medical man—it was before Dr. Ellkins came again that she had commanded me to swear that I would never tell the truth about the child, she saying—'Heaven sent it, Heaven sent it, though it was but a poor woman's daughter.'

"She told me," the poor lady continued, looking eagerly in my face—it was now half-past three, as I saw by the great French clock on the mantelpiece, so that if Sir Nathaniel had come up by the 1 P.M. train he would soon be at Shirley House—"she told me that it would break down Newton—Newton is Mr. Shedleigh—if he lost both her and his child together, and that he was doing the world good, and that nothing must stop his work. You know," she continued, breaking off, "she married my brother because she rather admired his intellect than himself.

"She said also I should save a poor child from destitution, and finally she declared that she willed that her uncle should not have her property—that he was wicked and wasteful, and that her husband ought to have it to do good with.

"And then, as I heard the ring at the hall-door, and as *she* knew it was the doctor returned, she raised her

right hand, looked wildly at me, and said—' I command
—in the name of God.'

"She never spoke aloud again. She only whispered
messages to her husband, and taking the doctor's head
between her hands, whispered something to him which
made the poor gentleman tremble.

"Then she died as the servants came trooping into
the house from the school treat.

"I knew how wrong I had been long before the
next day. But when I looked at her still face, my
dear, I could not disobey her; and I felt more unable
to oppose her last wishes when our housekeeper, Mrs.
Dumarty, whispered to me that she looked in her sleep
as though *she* had done her duty.

"I know how wicked it all was, but as the years
have rolled on I hoped I had done all for the best.
My brother, when he came home at the end of those
two days, found a deep consolation in the little child
—and I could not tell him he was weeping over a
stranger.

"I fell very ill myself, my dear, after the burial,
and they thought it was grief which had overpowered
me. But I am afraid it was more my conscience than
my sorrow, though I am sure I loved my sister very
dearly.

"As the years have gone on I have thought I had
done all for the best. Sir Nathaniel has received a
large income yearly from me; for I came into a good
property very soon after Mrs. Shedleigh's death. And I
have made my will in his favour, so that he could
never have been poor through my action—whereas had

he inherited the estates he would soon have wasted them, for he is quite a prodigal.

"Now you know all. You tell me, my poor woman, you wish to save me. How can you?"

Long before the good lady asked me that woful question, I had hung my head in sorrow and regret.

Don't suppose we detectives have no soft places in our hearts because we are obliged to steel them against the daily wickedness we have to encounter. It is not long since that one Tom White, a detective of the R Division, was shocked by seeing a young thief, whom he was pursuing, fall dead at his feet. Tom White never was the thing after that; so he must have had some soft place in his heart, poor fellow.

I confess I was sorry I had shown Sir Nathaniel the cards he now held.

Could I save her?

I was determined to do my best.

"Well?" she said, a little wearily, and coming to me, she put her hand lightly on my shoulder.

I confess I never felt a hand rest so heavily upon me, though her touch was as delicate as that of the lady she must have always been.

"I am very sorry——" I said.

"There is no need," she replied.

"And very much ashamed——"

"Why, my dear? *You* have done your duty, whatever I may have omitted."

"I would rather be you," I said.

I confess these replies of mine were sentimental for a detective. Still, as they were uttered, I repeat them.

And lo! as I spoke, there came a sudden, fierce, imperious peal upon the great gate-bell.

As I glanced at the great clock, and read "a quarter to four," I felt certain the visitor was Sir Nathaniel Shirley.

He did not even send a card up; only his name, with the statement that he must see either Mr. or Miss Shedleigh.

The man added that he had replied his master was out in the grounds, but that his lady was in the house.

Positively Sir Nathaniel felt himself already so much master that he had not waited for permission to come upstairs.

"Good day, Catherine," said the baronet, entering; "I heard you were in, and so I did not wait for the man coming down again."

The coward! he was afraid she would gain the more advantage the longer the time before he saw her.

As he spoke, he glanced at me as though I stood his enemy. He had held out his hand to me, taken what I offered without remark (like my friend the ring-tailed at the gardens), and now he was ready to snarl because he supposed I had nothing more to give.

When the man had left the room, he turned to me and said the following words, in as sweet a tone as he would have used for inquiring after my health.

"I thought I should find you here, you baggage!"

"Sir!" said I, and I think I was justified in the exclamation.

"Now, you don't get from me a rap," he said, still in

a sweet voice, but with one of the ugliest countenances ever I remember to have remarked.

It is certain he was a miserable tyrant—infinitely more dangerous to his friends (if he had any) than to his enemies.

"And what have you got to say?" he asked, turning to Miss Shedleigh.

"What have you?" she asked, and her voice was as surprisingly steady as her manner was collected.

"You know what I have come for."

"Yes," she said, quite gently.

"So I have found you out at last?" he said.

It was clear he had passed *me* over in the matter as though I had never known of it.

Here I looked at him—perhaps a little keenly—and then it was that I noticed the blackness I had marked on the previous night round his mouth was still more observable as he stood confronting his niece's sister-in-law, and with as ugly a look of victory upon his face as a man could wear.

"One moment!" here I interposed with.

"Well?" he said, speaking sweetly, but looking at me as though I was one of the worst kind of dogs.

"I'm not wanted here. I will leave the room."

"You will do no such thing!" said he, brave I presume because he had but to do with a couple of women.

"Indeed!" said I, "take care. You know I'm a police-officer; impede me in the execution of my duty at your peril. I say I am not wanted here, and I think fit to leave the room."

As I moved towards him another change in his face became apparent. Whether it was that he turned more generally pallid, and so he looked darker about the mouth—or whether the blackness around his lips did increase, it is certain that a change occurred.

He stood in my way till I came near him, and then he fell back almost as though I had touched him.

I left the room, but before I did so, I said to Miss Shedleigh—" I shall be outside. If you call to me I shall hear you. Don't be afraid of this gentleman."

Then I left the room.

What was said I never learnt.

The need of my attendance was brought about by a scream on the part of the lady, whereupon I thought fit to run into the room, where I found——

But before I reach that last scene but one in this narrative I should make the reader acquainted with some observations I made.

Upon reaching the corridor beyond the room in which the war was to be fought out, I found myself near a window which, with the ordinary eyes of a detective, I knew must be in a plane with the windows of the room I had just left, simply because the view from it was such as I had noticed, without much intention of doing so (for observation of all before him becomes a habit with the detective), from those openings.

The whole of these windows looked over the sweep before the house, which was enclosed by a wall in front, and two heavy solid wooden gates. In each gate, however, was a wicket, one of which was open,

and through it I saw the faces of two men who were
peering from the cab, the top of which only I could
see beyond the wall and gates.

Faintly as I saw their faces, and under such disad-
vantages, I recognised one of them as that of a policeman known to me.

Beyond any question the other individual was also
an officer.

So, he had shown no sign of mercy.   He had not
sought to compromise with the Shedleighs, by having an
interview with them.   Cruel as he was, he had brought
down two policemen with him, and it struck me at
once that it was the time necessary for the procuring
of these officers which accounted for the half hour's
grace he had shown before he arrived.   To arrest
Miss Shedleigh at an earlier hour than that at which
now he was proceeding to accomplish that act, he
must have got up early in the morning—a piece of
severity which, doubtless, he could not force upon
himself, though it was to lead the earlier to the exhibition of his cruelty.

I had been watching the faces through the open
window—for it was the end of July, fine weather—and
the gate-wicket, and without being seen myself, for
about two minutes, when I heard the officer I knew say—

"There he is—he's coming."

It was not much above a whisper, but the breeze
set my way, and my ears are uncommonly fine and
sharp ; indeed, I believe it is admitted that we women
detectives are enabled to educate our five senses to a
higher pitch than are our male competitors.

Clearly, the officers could see across the gardens, and round by the house over the grounds, whilst I was only to make observations in an opposite direction.

But in a moment I heard a clear light voice singing lowly and sweetly. I recognised it in a moment for that of the master of the house.

There was no sound but the rustle of the light wind (twittering the leaves and rippling patches of wheat) to interfere with his voice, and indeed it seemed to me as though the murmur made with his voice a sweet chorus.

He came round by the house, the volume of his voice increasing as he did so, and then he passed away on the other side, his voice dying away till the note of the wind was louder than his hymn.

The policemen followed him with their sight as far as they could, and if you have seen a cat lose a mouse you can comprehend the style of look upon the officers' faces as their charge went round the corner of his own house.

I suppose this episode had taken up about two minutes of time.

But this is only guesswork.

Suddenly a quick, sharp, shrill scream.

Then—silence.

As I heard the officers leaping from the cab and cranching over the gravel, I ran forward and broke in rather than opened the door.

There lay Sir Nathaniel on his face.

Two or three yards away from him knelt Miss

Shedleigh, her hands as tightly clasped as they could be, and pressed against the wall.

I may say at once—he was DEAD.

Afterwards, when the lady could speak calmly, she told me she had been certain it was death as he fell. She knew the family disease had grasped him—that fell heart disease which had killed his brother, which had helped in a measure to destroy his niece, Mrs. Shedleigh.

She declared she saw upon his face as he fell that expression which she had seen in death upon the countenance of her sister-in-law, and of that lady's father, at whose bedside she had been at the time of his death.

The policemen, I need not say, were in the house almost before I entered the room, into which they got quite as soon as the servants.

But before they had reached their client's dead side I had found a line of conduct to take.

The baronet was deceased. Very well—then all things were as they were before I told him of what was, perhaps, his good fortune, though he died over it; for, from what I heard, I doubt if he would have expired in his own bed but in a government one, had he been at liberty much longer to carry on his very bad life.

This question only stood in my way—

Had he told the police the exact state of affairs?

I guessed he had refrained from doing so. I felt sure he was a man who would say no more than was needed. It could not have been necessary to report at the station the history I had given him.

The course I took will perhaps be most quickly understood by a report of the words I used.

You may guess that the officer of the two who knew me was considerably taken aback by finding me in the room when he entered it.

"Blackman," said I, when the doctor had been, when he had pronounced his opinion (which did not take long), and when there was breathing time for the household once more—"Blackman, what on earth were you here for?"

"*He* brought us."

The emphasis on "*he*" plainly proved it was the dead man which was meant.

"What did he say?"

"Why, that he wanted to give his brother and his sister-in-law into custody for robbing him."

"Yes—he was MAD," said I.

Blackman turned all manner of colours.

"Lord!" said he, turning at last quite red, "and to think that though I thought him such a queer customer, and the job such a queer job—to think as *I* didn't see that. Of course, G. (I am called G. by the force), *you* is here on that business?"

"Precisely," said I.

"Of course—*I* see it all."

"Of course you do," said I.

And it is astonishing how my explanation was accepted by all concerned in the inquest, and even by the general public.

[I have not much hesitation in telling this tale, however, for now, by certain events, no one has been wronged by the substituted child, for she has played *her* part out in the play of this world.]

Sir Nathaniel's pocket-book, however, gave me a fright, for it contained the addresses of Flemps the cabman, and Mr. Geffins the medical student. However, Miss Shedleigh was out of the way when the cabman gave his evidence, she having been a witness at the opening inquiry (together with myself), and the cabman offering his evidence at the adjourned examination. Flemps's evidence was not full. He had to look at the deceased gentleman for identification, and his evidence ran to this effect—" Which if ever I sord the gent afore, take my badge away and give me three months."

I was out of the way when this evidence was adduced, nor did I show myself when the following witness, Mr. Geffins, deposed that he had never seen the " subject before in life."

Sir Nathaniel's medical adviser was called, and I have no doubt this gentleman, of great note—for Sir Nathaniel would have everything of the best of its kind, from his medical adviser to his blacking—I have no doubt that this gentleman considerably tended to close the inquiry quickly. He deposed, with some degree of pain evidently, a condition which gave his statement more weight, that the deceased gentleman had been suffering for some time from disease of the heart—a family complaint ; that this disease had been much accelerated in its progress by the loose mode of life in which the baronet had lived, and that he had warned him only a few previous days to avoid any great excitement, as it might be dangerous. "I added," said the witness, "that if Sir Nathaniel kept himself quiet he might live into a green old age—a result of which there was a possibility, but little probability."

Hearing this evidence, to which was added that of the *post-mortem* examination, I could readily comprehend why his face, and especially the skin about his mouth, assumed such appearances as they did each time I saw him ; and I could also understand how thoroughly well-fitted by nature he was to agree with his doctor's direction to avoid excitement.

It was clear his was a nature where selfishness provokes a man, habitually callous and insensible, till his natural licentiousness moved and carried him beyond himself.

I say I have no doubt the medical evidence against Sir Nathaniel blunted the inquiry—a result not proceeding from any wilful hoodwinking of justice, but simply from the fact that human judgment must be made up of previous impressions. When men hear a dead man has been bad, they surely are not so desirous of talking over his coffin as they would be did they learn he had lived an honourable life.

The coroner's "Oh !" showed how much even an old legal official could be impressed by a witness deposing against the gentleman on trial. I know that coroner. He is not a very moral man, but he offered that hypocrisy of faultiness, open respect for virtue.

Miss Shedleigh's evidence, under my direction, had been given to the effect that Sir Nathaniel came about money matters ; that when he fell he was about to seek Mr. Shedleigh, and that she had run forward entreating him not to carry out his intention.

And when the coroner and the jury learnt that Sir Nathaniel had for some years been supported by the Shedleighs, Miss Shedleigh was asked no more questions.

My tale of a "Tenant for Life" is done. It has been told to show how simple a thing may lead to most important consequences. Had I not taken that ride in Flemps's cab on a Sunday, I never could have learnt that Sir Nathaniel Shirley was the actual heir to the Shirley estates.

However, I am glad the baronet never possessed them.

When the little girl died (about eight months since) Mr. Shedleigh gave up the estates to the next heir after Sir Nathaniel. As it had never been proved that the child was not his, he by law was Tenant for Life; but he waved his right, not because he had learnt the secret of his sister's life—for we kept it to ourselves—but because he felt that the only owner of the Shirley property should be one who claimed to be of the Shirley pedigree.

So it all came right at last, and no man was punished in order to procure justice.

# GEORGY.

I AM about to relate here a tale which, as far as intricacy goes, has little to recommend it. But though it is a narrative of plain-sailing, I am inclined to give it a place here, because it once again illustrates pretty clearly how often it happens that popular and perhaps justly-grounded beliefs are in practice contradicted.

It is generally believed that a detective is not to be taken in. There is no greater error in relation to the police force. Once get the confidence of an individual of the home-blues—and I know no man (or woman) so easily and persistently deceived. I grant you that it is not often we yield our confidence, but when we do the action is perfect.

Then again, it is generally supposed that boys in their crime are audacious rather than cunning. This is a great error. The cunning of a boy-criminal is generally brilliant.

Again, it is frequently stated that the young in crime suffer a good deal more from remorse than their brethren in rascality of a riper age. This is a belief which is not always borne out in practice.

I give this narrative because it combines, in a very simple form, the facts of a deceived detective, a cunning boy, and a young criminal quite destitute of remorse.

The deceived detective was myself.

The cunning boy was Georgy.

The young and utterly remorseful criminal, Georgy.

As I said before, Georgy is not the hero of a good plot ; but perhaps his tale is worth hearing nevertheless, as showing what can be done by nineteen years and a cool hand.

This George Lejune was a dashing young gentleman indeed, and charming also. You could not be in the company of the boy for half an hour without taking a liking to him.

Bright-eyed, bright-lipped, laughing, clever (in his way), earnest, and upon the whole gentlemanly, he was rather a superior kind of lad.

Moreover, he was fairly modest ; and during the few short months I knew him, I never found out that he had any pet weakness.

He dissipated in no form ; he was too healthy-looking for that. The only approach to weakness which I observed was now and then a tendency to Hansom cabs, which I used to hear roll up to the house next door after I had gone to bed.

I taxed him once with the cabs, but he had so good an answer for me that I dismissed those vehicles from my mind at once.

"You see," said he, " I don't pay full fare, or anything like it. I wait till a cab is going my way, and then I tip cabby a tanner or a bob ; and so I ride home for next door to nothing."

What could be plainer than that statement? Only it wasn't true.

Then, again, when he told me that though he made but thirty shillings a week, he had it all to spend in pocket-money, as his mother had an annuity, that was an answer to his being well-dressed, and to his spending a little money. For upon thirty shillings a week pocket-money, you can have a decent coat to wear and carry clean gloves. Thirty shillings a week pocket-money—a plain statement enough.

Only it wasn't true.

I was living at the time (on business) at a small house at the east-end of London, and next door to the young man's mother. I took a liking to the boy from his turning out early of a morning, and singing like a lark as he looked at his flowers and fed his linnets. I defy you, if you have any heart, to mark a handsome boy, blithe, frank, and courteous, and not feel inclined to shake hands with him. I assure you this George shook you by the hand in the jolliest manner possible.

As I can make acquaintances very quickly, I was soon friendly with the mother; and finding her a very plain, simple-hearted woman, I was frequently in her house whenever my business would admit of my taking an hour to myself.

"I'm afraid Georgy spends too much money," said she to me one night.

And so I, the detective, who by such a speech should have been put upon my guard at once, I said—

"No, Mrs. Lejune, the boy doesn't. He is young, and while he keeps his eyes bright and his spirits up, you need not be afraid."

It is true he sometimes came home late, but I argued with myself that Bow was a long way from the theatres, and that he might be in the habit of going half-price to the pit.

But one evening, when I was at the house of his mother, who did not appear to be superabundantly well off, I confess the boy did startle me by appearing with what was evidently a diamond ring set open, and circling his little finger.

" Dear me, Georgy ! says his mother," " what a fine ring you've got there. You've been wasting your money again. What is the use of your working extra time and making extra money if you spend it so wastefully."

"Indeed !" I said, "he must have given quite a handsome amount for that ring—it is a diamond."

" Dear me, Georgy !" says his mother, " why whatever have you been buying diamonds for ?"

" It's only one, mother; and besides, I didn't steal it, it was given to me."

" Dear *me*, Georgy, who could have given you a diamond ?"

" Why, mother," says he, laughing gaily all the time, "don't you remember I told you Lieutenant Dun, Mr. Clive Dun's brother, had come home on furlough ; and don't you remember that I went to Dun's with Dun's friend, Will, on Friday, to a night at cards—well, Lieutenant Dun gave me the ring."

*N.B.* This conversation took place on the Monday.

" But, my dear Georgy, you've only seen the gentleman twice !"

" Well, mother, I can't help that ; but the lieutenant said I was a very jolly fellow, and he gave me the ring."

As I said before, this was on the Monday.

He was only nineteen.

On the Friday following, as I learnt afterwards, he said to his mother at breakfast—

" Mam dear, you must give me a kiss after breakfast, because you wont see me till to-morrow."

" My dear Georgy," I am quite sure she replied, " where are you going ?"

" Oh, the Duns have asked me to their uncle's to dinner, and it's ten miles out of town, and they will give me a bed."

So he kissed his mother. " My dear," said she, " as light hearted as ever he kissed me, and he went out and talked to the linnets, and plucked two or three flowers and put them in his coat, and he went away down that front garden, which there it is, singing as happy as any one of those dear linnets."

And yet he had taken the long farewell of his mother.

He has never seen her again.

I think in all probability he never will see her again—and this probability he must have been aware of as he went singing down the garden—singing, not because he had a light heart, but because he was cunning enough not to show the least suspicion, and because I suppose he could not feel remorse.

When Friday night came he was not missed because he was not expected home.

When Saturday morning came he was not missed because it was supposed that he would go straight to office from the hospitable country house.

Therefore it was only when the mother had waited up all Saturday night and Sunday morning had arrived, that any distinct notion would be come at that perhaps something had happened.

But now it was Sunday, and upon that day the innocent mother could give no warning of the actual state of things, no warning, that is, *at the office of the boy's employers.* So another day passed, and it was only on Monday morning that the firm got their shock.

For "Georgy," the gay, singing lad of nineteen, had managed matters so well both at home and abroad, that no suspicion of the truth could be taken at the office till the Monday.

This was his little arrangement.

Arriving on the Friday morning at his office, (after giving the very last good-bye to his mother) he asked permission to leave at noon, as he wanted to go into the country, and he further requested leave till the Saturday (the next day) at noon.

The firm, or rather its representative, gave way, being a sufficiently easy-going man.

"Oh, by the way," says Georgy, "as I'm going in the country, sir, I may want a little money—if you will give me a cheque for the month I shall be glad."

"Oh, certainly," says the principal, and I have no doubt the request for that poor little cheque helped to put off the uneasiness that principal was to feel sooner or later.

The whole business was so plausible—the visit to the country on the Friday, the permission for a couple of hours' grace the next morning, and finally, the request for the month's small salary, were all so rational and all so agreeing in themselves, that there was no room for suspicion—not even for that of a detective.

Now mark how well the plan was laid.

He had got clear till the Saturday at noon. Then he was not expected till noon on Saturday. But the office, in common with most others, was closed on a Saturday at two; therefore, when the closing hour for the week came, Georgy would but be two hours behindhand, a space of time which might be accounted for by supposing he had missed a train.

This was the literal construction put upon his absence, and therefore the firm went home with a serene breast, and passed Sunday without any doubt or uneasiness in reference to Georgy.

Now it will be seen that had this singing innocent of nineteen absconded on any other day than Friday, suspicion would have been aroused within twenty-four hours, or at their expiration; whereas by choosing Friday he got nearly *three* days' clear start before he was missed at his office, or any warning of his departure from his innocent mother could reach the city establishment.

In my detective experience I have come across much fine delicate management, but I never encountered an instance of more decided and well plotted rascality than that of George Lejune.

Of course within an hour of suspicion being raised, it came out that there were defalcations. Before the day was out a deficit of nearly £300 was discovered; the existence of which deficit was clearly attributable to the young man.

He had deceived every soul about him—me amongst the rest.

At any moment during the previous two months he had been liable to be taken into custody; at any moment he might have found himself ruined for life, and yet, to my certain knowledge, he was apparently happy, and evidently healthy, bright-eyed, and bright-lipped to the very last.

The young man could not have had any comprehension of morality, and, at the same time his bodily health must have been wonderful.

Of course the very pretty facts spread with great rapidity. The city detectives were especially busy in circulating the news.

The felonious performance had been effected in the most delightfully simple way.

The firm was careless in money matters — rarely checking its banker's book. This the very young gentleman discovered almost directly he had taken possession of his office-stool, and, it is possible, at once he made up a felonious mind. I should add that he was not altogether more than three months in the employment of the firm he robbed.

The whole of the large embezzlements were effected within two months of his absquatulation. His plan was marvellously simple, but ingenious.

My readers may know that it is the plan in the city, when paying into the bank, to send a paper with the amount to be put to the account of the customer, which amount is the total of the bills, cheques, notes, gold, and silver paid in—such items being put down separately, and the whole added together.

This draft, of money to be paid in, was made out by the cashier of the office honoured by the young Lejune, and then Georgy became the porter to the bank. His operation was very simple—suppose the draft stood thus :—

## The City Consolidated Bank.

### LIMITED.

............................................186

*Credit* ......................................................

| Bank Notes ................... | ¯50 | | |
| Country Notes .............. | 40 | | |
| Gold ......................... | 125 | | |
| Silver ....................... | 20 | 19 | 6 |
| Cheques, etc. ................ | 35 | | |
| *Country Cheques and Bills* NOT DUE— | | | |
| TOTAL £ | 270 | 19 | 6 |

JAMES HOOGLEY (*the Cashier*).

It is particularly requested that the DRAFTS may be paid in before HALF-PAST 3 O'CLOCK, and on Saturday by HALF-PAST 2.

The first manœuvre was to forge the cashier's name to a new draft, made an exact counterpart of the last, except that the gold item instead of being £125 was £25, so that the total stood £170 instead of £270.

Now mark the brilliancy of the felony.

It was he who had the carrying to and fro of the bank-book.

At the bank they would discover no fraud because the book agreed with the draft, while as soon as anything like suspicion were raised in the office he would be the first clerk applied to, to ascertain what had happened.

Now suppose in the given case the cashier had discovered that only £170 19s. 6d. instead of £270 19s. 6d., had been paid in, and suppose that cheerful young man, Lejune, had been called to explain the matter, what would his reply have been?

"Oh, I see; it's only a mistake in a figure—a 1 for a 2;" and this argument would have stood very well, because all the rest of the figures would tally in the bank-book and office cash-book.

"Dear me!" the cashier would have said; "go down to the bank and have it altered."

"Yes, sir."

He would then have gone, and never come back again.

It is true he would have had a poor start, but that was a risk he ran.

When I came to examine the case I found it ex-

hibit such thought and study that it was some time
before I could persuade myself that he had not been
helped by an old and experienced hand.

I am now convinced that Georgy was not only quite
capable of managing without help, but I am quite
sure he relied upon his own abilities.

It must have been very far from pleasant for all
George Lejune's young friends, but they had mutually
to endure that agony. I refer to their examination
and the investigation of their premises by the detective force of the city of London.

One gentleman was so shocked that he took to his
bed over the business.

Meanwhile, George had got clean away, and the
police (they were the city police be it remembered)
could gain no tidings of him.

His ability in deception was wonderful.

He had deceived his mother as to his expenditure
by saying he worked and was paid for overtime. This
accounted for his absence and his ease in the matter of
cash-payments.

And his companions, his fellow-clerks, and also myself, he had blinded by the statement that he had all
the money he earned to spend on himself, his mother
being in the receipt of an annuity.

The annuity statement—*as* a statement—was strictly
true, but he neglected to add that the income did not
go beyond seven pounds ten per annum.

This explanation had of course served to cover his
ordinary expenses. But he had to manage to avoid ex-

hibiting any remarkable flush of cash before his companions. He would never spend more than they. This was ascertained beyond any question.

But as the slow discoveries of the police were pieced together, it came out clearly enough, that when alone, or in company who were not aware of his actual circumstances, he would launch out into handsome extravagances, always, however, liking to have something for his money.

He would take a private box, it appeared, after a nice quiet dinner at the Tavistock—which he rather patronized than otherwise—or he would take his ease in a stall at the Italian, dressing at the Tavistock. He had much musical taste.

The opera or play over, he would take a quiet chop, it appeared, at Evans's, where he was rather looked upon as a gentleman. Then taking a fast cab home to Bow he would to bed, and rise cheerfully, and to all appearances contentedly, to coarse coffee and thick bread and butter, beyond which plain breakfast the rigid economy of the household would not go.

I doubt if anybody suspected George Lejune. When he was found out there was no need for suspicion.

He spent his money, or rather his employers', so judiciously, that nobody could suspect him. For instance—he had one pair of opera-glasses which were left at the Tavistock, and another pair at an establishment much affected by him—a place I will call Aggerney Vick—an establishment which is not much to look at, but where you can pay half-sovereigns to

see prize-fights, or running matches, or walking en-
counters.

I have heard that he would take his *lorgnettes* and
seat at this place with the air of a self-conscious and
well-bred prince.

There was no *blague* about him. He did everything
in a gentlemanly and an effective manner. He was
always brilliantly civil, courteous, attractive, and
never exceeded the margin of good language, while he
bore with much friendly patience the strong expressions of others.

And to think that all these social good qualities
should end in his printed description all over the
walls of London—his height, the colour of his hair,
eyes, and finally, the statement (which was emi-
nently untrue) that he had a slightly Jewish cast of
countenance.

He had appropriated the money he had taken in
three divisions. The first, a month before he said
*bon voyage ;* the second, a fortnight previous to that
event ; and the third, on that very fatal Friday
morning.

The last appropriation was the most audacious, and
this he covered with the meek request that as he
was going into the country he should be, glad of his
month's salary.

On the Thursday, so great was the laxity evident
in the conduct of affairs at the office, no smaller a
sum in gold (Georgy was too wise at any time to take
anything but gold, though it is evident he was too
luxurious a rascal to be bored with a weight of metal,

for it was found out he exchanged his gold for notes in several instances)—no less a sum in gold than £75 was left unbanked and in the office safe.

Georgy was last in the office, after the others had gone, and he showed this gold to a friend—one of those to whom the police were so specially unobliging after the catastrophe—commenting upon the bad management which allowed such a sum to remain at the office.

It went next morning.

Wherever he passed that evening, it is very clear he plotted those next days' performances, which ended, as far as he was concerned, so successfully. It is possible he saw that the game could not be carried on much longer, that the difference between the cash and bank-books must terminate in discovery, and the result be his fall. Therefore, no doubt he argued, as there was a good golden haul in £75, it was a fine opportunity to be off, as the next day was Friday.

Hence that little arrangement by which he got clear away, with three days' clear start. On that Friday morning, as he expected, he was sent with the £75 of gold to the bank. He forged his draft, he paid in the money this time without any nice reference to figures, he left the pass-book to be made up, he returned to the office (in all probability with the gold in his pocket) he asked for his leave of absence till two o'clock the next day, as he was going in the country. Then he suggested a cheque for his month's money, with the idea, it may be presumed, of getting all he could, and then he said " good day, sir." And went.

I believe the business of that four pound cheque as

the month's wages was a more difficult pill to swallow on the part of the principal than any bolus in the case. " It was *so* cool," he said.

But Georgy being now safe for three days, the accusing bank-book being at the bank, and he himself having laid his little plans so cleverly, he was in no hurry to quit the city ; and, indeed, to set out the better, he went round to his usual dining place and had a very festive little lunch, finishing up with black coffee after the French fashion.

He was in no hurry to go.

Here he was very gay, brilliant, charming, setting out he was going down into the country to dine with Lieutenant Dun. He was very gay with Amelia, the waitress, and gave her a florin for herself.

He chatted with all those he knew, and he made several small engagements for the following week, and one for Sunday to hear his favourite preacher—a Mr. Mellow.

Then he went, gay to the last, nodding through the plate glass window, and showing some of the very handsomest teeth in the city.

He had deceived every one.

He had told me and others his mother left him his money to spend as he liked—on the contrary she was poor, and took three-fourths of it.

He informed his mother what money he spent was the result of overtime ; he had never been paid for overtime.

He had given his friends to understand he had eight pounds a month ; he was paid four.

He spent modestly before his old friends—when he was by himself he would pay a guinea for a stall at the opera, and a similar sum before taking possession of that stall, as the price of a dinner.

But the most fallen trait in his character was the appropriation of the diamond ring.

The detectives beginning to make inquiries, the name of Lieutenant Dun, as a gentleman who had given Georgy a diamond ring, was mentioned. The lieutenant was found out, and then he discovered where his diamond ring had gone to.

This cheerful Georgy had left the card-party to which reference has been made, and gone into a bedroom, and after coolly taking the ring off the glass, he had returned to the card-table and played more cheerfully than ever.

"I do assure you," said the lieutenant's brother to me—for the sake of the mother I had made some inquiries—"I do assure you he ate quite a handsome supper (he having the jewel in his pocket all the time), and he must have been perfectly at his ease, because I remember his discussing, with perfect justice, the merits of two varieties of cream in our *soufflé*."

Just think of it. He was so fallen that he could even appropriate a ring, and yet he must have cared much for the world's opinion or he never could have taken such pains to charm it.

He got clean away.

I have given this narrative as an instance of the error of the absurd belief that young men when they are guilty can be neither cunning nor cheerful, and the farther mistake which lies in the belief that a detective is never hoodwinked.

The city police got to Gravesend three hours after Georgy had left that town.  I never had any doubt about him being George after hearing what the boatman said when describing the lad.  He added—"He was a main fine young gentleman, werry taking and smiling, and with a diamunt ring on his finger, an' as I was rowin' on him he steered his hand out Lunnonways, an' he says, says he, 'There's a many there 'ud like to see me.'"

Well, he got away.  I am afraid he will not make a figure in the world, but I am pretty certain of this, that he will be moderately happy wherever he goes, and will not be over-much troubled with his conscience.

# THE UNRAVELED MYSTERY.

WE, meaning thereby society, are frequently in the habit of looking at a successful man, and while survey- ing him, think how fortunate he has found life, how chances have opened up to him, and how lucky he has been in drawing so many prizes.

We do not, or we will not, see the blanks which he may have also drawn. We look at his success, think- ing of our own want of victories, shut our eyes to his failures, and envy his good fortune instead of emu- lating his industry. For my part I believe that no position or success comes without that personal hard work which is the medium of genius. I never will believe in luck.

When this habit of looking at success and shutting our eyes to failure is exercised in reference, not to a single individual, but to a body, the danger of coming to a wrong conclusion is very much increased.

This argument is very potent in its application to the work of the detective. Because there are many capital cases on record in which the detective has been the mainspring, people generally come to the conclu- sion that the detective force is made up of indivi- duals of more than the average power of intellect and sagacity.

Just as the successful man in any profession says nothing about his failures, and allows his successes to speak for themselves, so the detective force experiences no desire to publish its failures, while in reference to successes detectives are always ready to supply the reporter with the very latest particulars.

In fact, the public see the right side only of the police embroidery, and have no idea what a complication of mistakes and broken threads there are on the wrong.

Nay, indeed, the public in their admiration of the public successes of the detective force very generously forget their public failures, which in many instances are atrocious.

To what cause this amiability can be attributed it is perhaps impossible to say, but there is a great probability that it arises from the fact that the public have generally looked upon the body as a great public safeguard—an association great at preventing crime.

Be this as it may, it is certain that the detective force is certainly as far from perfect as any ordinary legal organization in England.

But the reader may ask why I commit myself to this statement, damaging as it is to my profession.

My answer is this, that in my recent days such a parliamentary inquiry (of a very brief nature, it must be conceded) has been made into the uses and customs of the detective force, as must have led the public to believe that this power is really a formidable one, as it affects not only the criminal world but society in general.

It had appeared as though the English detectives were in the habit of prying into private life, and as though no citizen were free from from a system of spydom, which if it existed would be intolerable, but which has an existence only in imagination.

It is a great pity that the minister who replied to the inquiry should have so faintly shown that the complaint was faint, if not altogether groundless.

I do not suppose the public will believe me with any great amount of faith, and simply because I am an interested party ; yet I venture to assert that the detective forces as a body are weak ; that they fail in the majority of the cases brought under their supervision ; and finally, that frequently their most successful cases have been brought to perfection, not by their own unaided endeavours so much as by the use of facts, frequently stated anonymously, and to which they make no reference in finally giving their evidence. This evidence starts from the statement, "from information I received." Those few words frequently enclose the secret which led to all the after operations which the detective deploys in description, and without which secret his evidence would never have been given at all.

The public, especially that public who have experienced any pressure of the continental system of police, and who shudder at the remembrance of the institution, need have no fear that such a state of things municipal can ever exist in England. It could not be attempted as the force is organized, and it could not meet with success were the constitution of the detective system invigorated, and in its reformed character pressed upon English society, for it would be detected at once as unconstitutional, and resented accordingly.

With these remarks I will to the statement I have to make concerning my part, that of a female detective, in the attempt to elucidate a criminal mystery which has never been cleared up, which from the mode in which it was dealt with, ran little chance of being discovered, and which will now never be explained.

The simple facts of the case, and necessary to be known, are these :—

One morning, a Thames boatman found a carpet-bag resting on the abutment of an arch of one of the Thames bridges. This treasure-trove being opened, was found to contain fragments of a human body—no head.

The matter was put into the hands of the police, an inquiry was made, and nothing came of it.

This result was very natural.

There was little or no intellect exercised in relation to the case. Facts were collected, but the deductions that might have been drawn from them were not made, simply because the right men were not set to work to—to sort them, if I may be allowed that expression.

The elucidation, as offered by me at the time, and which was in no way acted upon, was due—I confess it at first starting—not to myself, but to a gentleman who put me in possession of the means of submitting my ultimate theory of the case to the proper authorities.

I was seated one night, studying a simple case enough, but which called for some plotting, when a gentleman applied to see me, with whom I was quite willing to have an interview, though I did not even remotely recognise the name on the card which was sent in to me.

As of course I am not permitted to publish his name, and as a false one would be useless, I will call him Y——.

He told me, in a few clear, curt words, very much like those of a detective high in office, and who has attained his position by his own will, that he knew I was a detective, and wanted to consult with me.

" Oh, very well, if I am a detective, you can consult with me.   You have only yourself to please."

He then at once said that he had a theory of the Bridge mystery,. as he called it and as I will call it, and that he wanted this theory brought under the consideration of the people at Scotland Yard.

So far I was cautious, asking him to speak.

He did so, and I may say at once that at the end of a minute I threw off the reserve I had maintained and became frank and outspoken with my visitor.

I will not here reproduce his words, because if I did so I should afterwards have to go through them in order to interpolate my own additions, corrections, or excisions.

It is perhaps sufficient to say that his entire theory was based upon grounds relating to his profession as a medical man.   Therefore, whenever a statement is made in the following narrative which smacks of the

surgery, the reader may fairly lay its origin to Y——;
while, on the other hand, the generality of the conclusions drawn from these facts are due to myself.

I shall therefore put the conversations we had at
various times in the shape of a perfected history of the
whole of them, with the final additions and suggestions
in their proper places, though they may have occurred
at the very commencement of the argument.

As our statement stood, as it was submitted to the
authorities, so now it is laid before the public, official
form and unnecessary details alone being excised.

1. The mutilated fragments did not when placed
together form anything like an entire body, and the
head was wanting.

The first fact which struck the medical man was
this, that the dissection had been effected, if not with
learning, at least with knowledge. The severances
were not jagged, and apparently the joints of the body
had not been guessed at. The knife had been used
with some knowledge of anatomy.

The inference to be drawn from these facts was this,
that whoever the murderer or homicide might be,
either he or an accessory, either at or after the fact,
was inferentially an educated man, from the simple
discovery that there was evidence he knew something
of a profession (surgery) which presupposes education.

Now, it is an ordinary rule, in cases of murder
where there are two or more criminals, that these are
of a class.

That is to say, you rarely find educated men (I am
referring here more generally to England) combine

with uneducated men in committing crime. It stands evident that criminals in combination presupposes companionship. This assertion accepted, or allowed to stand for the sake of argument, it then has to be considered that all companionship generally maintains the one condition of equality. This generality has gained for itself a proverb, a sure evidence of most widely-extended observation, which runs—" Birds of a feather flock together."

Very well. Now, where do we stand in reference to the Bridge case, while accepting or allowing the above suppositions?

We arrive at this conclusion :—

That the state of the mutilated fragments leads to the belief that men of some education were the murderers.

2. The state of the tissue of the flesh of the mutitilated fragments showed that the murder had been committed by the use of the knife.

This conclusion was very easily arrived at.

There is no need to inform the public that the blood circulates through the whole system of veins and arteries in about three minutes, or that nothing will prevent blood from coagulating almost immediately it has left the veins. To talk of streams of blood is to speak absurdly.

If, therefore, an artery is cut, and the heart continues to beat for a couple of minutes after the wound is made, the blood will be almost pumped out of the body, and the flesh, after death, will in appearance bear that relation to ordinary flesh that veal does to ordinary beef—a similar process of bleeding having been gone through with the calf, that of exhausting the body of its blood.

What was the conclusion to be drawn from the fact that the fragments showed by their condition that the murdered man had been destroyed by the use of the knife ?

The true conclusion stood thus—that he was mur dered by foreigners.

For if we examine a hundred consecutive murders and homicides, committed in England by English people, we shall find that the percentage of deaths from the use of the knife is so small as barely to call for observation. Strangling, beating, poisoning (in a minor degree)—these are the modes of murder adopted in England.

The conclusion, then, may stand that the murder was committed by foreigners.

I am aware that against both the conclusions at which I have arrived it might be urged that educated and uneducated men have been engaged in the same crime; and secondly, that murders by the knife are perpetrated in England.

But in all cases of mystery, if they are to be solved at all, it is by accepting probabilities as certainties, so far as acting upon them is concerned.

3. There was further evidence than supposition to show that the remains were those of a foreigner.

This evidence is divided into a couple of branches. The first depends upon the evidence of the pelves, or hip bones, which formed a portion of the fragments ;

the second upon the evidence of the skin of the fragments.

First—

It may be remarked by any one of experience that there is this distinctive difference between foreigners and Englishmen, and one which may be seen in the Soho district any day—that while the hips of foreigners are wider than those of Englishmen, foreign shoulders are not so broad as English ; hence it results that while foreigners, by reason of the contrast, look generally wider at the hips than shoulders, Englishmen, for the greater part, look wider at the shoulders than the hips.

This distinction can best be observed in contrasting French and English, or German and English soldiery. Here you find it so extremely evident as not to admit discussion.

Now, was there any evidence in the fragments to which this comparative international argument could apply ?

Yes.

The medical gentleman who examined the fragments deposed that they belonged to a slightly-built man. Then followed this remarkable statement, that the hip bones, or pelves, were extremely large.

The second branch of this evidence, relating to the skin, may now be set out.

The report went on to say that the skin was covered with long, strong, straight black hairs.

Now it is very remarkable that the skin should exhibit those appearances which are usually associated with strength, while the report distinctly sets out that the fragments belonged to a slightly-built man.

It strikes the most ordinary thinker at once that his experience tells him that slight, weakly made men are generally distinguishable for weak and thin hair. Most men at once recognise the force of the poetical description of Samson's strength lying in his hair.

There is, then, surely something contradictory in the slight build, and the long, strong black hair, if we judge from our ordinary experience. But if we carry our experience beyond the ordinary, if we go into a French or Italian eating-house in the Soho district, it will be found that scarcely a man is to be found who is destitute of strong hair, for the most part black, upon the face. It need not be added that hair thickly growing on the face is presumptive proof that the entire skin possesses that faculty, the palms of the hands and soles of the feet excepted.*

Now follows another intricate piece of evidence. The hairs are stated to be long, black, and strong— that is to say, black, thick, and without any curl in them.

Any man who, by an hospital experience, has seen many English human beings, will agree with me that the body hair here in England is rarely black, rarely long, and generally with a tendency to curl.

Now, go to the French and Italian cafés already referred to, and it will be found that the beards you shall see are black, very strong, and the hairs individually straight.

* It should be here again pointed out that it is to the doctor that these physiological remarks are to be attributed,

The third conclusion stands thus :

That the bones and skin of the fragments point to their having formed a portion of a foreigner rather than an Englishman.

EVIDENCE OF THE FRAGMENTS. The evidence of the fragments, therefore, goes problematically to prove that the murdered man was an educated foreigner, stabbed to death by one or more educated foreigners.

Now, what evidence can be offered which can support this theory ?

Much.

In the first place, the complaints of the French Government to England, and the results of those complaints, very evidently show that London is the resting-place of many determined foreigners. In fact, it is a matter beyond all question, that London has at all times been that sanctuary for refugees from which they could not be torn.

Hence London has always been the centre of foreign exiled disaffection.

Then if it can be shown that foreign exiled disaffection is given to assassination, it stands good that we have here in London foreigners who are ready to assassinate.

Experience shows that this tendency to assassinate on the part of foreign malcontents is a common understanding amongst them. There is no need to refer to the attempts upon the life of the Emperor of the French, upon the life of the father of the late King of Naples—there is no need to point out that in the former cases the would-be assassins have lived in

London, and have generally set out from London. All required is, to talk of tyranny with the next twenty foreigners you may meet, good, bad, and indifferent. It will be found that the ordinary theory in reference to a tyrant is, not that he shall be overthrown by the will of the people, but by the act of assassination.

This theory is the natural result, possibly, of that absence of power in the people which we English possess. We take credit to ourselves for abhorring assassination in reference to tyrants; but it should never be forgotten that here we have no need of assassination — the mere will of the people (when it is exerted) being quite enough to carry away all opposition.

Once admit assassination as a valuable aid in destroying tyranny, and you recognise by inference its general value as a medium of justice and relief.

Now apply the argument to the treachery of a member of a secret society, and you will comprehend the suggestion that the murdered man was a member of a secret political society, who was either false, or supposed to be false, to the secret society to which he belonged.

The question now arises—are there foreign secret societies established in London?

Have they an existence abroad? Unquestionably. Even here in open England there are a dozen secret societies of a fellowship-like character—Masons, and Foresters, and Odd Fellows, &c. &c.

And if foreigners have secret societies abroad, in spite of the police, why not here, where they have perfect liberty to form as many secret societies as they like?

Where has the money come from which has rigged out various penniless men, and sent them on the Continent to assassinate this or that potentate?

The inference is good that the money is found by secret societarians. Where else could it come from? Exiles personally are not rich; but if twenty economical professors save two pounds a-piece in six months, there is forty pounds to be applied to a purpose.

Is there any solid evidence beyond that of the fragments to suggest that the murdered man was a foreigner? There is.

In the first place, the state of those fragments showed that death had been recent—say, within two days.

Now, was any man missing during those two days who was in any way suggestively identifiable with the dead man?

If so, no application was made to the police.

Now, if the dead man were an Englishman, and all who knew him were not implicated in his death (a most unlikely supposition), it seems pretty evident that the discovery of the murder following so swiftly on the fact, some clue to the mystery must have been gained.

Granted the supposed Englishman had no relations in London (for it must be accepted as certain that the murder was committed in town, it being hardly within the bounds of possibility to suppose that the remains were brought into London to hide)—granted he had no friends, he must have had either servants, landlady, or employers. If any of these had existed, how certain it is that the publicity of the crime would have been followed by some inquiries by some of these people.

Not one was made.

Not any evidence was offered to the police that could for a moment be looked upon as valuable, although it is not perhaps going too far to say that every soul in London who could comprehend the affair had heard of and talked it over within twenty-four hours of its discovery, thanks to the power and extension of the press.*

But see how thoroughly this absence of all inquiry will fall in with the murdered man having been a foreign refugee resting in this country.

Firstly—these refugees lodge together, and make so free with each other's lodgings, and visit so frequently and so generally, that an English landlady would have some difficulty in telling who was and who was not her lodger. It would be most unlikely that she would miss a foreigner who had been staying with her foreign lodger some weeks. Hence it might readily happen that a man having no locality with which he could be identified, no suspicion would be aroused by his absence from any particular place.

Then see how this supposed poverty of lodging would accord with a refugee who, broken down by

---

* I point out as an instance the late case of poisoning a wife and children in a cab. The culprit was discovered within twenty-four hours of the publication of the crime, and by several people in no way connected with the family in which the catastrophe occurred.

want, might betray his society in order to gain bread,
by selling their secrets to his home-police.

Or, on the other hand, he might be an actual police
spy, sent by his government to play the refugee and
the poverty-stricken wretch, in order the better to
penetrate the secrets of conspirators.

Then mark how all chance of recognition is avoided
by the absence of the head. In disposing of the
fragments, and slinging them over the bridge by means
of a rope, it was intended silently to drop the ugly
burden into the Thames. The idea of the bag resting
on the abutment of the bridge could never have entered
into the precautionary measures perfected by the murderers, and yet the necessity of strict secresy was made
wonderfully evident in the fact of the head being kept
back.

For what purpose? Probably that the chief actors
in the murder might be sure of its destruction—per-
chance that it might be forwarded to the president of
a secret society, that the death of the traitor might
be proved beyond all dispute.

Another very important line of consideration is the
inquiry why such a means of disposing of the remains
as that taken was adopted. It will be remarked that
the objectionable process of cutting up the body had
to be gone through, and that then the dangerous act
of carrying or riding with a bag of human remains
through the streets to the river had to be effected.
And effected *in the night time,* when it must be notorious to all parties the police are particularly alert in
inquiring into the nature of the parcels carried past

them. It will frequently happen that the police stop and justifiably examine heavy packages which they find being carried in the streets during the night.

The encountering of all these enormous risks, to say nothing of the fear of interruption during the final act of lowering the carpet-bag, all go to presuppose that the murderers were unable to dispose of the body in any less hazardous manner.

What is the mode in which murderers usually seek to hide the more awful traces of their guilt in the shape of the murdered man? They generally adopt the simplest and safest mode—hiding under the ground.

A body buried ten feet in the ground, even though in the close cellar of a house, would give no warning of the hidden secret. A body buried in quicklime, under similar circumstances, would give no warning, though only four or three feet below the surface.

Burial is the most evident and simplest mode of disposing of a dead body. How is it, then, that the murderers in question did not bury, and ran a series of frightful risks, which resulted in the discovery of the remains?

The answer is obvious—they had no means of burial. In other words, the murder being done in a house where there was no command of the ground floor it was impossible to bury the body, and so it had to be disposed of in some other way. The inference therefore, is, that the occupier of the place was a lodger—not a householder.

Now make inquiries in the Soho district and you will find that refugees rarely become householders.

Always hoping, perhaps, to return to their countries, never possibly desirous of taking any step which shall appear to themselves like a settling in a foreign land, it will be found that they prefer lodgings, and that the householders in most of the streets frequented by this sort of people are either English people or foreigners who do *not* belong to the refugee class, such as Swiss (chiefly) and the world of waiters, who with their savings have gone into foreign housekeeping.

I am aware that there is one good objection to this part of my scheme, in the remark that the murder might have been committed in a house occupied by the murderer or his friends, but that there might be no yard attached, or a yard too much exposed, or that the ground-floor was too publicly in use to admit of time for the removal of the boards, the replacing of the flooring, and the burial of the body.

However, I beg again to urge the doctrine of probabilities. Accepting the theory that it was a murder by foreigners, and not denying the statement that foreign refugees, as a rule, rarely become householders, the probability is greater that the murderers had no ground in which to bury, rather than they had ground at their command, but that circumstances prevented them from using it.

It is true that there is one awkward point in the fact that the bridge selected from which to throw their burden was not so near to the refugee district as the late Suspension Bridge. At first sight it would appear strange that a longer risk should be run by taking the remains to a bridge not the nearest to the scene of the murder. But it must be remembered that the Suspension Bridge had no recesses, while the actual bridge used has many—that the Suspension Bridge was altogether more open and better lit than the other. These suggestions must be taken for what they are worth. I am willing to admit that it still remains extraordinary that the attempt to dispose of the body should have been made at the more distant of the two bridges, and I acknowledge that the apparent advantages of the bridge used over the Suspension do not appear to compensate the extra risk incurred.

Let those who object thoroughly to the whole of this theory, advanced to account for a mystery which has never been cleared up—let them make the most of a weak point.

The probability seems to me that the murdered man was a spy amongst men who, holding to the theory of the justice of assassination, very necessarily recognised its value in relation to a spy in the pay of a tyrant. Nay, to be at once exhaustive in reference to spies, few people will be inclined to deny that the spy, whatever the shape he has taken, has always been dealt with most implacably.

The supposition once accepted that the murderers had no power of burial, the use of the Thames as a hiding place follows almost as a natural consequence. To hide below the water when the earth is not to be opened for the purpose of concealment appears to be a very natural thought. In what other way could the body be so readily disposable ?

The Thames offered secresy, the risk of carriage was

surmountable; this means therefore of concealment, though it involved danger to those concerned in the work, was far preferable to leaving the remains in the street—a mode which only a madman would adopt.*

Had the bag not lodged on the abutment of the bridge not one hint of the crime, it is evident, would ever have been made public. Or two or more may have been concerned in this crime, but they all kept their counsel well. Whether this silence was the result of brotherhood or fear it is impossible to say— possibly the latter. The very success of this one murder would intimidate any societarian who contemplated betraying his companions.

There has but to be added to the statement already put before the reader, two facts which, however, call for little or no comment.

1. The toll-keeper at one end of the bridge recognised the carpet-bag as a heavy one he had lifted over his toll-bar during the night.

2. He stated that he did this kindness for a woman whom he afterwards thought must have been a man in woman's clothing.

I see no value in this evidence.

1. The identification of the bag was of no value.

2. It does not appear that the man remarked upon any peculiarity of the carrier of the bag till after its

---

* Such a mode was exercised a few months since with several still-born children. Inquiry was set on foot, and the perpetrator of this open mode of disposing of human remains turned out to be a doctor who had suffered so much from delirium tremens that he might be called a madman.

discovery on the bridge abutment. And therefore his evidence is not reliable.

All I have now to do is to put in form the result I drew from the above theoretic evidence.

The result in question may be put thus :—

DEDUCTION.—That a foreign man, of age, but not aging, was murdered by stabbing by the members of a secret foreign society of educated men which he had betrayed. That this murder was committed by lodgers and most probably on some other floor than the basement, and of a house situated in the Soho district.

A copy of this statement now made to the reader, but somewhat more abridged and technical was forwarded to the authorities—but so far as I have been able to learn it was never accepted as of any value.

The inquiry, as all the world knows, failed.

I do not wonder that it did.

Left in the hands of English police, who set about their work after their ordinary rule, it is evident that if the murder was committed by foreigners, in a foreign colony, there was little chance of discovery.

I believe the chief argument held against me at the time I sent in my report ran as follows : that if my supposition to the effect that the murdered man was a foreign police spy were correct, the publicity given to the discovery of the remains would have led to a communication sooner or later from a foreign prefect of police stating that an officer was missing.

I did not make a reply to the objection, but I could have announced that the French police, for in-

stance, are not at all desirous of advertising their
business, and that a French prefect of police would
prefer to lose a man, and let the chance of retribution
escape, rather than serve justice by admitting that a
French political spy had been in London.

The silence of continental police prefects at that
time is by no means to be accepted as an evidence that
they missed no official who had been sent to England.

The case failed—miserably.

It could not be otherwise.

How would French police succeed, set to work in
Bethnal-green to catch an English murderer?

They would fail—miserably also.

There can be no question about it, to those who
have any knowledge of the English police system, and
who choose to be candid, that it requires more intellect
infused into it.    Many of the men are extraordinarily
acute and are able to seize facts as they rise to the
surface.    But they are unable to work out what is
below the surface. They work well enough in the light.
When once they are in the dark, they walk with their
hands open, and stretched out before them.

Had foreign lodging-houses, where frequent numbers
of foreigners assemble, been inquired about, had some
few perfectly constitutional searches been made, they
might have led to the discovery of a fresh blood-stained
floor—it being evident that if a spy were fallen upon
from behind and stabbed, his blood must have reached
the ground and written its tale there.

These blood-stains must still exist if the house in

which the murder took place has not been burnt down, but I doubt if ever the police will make an examination of them at this or any other distance of time, owing to the distant date of the crime.

Experience shows that the chances of discovery of a crime are in exact inverse proportion to the time which has elapsed since the murder. Roughly it may be stated that if no clew is obtained within a week from the discovery of a crime, the chances of hunting down the criminal daily become rapidly fewer and fainter.

Let it not be supposed that I am advocating any change in the detective system which would be unconstitutional. Far from it. I am quite sure any unconstitutional remodelment of that force would not be suffered for any length of time to exist—as it was proved by that recent parliamentary protest against an intolerable excess of duty on the part of the police to which I have already referred.

My argument is, that more intellect should be infused into the operation of the police system, that it is impossible routine can always be a match for all shapes of crime, and finally that means should be taken to avoid so much failure as could be openly recorded of the detective police authorities.

Take in point the case I have been mentioning.

What evidence have the public ever read or learnt to show that any other than ordinary measures were taken to clear up any extraordinary crime?

It is clear that while only ordinary measures are in

force to detect extraordinary crime, a premium of im-
punity is offered to the latter description of ill-doing,
and one which it is just possible is often pocketed.   Be
all that as it may, it is certain the Bridge mystery has
never been cleared up.

# THE JUDGMENT OF CONSCIENCE.

HE was in great poverty—yet a good citizen.

I came to know John Kamp over a very trifling affair—as you shall hear.

He was then about thirty years of age, and unmarried. I learnt very soon that he had a great desire to marry. Not any particular person. The desire appeared to be the result not of any individual passion, but the effect of reason.

I do not think I have said he was a shoemaker.

I am about to tell a romantic tale of this shoemaker, out I will not surround the narrative with any of the ordinary plaster-of-Paris conditions of romance. He was a plain, ungainly, and not remarkably tidy London shoemaker, earning a poor living, having but meat once a week—on Sunday to wit, and mealing on herrings, sprats, winkles, and such poor man's blessed food, all the week. Why do I call winkles, and herrings, and sprats blessed food? Simply because they are cheap and plentiful, and uphold the poor when otherwise they would sink under their low diet—sink not under the weight of it, but under its meagreness.

I never saw him drunk during the many months I knew him, I never heard a violent word pass his lips, and he was always following out some new train of thought.

He was one of the lower classes.

Perhaps there are many such men as he amongst the lower classes. I hope there are; for though many live and die without making their mark in the world's history, they have honoured their lives—and seeing what we see daily amongst all classes, why, the memory of a well-spent, if lost, life must be a very great comfort on a death-bed.

He was not a happy man, though his unhappiness it appeared to me did not arise from the injustice the world did him, but from the consciousness that he was debarred from doing good in his generation.

Pray do not misunderstand me—or him.

He did not go about like a man who has a grievance with the world because it has failed to comprehend him. He had nothing in his constitution of the cynic, either lachrymose or scoffing. But I am quite sure he was generally sorry that he could do the world no good, beyond that of living the life of a good citizen (a condition which he did not sufficiently value), and that the world had so treated him he could not benefit society.

I do not say he was right in feeling that the world had not treated him well. I am quite aware that society cannot go about finding youthful genius or guessing at it. I am not destitute of the knowledge that the world is willing to pay for certain genius, and handsomely; but that it is not disposed to foster it before it is known. But, nevertheless, I do not condemn

John Kamp for feeling more bitterly towards the world than he spoke generally of it, and clinging to the belief that it had injured in neglecting him.

It is true men make themselves or are helped by their friends; but it does not follow that a poor, ignorant man, who suffers in after life because the powers of the land did not foster him when neglectful parents let him run wild—it does not follow such an one shall reason in this fashion.

Take his argument.

"I know I have that in me which would benefit the world, but my hands are tied with the ignorance of my youth, and I am powerless; and I must live powerless; and I must die powerless."

What do you say to that argument? A wrong one to hold, but a very natural one.

It may be urged, however, that many men have raised themselves to eminence who held no higher social position than this John Kamp. But in their cases their early youth had as a rule been cared for— and a foundation to build upon had been made. Take Bloomfield, for instance—a genius who rose out of the menial trade to which Kamp belonged.

Again—the shape of his genius was one which called for help to demonstrate it. A man who has a genius for writing is set up with a quill, a quire of paper, an ink-bottle, and a penknife. A painter has to go farther in the way of an expensive nest of colours and a canvas; but when your genius takes the Esculapian shape—when your thirst is to be a doctor, you cannot at once launch into the exercise of your genius—you must work through patient, expensive years, and then begin lowly and humbly to climb, not daring at first to use your knowledge, lest its novelty shall appear like ignorance, fighting for years and years, perhaps for a lifetime, before the world can look towards you, and cry out, "Behold him! he has benefited all men."

To benefit the world—this it was for which John Kamp, shoemaker, and indeed cobbler, aged thirty, thirsted.

And as I write I remember the occasion upon which we first met. A crowd in the street is always an attraction to a detective, for it may happen, indeed generally does, that he is wanted to complete the performance.

I saw a crowd one night in the classic regions of Whitechapel, and making one of it directly, I found a woman in a fit, with a weakly-looking but clear-brained man superintending the unfortunate.

Neither born to command, nor used to that luxury, I felt certain directly I saw him, here he appeared to be in his element—to be doing what he knew it was within his province, and without that of those about him, to effect.

"Stand aside, mates!" I heard him say, as I approached; "if there's one thing more than another she wants, it's fresh air. Do stand aside, mates!"

This the "mates" proceeded to do by falling back about two feet, and then immediately advancing over one and a half.

"Look here, mates—don't hold her back like that." These remarks were addressed to the men who were holding the wretched woman with an energy which would have arrested the vigour of a grenadier. "Hold her well up," he continued, "and a little on one side, so that her head hangs a little on one side; if she gets anything in her throat she will choke if you hold her back, mates. P'r'aps it's one of them fits which comes on through want. Will one o' you, mates, go and get three-penn'orth of brandy?"

One of the mates did; a raffish-looking young man, whose true vocation very much I fear was that of the general thief; but, to the credit of humanity, even amongst thieves, I am bound to say he returned with the spirit (and some water) in a public-house basin.

The case was one of those ordinary fits which are in truth the result of want acting upon a frame which tends to epilepsy. Poor creature—dank, thin, ragged, haggard, we police people see such miseries daily, and until we get so used to it that the less amiable amongst us look upon them as nuisances.

I waited till the poor woman "come to," as the expression goes, till once more she looked about her, as though she had been born into a strange world—till once more she recovered her poor wretched senses, and putting herself together, uttered some few shamefaced sentences, which sounded like excuses, and prepared to slink away.

"Come, mates," said the impromptu doctor, "let's give her some coppers—let's make a collection."

I grieve to say that doubt was rife in a moment, and

that calumny, looking the good Samaritan in the face, said it was "all a do."

And as every grain of calumny tells, the collection, I remember, amounted only to twopence-halfpenny, which he who had spoken handed (with some scorn flashing from his eyes at the crowd), to the poor old woman, who appeared more shamefacedly apologetic than ever upon receiving this douceur.

As for me, I followed the Samaritan, whom I saw by his clothing was a mechanic of a very ordinary character.

I followed him with no bad intent to the neighbourhood of the Tower, when he entered a house which was so poor and so temptationless that the door swung idly and without a lock.

That same evening I made some inquiries at the parlour-shop of a widow, who exhibited so little a desire to sell, and so great a desire to talk, that I looked upon the hundred and one articles she had for sale as mere commercial excuses—a kind of business-like umbrella for harbouring scandal.

I was not wrong. When I came to know the vicinity better, I ascertained that the Widow Green's was the street club, and one which emulated any social gathering of the sort at the west end, as far as dealing with reputations went. I calculated that a character was ruined per sixty minutes during business hours.

I learnt a good deal from the Widow Green, who by the way also played upon that piano of the poor, the mangle.

It appeared he was John Kamp, a nice young man,

but objectionable on this score—that he was "a little orf 'is 'ed."

This statement inquired into, it appeared that he was a respectable young man, looking after his sister, never getting too much (this was a delicate east-end mode of reference to strong drink), always paying his rent, though rather despising credit (this was a reference to his want of patronage of the parlour-shop, I saw); but what "were agin him were this—that he were crotchetty," though nevertheless mending a shoe with punctuality to time and the best of thread and leather.

I need not say it was no difficulty for me to make acquaintance with the Kamps. I was engaged at that time (though it may appear to my reader an odd case to call for the operations of a woman detective) upon what has since taken the name of the great sugar-baking case, and therefore I was living in the neighbourhood of Aldgate and Whitechapel. And inasmuch as my professional abilities could only be exercised at certain hours, I had a good deal of time at my disposal.

The meeting with Kamp took place on the second day of my sojourn in that quarter of London, and it was on the third that I made his acquaintance, with the help of a pair of mendable shoes, which I bought of my landlady to her eminent suspicion, for my act was unusual.

I knocked as well as I could the two knocks which I had learnt was the dose for the Kamps; and, after some time, for the knocker was loose and askew, to say nothing of its having no anvil, the sister, as I afterwards learnt, came down to the door.

She was not pleasant to look upon, her jaw being so underhung as to give her at first sight that malevolent expression which is too suggestive of the bull-dog—but accustomed to search rather than glance at faces, I perceived very quickly that she was a pleasant, and (her mouth and jaw apart) an attractive young person.

I need not here dilate upon my first interviews with John Kamp, because I have more important matter to write about. Let me, therefore, but just say that I found he was an earnest-looking man as he sat at his hard work, and the faint, fog-drenched light fell upon his forehead, which was wide and massive, though coarse-grained, and framed with rather dull-looking and not too well kept soft, black hair.

It is a part of my profession to bring people out, and I soon effected that object with Kamp.

After a few days we got on very pleasantly together. He accepted perfectly my position as a visitor, and not a customer. He would look up from his work when I went in, and give a pleasant but rather worn smile, and then he would drop over his lapstone, and tap away at his work.

He was assuredly very unfortunate in many ways. Certainly superior to his trade, and not inclined to rest content in that place in which chance and his own will had placed him : he was forced even to yield an outward respect to his poor trade which he could not feel. He never attempted to take a high place in his trade, because, though a good workman, he had not

regularly served his time to shoemaking. Forced
early in life from a bad home, he had become errand-
boy at a shoe-shop, and here he watched the trade and
ultimately practised it.

And as there are always men who avail themselves
of all advantages, many of those master-makers who
employed Kamp, had given him the worst pay for the
best work, simply because he could not show an ordinary indenture.

I am afraid this system tended to make him more
discontented with his lot than he would even otherwise
have been.

On my third visit I found him operating on a thick-
headed loading labourer, and pulling a back tooth from
his heavy jaw with the ordinary pair of pincers with
which he stretched his leather.

For you see, exactly as at an evening party, the
gentleman most rallied and patronized is he who does
more than anybody for the general amusement, so
with John Kamp. The general neighbourhood pitied
him in a small-beer kind of way as an oddity, and
availed themselves of all those oddities which they
could turn to their own advantage.

" Thank ye, mate," said the heavy-headed labourer ;
and without a word to the sister he left the room.

" He did'nt pay you !" said I.

" No ; I never take any payment for medical advice," he replied.

I admit the answer was a little bumptious, but he
was a poorly-informed man, and it is not always the
unlearned who alone are vain. And I would have you

remark that when a poor man who makes but from fifteen to eighteen shillings a week refuses a payment which is justly *his*, there must be more in the abnegation than at first we see.

"But he would have had to pay a shilling," said I, "had he gone to a dentist; you ought to have charged him sixpence."

"Oh, he could have got an order from the relieving officer to the parish doctor, and had his tooth extracted for nothing."

"But then he would have lost his time."

"Yes, he would," said Kamp.

By the way, it was the dinner hour, and Kamp had left his meal gratuitously to take out the labourer's tooth.

The sister and I did not get on very well together. It appeared to me that she resented my intrusion, though I am sure I in no way impeded them. The curse of poverty was evident in her, whereas the brother had gained a victory over it by his wisdom. For he was wise though he had little knowledge. I am aware that wisdom presupposes knowledge, but my experience tells me that much wisdom may exist accompanied by very little knowledge. Farthermore, my experience tells me that it too frequently happens that an immensity of knowledge is accompanied by no wisdom whatever.

Somehow I grew to like this John Kamp.

But his vanity was by no means flattered.

And by this sentence perhaps the reader apprehends a personal secret which may not already have been very difficult to learn.

He knew much of medicine, and more of its philosophy. His favourite work was "Johnston's Chemistry of Common Life." He knew the book almost by heart, and he would dilate upon it in a manner which was almost touching, when was taken into consideration his hopeless passion for a profession in which in all probability he could never practise.

In politics he was of course a thorough liberal, but he was not governed by those extreme views which it must be confessed are generally held by the self-educated. Self-educated this man wholly was. In after times I received letters from him, and I am bound to say they showed a height of education which was most praiseworthy. It could be seen he had been his own master perhaps. There were too many capital letters, and much faint obscurity in the composition, but it could be seen that the man was earnest and straightforward. Every sentence had bone in it, and every line had something in it, and every letter was a something perfect in its way, and in itself.

No, he was not in the ordinary sense of the word a chartist.

He has said to me—

"I once went to a chartist meeting, but I never attended a second. If chartism means anything it means that those who suffer shall suffer no longer. Well, I went, and found the men there were hearty hale mechanics, they were those especially who are luckiest amongst us workers—such as engineers and smiths—the men who get the best pay amongst us. *They* had little cause of complaint, whereas now those mechanics who are really down-trod—I mean all those that use the needle, such as shoemakers and tailors— they that can hardly get a bit o' bread, much less cheese, *they* weren't at the meeting at all. They had not got time to go. I was shouldered out of the way, and my voice could not have been heard amongst all those big men, shouting and yelling. It struck me I had never imagined so tyrannical a meeting as that. So I did not go to another of them, for they are a lie, and no better."

During these talkings, while he worked, and I also, the sister said nothing, but bent over her hard, hard work, which was military tailoring.

I have seen her fingers quite blue and rough through the action of the harsh serge used for artillery uniforms, and at other times I have seen her looking wonderfully faded and worn in the midst of red linesmen's tunics.

I think I have said she was very pleasant-faced, apart from the under-hung jaw; but the mass of people had not looked beyond her deformity, which was very apparent when she ate her poor meals, and they had been prejudiced against her. She had accepted this life-long condemnation in a quiet way, without resentment, but not without knowledge, and had fallen into a kind of meekly-repelling apathy which must have tended, in a general way, to increase that want of prepossession with which people I am afraid regarded her.

It was about two weeks after I came to know this far from ordinary man that, as I was talking with Kamp on one of the chapters of Johnston's Chemistry, a copy of which I admit I purchased and read up, and as Johanna Kamp was working under new conditions, as far as my experience went, for she was surrounded by the white flannel devoted to the summer wear of the marines—I say it was as we were thus occupied, it being at three o'clock in the afternoon and a pleasant April day, with the one window open and the light wind waving over a quivering penny pot of primroses, that a heavy, solid step was heard on the stairs.

Upon this Kamp looks up at his sister, and she at the door. And it may be it was only that her pale countenance was heightened in colour by being contrasted with the unordinary white materials about her, but it seemed to me a something like warm-hearted blood rose to the poor woman's face.

Without any preliminary tap, the door was rattled open, and a well-built but intolerably plain soldier of the line entered the room.

It may be that my presence made a difference in their meeting, but whether this was the case or not I am bound to say that the working woman met the soldier's "how do ye do?" with no enthusiasm, but with much pleasant, calm cordiality.

He was a very honest sort of man, this soldier, who, I gathered, had (like most of the soldiery) gone a little astray in youth, and been brought back again by the discipline of the army.

"My company's back at the Tower, Johanna," he said cheerily to the woman ; adding, to Kamp, "So you'll see plenty of me, Jack."

"Perhaps I am intruding," I said, at this point.

"Oh no, ma'am," replied the soldier, evidently with the air of having some proprietorship in the room himself—"it ull hold four on us"—looking about the premises with a soldierly air.

Then he slipped off his coat, unhitched his braces, and taking a seat at Johanna's table, he began to thread a needle.

For the poor have no time to waste, and I saw at a glance he was at an old office—he helped to gain bread in that poor place.

As he took up the pieces of cloth Johanna laid efore him ready basted together, he said, "And where's the table and them other things ?"

She pointed to a covered pile in the room, which had often given me cause to wonder of what it was composed.

"One half look," said the soldier (he was a corporal, I saw). "One half look"—already apologizing for wasting time—and he went in three strides to the pile, took off the dingy cover, gave a glance at a table, two or three chairs, and other matters, covered the whole again, and then returned with three more strides to his seat. I think these three strides were taller and handsomer than those which had preceded them.

As he sat down, he tapped himself with one hand upon the other arm.

"I shall get 'em soon now, Johnny, and then !"

Here a bright look came on his face, which made it momentarily prepossessing.

Of course, it did not require any profound detection to comprehend what was going on.

The soldier and seamstress were engaged to be married, some of the furniture had been bought, and they were only waiting till he got his serjeant's stripes upon his coat.

Well, well, it was very pleasant to see them hard at work. He was no bad needle-man, as indeed few soldiers are. Indeed, I believe the army contractor got better work out of him than any one. He did certainly appear to take every stitch with a will.

This was the only occasion on which I saw the soldier.

One day in the same week, and when Johanna was away taking home a huge bundle of completed clothing to her employer, a sub army clothing contractor, whom I had once seen (he was a kind of Hebrew Adonis)—on that day Kamp told me the history of the engagement.

Exactly as she had met with nothing but inattention from men during her life, so he had been made the butt of women. When they by chance met (in that little East London paradise, the Victoria Park), it was clear they had both felt grateful for the frankness with which each met the other, and the conversation had begun by his picking up her umbrella. They had experienced a good deal of pain at the way in which the world had treated them, and as it is the knack of mental pain to purify people, why they soon found out that they were fitted to each other.

When they walked out of a Sunday (this I learnt from Kamp) they were frequently laughed at. And I must confess at first sight they were an ugly pair, and their ugliness was all the more remarkable from the contrast between them, for his chin and jaw shelved away in a very remarkable manner. But I believe the public ridicule gave them the benefit of feeling a kind of mutual pity for the public unkindness, which after a time was a kind of satisfaction to them, as showing how much they ought to be to one another.

For my part I think, in a quiet, sad, earnest way, Johanna Kamp and Tom Hapsy were happy, and loved each other very truly in a poor, plain way.

I have said that I did not see the corporal again. This loss—I felt it one, for I had taken a liking to the ugly fellow—arose from the fact that I was recalled from the neighbourhood and set upon other business.

I heard nothing more of the Kamps. I may add that they had never learnt my true occupation, but supposed me a small annuitant, a little eccentric, but very kindly disposed upon the whole. .

Six months passed away—six months to me in my profession of very great importance.

I had been out of London, and it was the second night after my return, that, going down to the office, I found my fellow-workwomen very earnestly discussing a piece of news which had arrived. This was made up of the particulars of a murder in the east of London.

Two hours before, and at about eight o'clock in the evening, and when, therefore, the night had fairly set in, a tradesman in a large way of business had been shot dead. He had received the charge full in the breast, and therefore his enemy must have faced him; but though the alarm was immediately taken and the murdered man was alive when several people reached his side, he was unable to utter a word, and he died speechless as when found.

This affair had occurred at a place called New Ford, and very near to a running stream.

The spot upon which the unfortunate man fell was not many hundred yards from his own house, and he had been seen walking up and down a field as though waiting for some one. I may add at once that this was so—he expecting a young person who it appeared was notoriously in the habit of meeting him in the field where he was found dying.

The usual government reward in cases of evident murder was in this case very rapidly advertised.

Now, I need not tell the reader that detectives are as much excited by one of these rich government rewards as—as a ladies' school by the appearance of a new and an elegant master.

Every man or woman amongst us has an equal chance in the first place of gaining the prize, and as one hundred pound bank notes are not going begging every day in the week, we of the force look upon them with a considerable amount of respect.

I went down to New Ford and obtained a view of the dead man.

I knew the face, for I never forget features I have once seen, but I could not identify it, owing to that marvellous new expression which death lays on the human countenance.

For a full hour I tried to recall where I had seen the face, and what were the associations connected with it.

I confess I failed, and I turned once more into the station at which the chief particulars of the case were known—the station within the district of which the crime had been committed — and sat down more fatigued than though I had been walking half a score miles.

I was known well at the office, and therefore no impediment was thrown in my way in relation to this matter.

"Have you got any clue?" I asked in, I am quite sure, a worn and tired voice.

"Only a bit of a one," said to me a sergeant, who at horse and turf cases is supposed to be quite unapproachable.

The clue to which he referred is one which in cases of ordinary shooting has on many occasions brought home his guilt to the actual murderer. I refer to the wadding, or rather stopping, used to fix the charge in the barrel of the firearm. If this stopping is not a disc of pasteboard, or a material sold for charging purposes, it frequently happens that it is a piece of paper torn from a supply in the possession of the person using the firearm.

It has in many instances happened where this stopping has not taken fire and burnt itself out, that enough of the paper, either written or printed on, has been found to bring home the shot to certain parties; and indeed there are cases on record where the rough line of the edge of the bit of half-burnt paper has agreed so certainly with another morsel found in the pocket of a suspected man, that upon such circumstantial evidence as this to begin upon, murder has been brought home to the guilty man.

In the case under consideration a crumpled stopping, which had in all probability been in the barrel of a firearm, in company with the bullet that had been found in the body of Mr. Higham, was picked up near the spot at which the murdered man had fallen, and within an hour of the catastrophe.

It was the scorched blackened remains of the upper half of a printed page of what the printers would call a demy-octavo book.

It bore the title of the work in the running-head line—"Johnston's Chemistry of Common Life."

I knew now where I had seen the dead man when in life. Once accompanying Johanna Kamp, with a large bundle of work to her employer's (it was in the evening, and she feared she might have the work snatched away if she went alone), I recalled that we saw the dead man, and I further recalled that in taking her work he had paid her a kind of marked attention which was half mirthful and half real.

I recalled also that she said to me, it was hard how much poor folk had to put up with in order to get a crust.

I declare that the idea shot into my brain in the moment of seing the scrap of printed paper—had it been torn from John Kamp's copy.

This was a matter which, as far as I was concerned, could easily be found out. I had but to pay the shoemaker a visit to bring the conversation round to Johnston, and then ask to see the book.

Perhaps it was cruel to spy upon the man who had met me daily as a something more than an acquaintance ; but if such a consideration were always to arrest the course of justice the ordinary affairs of the world could not go on.

A man is your friend, but if he transgresses that law which it is your duty to see observed you have no right to spare him because he is so ; for in doing this you admit, by implication, that you did not spare other men because they were no friends.

I went down to Kamp's house next morning.

I did not knock at the swinging door of the house. The knocker was still hanging to the door all askew, and still wanting the anvil.

I went direct upstairs—something beating at my heart and saying, " cruel, cruel !" as I did so. I tapped at the door.

I remember how earnest and emphatic those sounds appeared to me. The last time I stood in that room I was there as the man's friend ; now I was entering it as his enemy—as one suspecting him of murder, for that was my errand.

Yes, I was about to use that past friendship as the means of prosecuting my profession. I know I was but doing my duty—I feel certain at this moment I was but doing my duty ; but something, which I suppose was conscience, told me that this was not well.

" Come in," said a weak voice.

Hearing a quick, beating sound—and which, indeed, was the rushing of my blood through my heart, I opened the door and entered.

My heart failed me as I did so, for hope sank within me.

He was sitting desolately upon his work-stool.

He had not been working.

As I came in he recognised me, but he did not rise or hold out his hand.

"How are you?" he said, abstractedly, and then in a distressingly absent manner he took up one of his most ordinary tools—one he used a thousand times a day—and looked at it with an odd, distant expression, as though he had never seen it before.

Then he laid this down and took up a piece of the wax used in his trade and began abstractedly pressing it into different forms.

The room looked very desolate, and though it had not been distinguishable for cleanliness when I had been in the habit of seeing it, the place now looked indescribably more dirty than it did, while there was a forlorn expression upon it which was totally absent when I had seen it daily.

There was no evidence of the sister—no threads, no shreds of cloth, no waiting chair, or draggled work-basket. The table at which she used to work was put away against the wall, and upon the spot where the covered furniture used to stand.

The linnet's cage still hung in the window.—Ah! I did not mention the tailless linnet the sister fed and called "Tweet." But the bird was dead surely; at all events the cage was empty, and dry, and dusty.

Kamp looked very worn and broken down; and, for we detectives have to look at everything, I saw that the silky, black hair, which had never had those proper pains taken with it which its natural beauty deserved, was all bestreaked with grey.

I think I need hardly tell the reader that not for two moments had I been in the room before I felt that the old life of that chamber had passed away never to return.

Between him and me, as I entered the room, there was the space of the dusty unswept floor. He was seated on his stool, listless and broken down.

There was an ugly stoop in his shoulders, which had not been there when I was a visitor. His hands, so adroit and earnest as I had seen them, lay inert and drooping one over each knee, and there was a substantial shadow on his face beyond the darkness of his room, for though the day was bright the glass was thick with old, old dirt.

"The sister has not been here for weeks," I thought, "and perhaps not for months."

The first volume of "Johnston's Chemistry of Common Life," lay open and face downwards, on a pile of work-a-day tools and scraps of leather at his feet.

I saw that the heap of dirt and rubbish round about him (and which seems to be a condition of correct shoe-making), was far larger and higher than when I used to come almost every morning for several weeks together, and, I hope, make the time pass pleasantly to him, while I listened to his half-learned and wiser talk.

He looked very desolate—poor fellow.

It seemed to me that his heart was bleeding.

All the brightness had passed from his face; and all the patience, and all the blunted hope. All his countenance sat with despair, all its desire seemed to be annihilation.

For my part I hardly knew what to say.

I looked about for some moments, and then I said—

"I hope you have been well since I saw you last?"

"Yes, well," he said, looking mournfully round the room.

A pause.

I found that my sense of justice could flag.

At last I said—

"Have you perfected your machine yet?"

For the poor fellow, amongst other ideas, had given his attention to the shaping of a machine at which shoemakers could do their work without bending and curving themselves over it in the ordinary way, to which is attributable so much of the lung and liver disease to which the men of his trade are subject.

"No," he said, with a dead wild look out beyond him —far past the walls of that narrow dirty room—"I've not thought of it lately."

And now I fell to my duty.

"But I see you still study your book," I said, pointing to the volume lying face down upon the ground.

"I've been trying to read," he said, "but I can't."

He was speaking like a sick, patient child. I know I might have struck him, say upon the cheek, and he would not have resented it.

I knelt down to take the book— feeling, I am afraid,

much like Judas when he held out the red hand for the thirty pieces of silver.

These words stopped my action:

"Those were very happy days when you came here and talked about old Johnston with me—wasn't they?"

I could not take up the book.

"But where is your sister?" I asked. I was going to add in a gayer tone—"married?" But a something, 'twas sympathy I suppose with the place and man, stopped the word.

He did not move, he did not look at me, as he answered, his eyes once more looking forward with that seeing blindness, if I dare use such an expression, to which I have already referred.

"DEAD."

"Dead!" I replied, something like an echo.

"Oh yes; Johanna has been dead a month or more, only I don't quite exactly know how time goes."

I hardly knew what to say, indeed I had a very great mind to confess to him what my errand was, and to ask him to forgive me for having wronged him.

As the history will show, I did well to keep my confession to myself.

"Indeed," I said. "It must have been a sad blow to Tom Hapsy."

A fierce look came over his face for a moment and then died again.

"It was partly his fault," said he, "since he would not trust her."

"Not trust her?" I said, and I confess that heartily

as I was pitying the poor fellow I saw before me, it struck me as wonderful that Johanna Kamp should have excited jealousy in her lover.

"No," said Kamp, "he would not trust her. He couldn't understand that she had to be civil at the warehouse, and that it only was civility."

"Surely they didn't quarrel, John?"

"Yes, they quarrelled."

"And did they part?"

"Yes, they parted."

He uttered these sentences with a patience of despair which almost made me love the man.

"And—and what happened then?"

"What happened—why what happens to most women when they are disrespected? Don't they disrespect themselves? She was a good woman," he continued, with a smile which was sweet though it was so ghastly; "a good woman," he repeated, with a sound something like a dry hard sob, "and Tom Hapsy should not have been so hard upon her, for she would have lost her work, and I'd give my life on it there was nothing to complain of till he left her."

"Did he leave her?" I asked.

"Yes; he set to watching for her one night outside the warehouse, and when she came out, laughing, though it was all in the way of business, poor thing, he caught her by the arm. I saw the marks black and blue the next day, and then he flung her away from him as he called her an under-hung ——," here he stopped and a something like a blush overcame his countenance, and he continued, "I beg your pardon, I was going to use a word you would not care to hear."

"But what happened?"

"What happened?" he asked, with a soft kind of fierceness; "what happens to any woman, whether she is under-hung or not, when she does not care what comes of her? She had lived patient enough, never thinking any man would honourably notice her, living here in my poor home, till Tom Hapsy took up with her—and then when he went off she did not care what became of her."

He stopped for a moment, and then he went on:

"I was ill at the time, and we were poorer than usual, or I would not have let her go still to the cursed warehouse. How did it end? There—I remember reading amongst the ancients that there was a woman who asked her husband to kill her, and she flung herself upon the sword. That was just the way with poor Johanna. He had not much trouble with her, and he flung her off as you'd fling away a down-at heel shoe."

"Who was he?" I asked, with my breath coming and going nervously. I was beginning to be afraid that I saw the whole tragedy, and in which I was to play a terrible part that I had brought upon myself.

His answer was as I suspected; *he* was the man who lay dead, shot through the left lung; *he* was the sub army tailoring contractor who had employed Johanna Kamp, and who, to my own knowledge, had distinguished her in a marked manner (whatever the cause) from the other workwomen.

Whatever the cause !

Can it be guessed at ?

I think it can.  The dead man had been a sensualist in the strictest sense of that term.  Now, what is the career of the sensualist ?   It will be found that as satiety approaches the appetite requires a stronger and stronger stimulation.   If it were possible I could here give some awful examples of what depths of depravity the professed sensualist can fall to, but their narration is not admissible.   Yet I can illustrate the sin by referring to the opening chapter of a tale of Eugene Sue's, in which the career of a sensualist is depicted. As he sinks and darkens in iniquity beauty palls upon him, innocence is contemptible, and his passions are aroused in exact proportion to the brutality and coarseness of the objects who surround him.

A purer and better-fitted comparison may be found in one's frequent experience of a very handsome man, or beautiful woman, mating with an extremely ordinary companion for life.

I assume that this wretched man—poverty having been the handmaiden of his sin—had luxuriated in so many instances in the youth and good looks of those who sought his employ, as a large army sub-contractor, that by a natural moral decay, or immoral progress, he became enamoured of poor, ugly, unprepossessing Johanna Kamp.

After a pause, a very long pause, the desolate man said—

" I see her there now when they brought her in wet and dead out of the dock.  I didn't know her at first, for it's black mud in the docks. I can't get away from poor Joan—there she is, *there*, with her poor hands that worked so hard, down on each side of her, and the black water coming from her closed eyes just like tears. They laid her down just here," he said plaintively, as he stooped upon one knee, and pointed to a spot with his hard right hand, the fingers of which were flattened with many hard, hard years' work ; " and she seemed to be smiling almost. And when I stooped forward to kiss her they pulled me back, and asked me if I was mad. Joan and I were all alone in the world ; our mother died when she was an hour old, and father never cared for us. There she was," he continued, pointing to the spot again, " and she and I was here four days together," and he pointed to the cupboard-room which she had used as a bedroom. " When they took Joan away, they took my heart and buried it with you, Joan—buried it with you."

He dropped forward on the ground, and over the spot where the ill-featured sister had been laid. But no tears wetted his face—his grief was too hard for that.

And now, what should I do ?

There lay the book ; there, farther off, perhaps lay a murderer.

What if he who had been shot had been a heartless wretch—what if he was better out of the world than in it ? In the face of the law all men are equal, and their lives are sacred.

Thou shalt not kill.

This rule stands whether it be godly man or fallen, true or false. Thou shalt do no murder.

The book was nearer to me than to him.

And he lay in a kind of stupor, with his eyes gazing in another direction than mine. Had he been looking on me I could not have stooped and turned the pages of the book.

The folios of the half-burnt fragment lying as witness at the station-house were 75, 76. I turned the pages of the book without noise and with the least movement.

Page 74—no pages 75, 76. Then followed page 77.

The leaf comprising the pages 75, 76, had been roughly torn from the book, leaving some jagged fragments about the thread used in the sewing of the sheets.

Certain now that he was a murderer, I looked upon him with dread.

And yet I pitied him.

What was I to do?

What could I do—except my duty.

I do not know how long a time passed from the moment of my discovery until that in which he spoke to me. But by rough calculation, really I think minutes must have elapsed before the silence was broken.

"Good-bye," he said, "we shan't see each other again."

"Why not?" I asked, a little shamefacedly.

"I'm going to give myself up to the police."

Of course there could be no doubt in my mind as to who was the murderer of the Hebrew army contractor.

" Why give yourself up to the police ?" I returned, awkwardly.

" Because I have done murder."

He uttered these words in the simplest and most immoveable manner, with no fear, no pain, no shame. It has since appeared to me that he was in that condition of which most men have had some experience, when a great shock has so stupified the mind that there appears to be no ability to exercise reason ; when the acts we commit ourselves, or those of others, affect us so little, that under such circumstances we may be declared in a sort of half-trance.

He was so despairingly callous that he did not notice the absence of all alarm on my part.  As for me I could play no double game with this man.  He was so candid with me that to lie to him would have been indeed the depth of meanness.

" I am a detective," I said.

He looked up, but did not by his face betray any astonishment or distrust at my words.

" Do you understand ?" I continued, my eyes upon the ground ; " I am a female detective."

" Are you ?" he said, with piteous simplicity.

" What made you kill him ?"

Suddenly he looked wild, as he replied—

" Why should bad men live ?"

I shook my head.  I replied—

" Why should better men kill the bad ?"

" They ought not to live—they are no good on the earth."

You see the poor creature had been so " hardly

entreated" by the world, that he had turned against it
when a common crime which the world does not
punish very rigorously had crushed *his* home.

It is very well, perhaps, to preach, but there are
times and places for sermons, and I felt that before
his despair there was no need for me to give out a
text. If despair outrages the law, well and good.
The law must be satisfied. But let us leave despair
alone, if we can only preach to it. For my part, whatever the man, I think I feel inclined to take his hand
if he is despairing.

So I turned to facts.

" How did you do it?" I asked.

He got up from the floor where they had laid down
the ill-favoured sister—the boards were still marked
with the black dock mud in which the body was
enveloped when brought to the poorhouse (for I may
add the dead face was recognised while yet the water
was streaming from it by a fellow-workwoman of the
deceased); he got up from the ground quite mecha-
nically, if that expression is allowable, and going to
the pile of dirt and leather cuttings which lay heaped
near his working stool, he put his hand in a wandering,
awkward manner into the rubbish, and after feeling an
for a few moments, produced a common rusty pistol.

*It was charged.*

The natural thought to occur to a detective was
this—" Why is the pistol loaded?"

So I said to him—

" Why, it's charged."

" Yes," he replied, with some appearance of stupid
confusion.

"Surely," I said, "you were not going to—to let anything happen to yourself?"

He looked up. And this was the only moment throughout our interview when anything like an expression which was not abject dejection appeared upon his face. And as he raised his face he said—

"Do you think I could kill myself? No! I know myself too well for that."

I will leave the reader to ponder on the apparent contradiction in his declaration of murder on the one hand, and his evident abhorrence of suicide on the other.

"Then, why is the pistol loaded?" I asked.

"I—I don't know," said he.

So I continued—

"But how came you to do this?"

"How?" he replied, relapsing into his apathy, "I thought he ought to be killed, like so much carrion, and I bought the pistol, and paid the shopboy to show me how to load it; and then I went to the field where I knew he was to meet another of 'em. I learnt that from one of the women at the warehouse, who knew all about it. I came up with him, that is near him, and then——"

Here he stopped, and appeared to fall into an abstruse chain of thought.

"Well?" I asked.

"Why—why, then he fell, shot!" he replied, in a quick, half-astonished manner.

His words even then appeared to me extraordinary, from the peculiar mode in which they were put together.

But the great question stood—Why was the pistol loaded?

I will pass over the actual giving of the poor fellow into custody, for there can be no need to launch into detail upon so painful a subject. Suffice it to say, that he exhibited no emotion whatever upon being charged with wilful murder, and went with many sighs, but no repugnance, to the dark cell.

For my part, I felt there was something, beyond what he had said, wanted in order to elucidate the matter.

Now, when we detectives doubt we question.

This was my plan in the case of which I am now writing.

The first person I questioned was the girl who was to have met Higham on the night when he was killed.

She only had benefited by that crime—she benefited but for a short time. She was a pert, saucy, bold-eyed, young person, who replied to my questions in a tone which clearly argued that she should much prefer slapping my face to answering me.

Had she seen a stooping man about the spot, with long black hair hanging quite to his shoulders? No, she had *not*. How should she? *She* had not been looking for persons with long black hair, *she* had been looking for poor Mr. Higham. What? Had she seen anybody about? No; of course not. She did not go there to be seen by *anybody* but poor Mr. Higham. What? Had she seen anybody about? Yes, if she must answer. She had seen a soldier. What? Could she describe him? No, she could not describe him.

She saw him once under the gas-lamp at the corner of the field near the road, and that was quite enough for *her*. Why was it quite enough for her? Why, because when *she* looked at a man a second time it was because he was worth looking at. Yes.

This was all the information I got from this extremely pert young person, who, I may remark, in quitting her at this place, came under my especial attention about two years after the termination of the case, "A Judgment of Conscience."

Now to the detective all people who by any chance may be guilty, are not considered innocent till they have been proved guiltless.

Therefore, the confession of the shoemaker apart, the unknown soldier who had been seen by the girl I had questioned was quite likely to be the guilty person.

The inquest was to take place that evening—the evening following the giving in custody of John Kamp. Of course I attended.

The case created some commotion, by the fact that the murderer had given himself up to justice; but I need not tell you that the inquest proceeded, as far as evidence went, precisely as though Kamp had been still at liberty.

I need here only refer to the evidence of the medical man, for his depositions alone affect the course of this tale.

He produced the bullet he had extracted from the body of the dead man, and then proceeded to describe the course the ball had taken.

Judge my surprise when upon asking for and fitting

the bullet to the pistol Kamp had given me, I found that it would not run down the barrel.

Therefore it was evident that if Kamp had shot the man, he had used some other weapon than the one he had given me. But if so, why had he deceived me in reference to the pistol? Not seeking to hide the crime, why should he seek to mystify me in reference to the weapon?

Nay, upon further consideration, I saw that he could not, of course, know that the evidence of the bullet would be in his favour.

I gave my testimony, which exhibited very fully the discrepancy between Kamp's statement and the evidence given by the doctor in relation to the bullet.

It was quite impossible to reconcile the contradictions, and, after much bald and unequal suggestion, the inquest was adjourned.

The night, however, was not to pass without the mystery being cleared up.

I was at the district station, and it was about eleven p.m., when the ears of all the officers at the station were pricked up at hearing a crowd of approaching footsteps.

We went to the door, the jailer, I remember, clashing his keys loudly, and there coming towards us was a stretcher carried by a couple of policemen and surrounded by a number of people—for the greater part, of the lowest class—the hum of whose voices on our practised ears told us that it was no drunken case which was being carried in.

A policeman leading the *cortége*, and who had an air

of startled dignity upon him, stopped as he approached
the office-door.

"It's sooicide for a pot!" said the jailer, who stood
behind me.

"Sooicide!" said the sergeant, as he stopped, and as
the official part of the procession followed his example
—not followed however by the rabble, who flocked
round and gorged intelligence with all their eyes, their
mouths meanwhile being wide open with excitement.

"I know'd it," said the jailer. "*I* should have won."

"What is it, Brogley?" asked the inspector of the
sergeant.

"Military case, sir," said the sergeant; "soldier
shot hisself in a room in Hare's-street, in the room
where the prisoner Kamp, the shoemaker, lived."

It was no good guess on my part, after hearing
these words, to feel certain that the soldier was Tom
Hapsy.

I raised the poor quilt that had been thrown over
the body—a quilt that had been taken from "the
prisoner Kamp's" room—and there sure enough I saw,
as the eager crowd herded about me, glad of this
chance to see a horror—there I saw what remained of
the features of Tom Hapsy.

So in six months, I thought, as after some official
directions the body was borne on towards the dead
house, Johanna Kamp had destroyed herself, so also
had the cheerful soldier Tom Hapsy, and the third of
that humble trio, John Kamp, lay in prison self-
accused of murder.

Nor let the reader suppose this case untrue because

it may appear overdrawn. The poor and the wretched too often find death sweeter than life. And indeed in this particular case, the man and woman, by reason of their physical drawbacks, had been so desolate before they met, that it is no wonder they fell into despair when the love they felt for each other was broken down by a selfish, heartless man.

The searcher at the dead-house found that letter on the poor dead body which exculpated John Kamp, though I could have saved him had the letter fallen from the body in its passage to the dead-house.

For the bullet extracted from Higham's body exactly fitted the pistol found in Hapsy's right hand, and what is more, the bullet taken from Tom's temple, where it had lodged, had been cast in the same mould (as the mark of a fracture proved) as the lead which the doctor produced at the inquest upon the sub-army contractor.

Thereupon I went by permission to John Kamp's cell.

By the way I will not reproduce Tom Hapsy's letter found on his dead body, for it was badly spelt, and written in a highflown, sentimental style, which might appear ridiculous to the more unthinking of my readers. It is sufficient to say that he declared he had taken the law into his own hands, first in destroying " Johanna's seducer," and then himself.

I went, I say, to John Kamp's cell.

" John Kamp," said I, " you did not kill Mr. Higham."

He looked up amazedly.

And then I told him all the news.

He did not weep.  He was too thoroughly broken-down for that.  He did not betray any surprise when I told him about the cartridge-paper being a leaf from the work of which he was so fond.  He took little notice of my explanation to the effect that the soldier must have torn the leaf from the book when contemplating the murder.

All he said was—" Poor Tom."

Some time afterwards I comprehended how it happened that both men were at the same time in the field where the catastrophe occurred.

The young person who was to meet Higham, viciously proud of the interview, had confided the news to a companion (who of course knew all about the talk concerning Johanna's death), and she it was who informed the brother and soldier the of the coming meeting.  With what intention I have never learnt.  But I have surmised that she did so with some idea of that rough, terrible justice called vengeance, and which more or less lurks in every human heart.

Yes, all he said was, " Poor Tom !"

At last I said to him—" But, John, why did you say you killed the man ?"

He looked up to me with most weary simplicity, and he said—

" I went out to kill him, and should have done so if Tom had not.  I did not know who shot him at the time.  I was a murderer in intention, and I gave myself up."

So, there you have my tale of " The Judgment of Conscience."

John Kamp is in Australia now, and doing well. Nor am I sorry that I helped him to do well. He has long since paid me back; and he tells me if ever I want a pound or two I am to let him know.

I think he is happy for being in Australia, where they are not so socially particular as in England, even in the matter of doctors. He has long since managed to become a kind of under-assistant at a dispensary; and I am sure that I for one would not at all hesitate to swallow a prescription made up by him, even though he had put the dose together in the dark.

# A CHILD FOUND DEAD: MURDER OR NO MURDER.*

I HAVE had great doubts as to the desirability of printing the following narrative. I do so, because I think it worth record. Strictly speaking, it is no experience whatever of mine. It was given to me in manuscript by the medical man who induced me to follow up the Bridge mystery. Perhaps flattered by the respect I paid his first communication, he offered me a second.

* Many persons will find a surprising similarity between this tale and the particulars of the destruction of Francis Saville Kent, the little victim of the Road Hill tragedy. But there is a radical difference between the two cases, for it will be found that in this paper the perpetrator of the horrid deed was not a person that could be identified as representing any of the occupants of Mr. Kent's house on the night of the catastrophe. On the contrary, the principal character is a *visitor* to the house in which the action takes place; whereas, in the terribly real case near Frome, no visitor was in that house at the time of the tragedy. However, if readers are determined to see in this paper an attempt at an elucidation of the Road mystery, I am not amenable for being unable to blind them on this point. I may add, that until this most extraordinary of cases is cleared up, if ever it can be, all the occupants of that house must rest under a certain kind of suspicion; any attempt, therefore, to relieve the number by fixing the calamity of the act upon an individual, would be an act of great kindness and justice, however hard it might bear upon the latter.

I give it precisely as he handed it to me, believing this to be the only justifiable way in which to present it to the public. To begin [It is the doctor speaking] :—

I was sitting, perhaps a little sadly, looking out into the street from a drear tavern window, and thinking of a lost home, when I heard these words in a low soft voice—

" There's no reason in the whole business from beginning to end."

I knew the tones in a moment, or suspected I did, which is pretty much about the same thing, for suspicion is frequently but cautious certainty ; and starting up, I looked over the screen which separated my dismal dinner-table from the next.

It was Hardal beyond a doubt. Hardal himself— as frail, wild-looking, and attractive as ever—a man neither beautiful nor elegant, and yet one after whom clear-headed and observant passers-by generally looked with an inquiring and a puzzled air.

Hardal is a thin, short, sallow-faced man, with mournful-looking yet penetrating eyes, and he has a habit of looking at people, which as frequently irritates some as it awes others.

This peculiarity I marked at our school, and I have, during the last year or so, had ample opportunities of observing my old school-chum's odd qualification—for I need not say that, recognising him, I made myself known immediately. Amongst men who have gone to school and been thrashed together, there is always much mutual candour to be found, and plenty of the hail-fellow-well-met good fellowship.

Hardal was known at school as the queerest fellow out—he is known at this moment at the common-law bar as the most eccentric barrister who ever donned a stuff gown and a wig. At school he was doubted for his oddity—now he is questioned for his eccentricity. At school he never got on amongst his schoolfellows, and now he does not progress in the midst of his fellow-men. The man is the child of the youth, and the same prejudices pervade both. They but follow the law of hereditary transmission. It is the misfortune of unknown genius to be doubted, as it is the glory of known genius to be held in awe. Hardal was and is an unknown genius. As a boy he was thought to be mad, this being one of the privileges of genius, and as a man I doubt if his associates feel quite sure that he is sane. He knows his own position as well as any man, and he says—" I shall never rise out of nothingness (because I am not an ordinary man) unless extraordinary circumstances surround me, when nothing will impede my rise. I am a man who cannot make an opportunity, but who, having an opportunity given him, will use it to good account, unless pulled down by the vain or ignorant, or both kinds of fools, about him."

At school, nothing would turn Hardal from what he thought to be right. I remember the especial case which caused him to be dubbed a sneak, and which was really the cause of his abandoning the academy where we met.

A very mild, modest, junior Latin master had arrived, and as boys are cowards enough to be unable to forgive mildness and modesty, the new man was turned into a butt. The grossest questions were put to him, and letters of the nastiest character slipped into his desk through the crack on the top of it. He took all these performances very quietly, though it was whispered about that he had been heard to sob in his own room. But the hat business, at the end of his first week, outraged even his rosewater blood.

The poor man had quietly taken his hat from a peg and put it on his head, preparatory to going out with a copy of his beloved Persius under his arm, when down fell the body and crown of the hat to the ground, leaving above the junior Latin master's surprised countenance the rim, like a queer crown, turned up on the edge next the head with the leather lining of the hat itself.

Boys never spare the ridiculous, and this spectacle created such a roar of laughter, that Bargee, the *nom-de-ferule* of the immense doctor who governed us, came tramping out of his private room, to which we used to go for judgment, with the air of an outraged elephant.

There stood the young Latin master, still crowned. Of course Bargee, the unjustest of men, fell upon the junior master at once, and bullied him handsomely, and this bringing about a general explanation of the performance, Bargee delivered himself of this ukase — no boy to enter the playground till the culprit was found out, five shillings being offered as a reward to any Bargee's evidence, witness not being an actual accomplice.

Every community has its cowards, and within five minutes Seth Cundle, the stupidest and most thrashed of boys, was accused by Allen Buckenham of the crime.

Seth hadn't a word to say—he believed himself born to blows and injustice, and of course soon involved himself in such a whirl of contradictions, that ignorant old Bargee set him down as guilty at once, and being hoisted, he received thrashing number one.

Now this thrashing shook Bargee's state desk, at which the operation took place, and the hat-rim, which had been brought forward in accusation, fell with the shock upon the school desk below and close up to the Bargee's. This desk was shared by Hardal and myself. We sat side by side.

I saw Hardal pick it up ; turn it over and over ; then he smelt the leather.

All that morning he was, I saw, uneasy. He had said to me, " Look here, Roddy ; you know the rim was stuck on to the body with gum ; now you know Cundle isn't a dandy, and hasn't got any gum ; and besides, if he had, *he* would not have thought to stick on the rim. You know, Roddy, it *wasn't* Cundle ; and I mean to find out who it was."

Now I want the reader to mark this perception, forecasting as it does that which he applied to the discovery of a certain mysterious slaying of a child. Hardal knew that a number of our boys used gum-water, scented with various perfumes, for making kiss-curls, and sticking them on their foreheads. These were the boys we called dandies. Cundle certainly wasn't one of them ; his hair was always as rough as a long-haired mat. Hardal was quite sure, by smelling the gum on the inner part of the rim, that Cundle was not the guilty party—who was ? of this I felt sure, knowing him well, that he, if any one, would find out the culprit—and he DID.

It was in the afternoon, and poor old Seth was about to get his third elevation, when Hardal, as though unable to restrain himself, started up and said, "Sir, Dr. ——, Cundle didn't do it." The school became immediately as silent as the grave.

Hardal's case was opened, and looked into to the bottom in no time. He showed the gum marks, pointed out that only a few boys had gum-bottles, and then told Dr. —— that the gum on the hat, if wetted, smelt strongly of roses. Of course the reader sees the argument. Old Bargee, with the air of having found it all out himself, ordered every box to be searched. But one bottle of rose-scented gum was found—in the box of Dandy Buckenham, who, panic-stricken, admitted his guilt, and literally "got it."

"I knew it," said Hardal to me ; "and he fixed upon Seth because he is a fool." I saw tears in my schoolmate's eye as he spoke ; and *yet* the boys made such war against him for that evidence of his love of truth and justice, that actually he left the doctor's, and I never heard of or saw him till we met by the sign of his voice, in that dull dining-room in the Strand tavern.

I will pass over the meeting between us. I had always known Hardal to be no common man ; and therefore I was not disturbed by the extreme emotion he betrayed in seeing me. "It's like a dip in the past," he said; "and the past with me is always brighter than the present."

Of course our talk soon referred to the accident of our recognition ; the words Hardal had used, and what I had heard, "There's no reason in it from beginning to end."

"I suppose," said I, referring to the words, "you were at your old game again ?"

"Yes," said he, "I am trying to elucidate the mystery of that murder, if murder it was, in the house of that Mr. Cumberland, in the North of England. It is the most contradictory business I ever came across."

"It is," I answered. "But why did you say 'if murder it is ?' Surely there can be no doubt of that ?"

"Surely ?" Hardal returned. "You think there can be no doubt of murder because you think in ordinary channels. You hear of a body *found* under the ordinary conditions of a murdered person ; and therefore you jump at the conclusion that a murder has been committed. This is ridiculous, when the whole facts of the case are taken into consideration ; but, Roddy, as I used to call you, I noticed just now that when I mentioned the name Cumberland—there, you have started again—why ?"

"I know the Cumberlands," I said, "well, and pity them much. They are nice people, and are suffering horribly, as I know."

"You are acquainted with them ?"

"Well—thoroughly," I returned.

"Tell me," Hardal eagerly continued, "do they wish this affair of the loss of the child investigated ? or after the horrible investigations which have taken place, do they shrink from further examination ?"

"On the contrary," I returned, "nobody is more anxious than the father of the dead child to learn the cause by which he came to his death."

"Then you can give me an introduction to this Mr. Cumberland, if I assure you I think I have the clue to the catastrophe ?"

"I will go down with you to his place," I said, "and put myself at your service ; but in the first instance you must really convince me you have a good basis to rest your attempts upon."

For you see, even I, knowing Hardal well, doubted him. I do firmly believe that to be doubted is one of the inherent curses of genius.

"That's but rational," said Hardal ; "but don't be judicial," he urged, "or you will doubt. This murder, as I will call it for the sake of brevity, was no common crime, and must be accounted for by no common reasoning. When Newton made his great gravity discovery, he did not judge by ordinary efforts ; had he, he would have perhaps died nameless. Now listen. There are two conditions of absolute murder, which should be both present to exhibit absolute murder, and of which the first cannot be absent. The first is MOTIVE ; the second, CONCEALMENT OF THE BODY. If a man kill another without motive, then the act is not murder, which is wilful taking away of life ; while if a man kill another, motive being present, without taking either the precaution of concealing the body, or deflecting suspicion from himself, the plot is defective, and argues insanity, or a weakness which may be called insanity, in the perpetrator. For instance, if I kill a man in my office on a second floor by shooting him, is not the act weak ? I warn those about me with the pistol, and I have no means of hiding the body. I have been acting either in a state of permanent or temporary insanity ; I am no true murderer, who should not only show motive, but a perfectly logical self-preservation.

"Now what real *motive* has there been for the destruction of the child in this case ?

" Now what self-preservative means by the hiding of the body have been shown by the destroyer ?

"Let me lay the facts of this history before you. The family went to bed at the ordinary hours on a given night. In the nursery are three beds, one under the window in which a child about four years old is asleep, a second in which a younger child sleeps, and a third in which a nurse sleeps, generally by herself, but which, on the occasion of the murder, as I will still call it, is partly occupied by a friend of the nurse's.

" The nurse falls to sleep at eleven o'clock, and wakes at five in the morning, it then having been light two hours, for the catastrophe takes place towards the end of June. As would be natural, she looks over the room to the cot in which the boy is sleeping, and misses him from the bed. Supposing that the child has gone, or been taken, to the mother's

room, which is only across the passage, the nurse falls
asleep again, and only wakes when it is time to rise.
She gets up, dresses the little girl who sleeps in the
cot near her, and then very naturally goes to the
mother's door, and asks for the child. He is not there.
Supposed to be upstairs in an elder sister's room, application is made there without success. The alarm is
taken, and the house searched, with no results beyond
these—the drawing-room door and one of the drawing-
room windows are found open. The father immediately sets out in a vehicle for a police-constable,
believing the child to have been stolen, and the search
for the child is continued. While the father is still away,
the body of the child is found, thrust out of sight, not
concealed, just below the seat of the servant's closet,
and wrapped in a blanket.

"These are the broad outlines of the case, and
though we already find two far from comprehended
facts, we are not yet staggered. These facts are—
First, that one of the drawing-room windows is open ;
and second, that the concealment of the body betrays
as much *weakness* as that of the ostrich, which hides
its head in a bush and thinks itself concealed from the
hunter. The body was concealed—if concealment it can
be called—exactly in the place and in a manner where
it must be immediately discovered, and is thrust into
the closet under circumstances which could not remain
unseen. Indeed, this concealment is so weak that it
suggests idiocy.

"But when we come to investigate the many peculiar facts of this act, each one of which takes it out of

the list of ordinary sentient murders, we must feel that
to apply the ordinary rules of causes and effects to this
affair, is taking exactly that road which must lead to
nothing but disappointment.

"In the first place, it is extraordinary that any
human being could have entered the room without
waking some of the inmates. However, let this pass,
and come to the removal of the child. He was removed with *womanly* care, being wrapped in a blanket.
Now comes the question—Whence came the blanket?
The answer is—From between the sheet and counterpane which formed the upper clothing of the bed.
Well, we can understand that, in *stealing* a child, even
a man might think of removing it in a blanket; but
when it comes to a question of murder, this use of the
blanket is inexplicable.

"But the following eccentricity of this catastrophe
is the most marvellous in the whole history. The
counterpane and the sheet must have been very considerably displaced by the removal of the blanket from
between them. And yet we find them not only not
disrupted, but smoothed, and arranged as though the
bed had been made *after* the murder and before its
discovery. Yet this is not so, for the impression of
the child's body is found on the bed, and beneath the
smoothed sheets.

"Now, whether the child were removed living or
dead from the bed, the re-arrangement of the bed-
clothing is inexplicable. Would a sentient murderer,
or even a sentient child-thief, have remained to re-
arrange the sheet and counterpane? Again, if two

accomplices were not present, the one murderer would have had to lay the child down while the sheet and counterpane were smoothed. Could the child, if alive when removed from the room, have slept through all these extraordinary proceedings without waking?

"Now comes the removal of the body from the house. The drawing-room window is found open, and this is the only exit from the house discovered unfastened. It is a remarkable fact that this window is the most distant means of exit out of the house from the spot at which the body was found.

"To reach that closet, the person carrying the child had to pass round *the front* of the house, and between it and the road, then to pass the yard-gates, behind which was a watch-dog, and so reach the closet. The closet reached, the child's body is slashed in the most horrible manner, the head is nearly severed from the body, and a frightful stab is found through the body, and near the heart.

"The poor child's body, wrapped in the blanket, is then thrust down the closet for but a few feet, when it rests on the splash-board, and is there found. Also is discovered a small piece of flannel.

"Thus things stand to the inquest, at which all the facts above narrated are stated, and also the following. The nurse says of the arranged bed, 'the bedclothes were placed neatly, as if I or his mother had done it.' The dog is found to be quite in ordinary health on the morning after the murder. Next follows the evidence of the man who discovered the body, and he states that he found about two tablespoonfuls of blood of a *dark* *colour* on the ground of the closet. Outside the closet, a piece of bloody newspaper is found, and this is never identified as having formed part of any paper in the house. The evidence of the surgeon is exceedingly important as throwing light on many otherwise inexplicable circumstances of the case. He states that the mouth was discoloured, that the small quantity of blood on the floor of the closet does not represent anything like the entire mass of blood in the child's veins, and that the absence of blood from the walls of the closet goes to prove that the wounds were inflicted after death, or just as death was being consummated, and the action of the heart had ceased.* In fact, the evidence of the doctor goes to show that the child was smothered before the wounds across the throat and in the breast were made. The surgeon represented the

---

* To the general reader, perhaps not fully acquainted with the human blood circulation system, this sentence requires some explanation. The whole blood of the human body (nay, indeed, that of all living things in more or less time) passes in about three minutes throughout the body—leaving the heart by one series of veins, those which beat, or pulsate, and returning by a second series of veins, which do not pulsate. Now, the blood is forced forward by jerks, those of the heart, and at each jerk the heart-veins, or arteries, distend a little. Let one of these arteries be cut while life is in the heart, and the blood will spurt out exactly as water from a burst water-pipe, and fly all manner of ways around—and *at* the murderer, if murderer there be ; while if an artery be cut *after* death, or after the cessation of the heart's action, and while the body is yet warm, the still but partially congealed blood (for blood begins to congeal the moment it ceases to be propelled by the heart's motion) will gradually ooze out in a dark-coloured stream. Hence, in the case of this child, there being no marks on the wall or seat of the closet, and there being only a little dark blood on the floor, the certain conclusion is that death had taken place before the wounds were made.

wounds as of the most savage nature—the throat being cut to the bone, and the chest wound evidencing great force. The doctor, viewing the body at nine A.M., pronounces death to have taken place quite five hours previously—this gives four o'clock as the latest time of the murder (it having then been light one hour, and, it may be supposed, plenty of summer labourers about), while, as the family went to bed at about half-past eleven, midnight may be taken as the earliest hour at which the act could have been committed. This narrows the time of the deed from midnight to four—or more likely, from midnight to two in the morning.

"In summing up, the coroner, apparently a not too able man, lays most stress upon the drawing-room window being found open about a foot.

"Many events follow the coroner's inquest. The mysteries rather than the atrocities of the case attract public notice, and at last a splendid yet ordinary investigation is made—it fails entirely and quite naturally. To hope to discover extraordinary answers to ordinary questions is to be too rational.

"A boy of sixteen, an out-door servant of Mr. Cumberland's, is the first to be suspected, for he had been discharged the day before the murder; but he is shown to have slept at home on the night of the murder, and about two miles away from the scene of the catastrophe—and he is freed from suspicion.

"A daughter of Mr. Cumberland is then taken into custody, because one of her night dresses is missing, and this investigation failing, the nurse herself is literally put upon her trial, apparently because she

has said the boy was 'killed for vengeance,' and because a fragment of flannel is found in the water-
closet, and under the body of the child, and which
might or might not have been there before the murder.
This accusation fails as did the other, though it is
conducted magnificently—upon the basis that the
murder is one of an ordinary character, committed
with ordinary motive and action, but about which
many extraordinary circumstances cling. The lawyer
who conducts the case points out many valuable facts.
He urges that, as there are no marks of external vio-
lence about the house, did any one from *without*
commit the crime he must have had an accomplice
within the house. He then points out that the window
is found only a foot wide open—not wide enough for
the passage of any one carrying a child—and as the
window upon being raised higher makes a noise, He
suggests, not only that this proves it was raised by a
member of the household, but that it was raised as a
blind—he does not, however, tell us of what character.
He then argues from the state of the bed that two persons were engaged in the murder, not questioning the
eccentricity of this needless act, or doubting if the
boy is alive when removed from the room. In fact,
this gentleman's argument is, the murder was com
mitted by an inmate of the house, and the nurse is
most likely to have committed it.*

"The case fails entirely—the girl is liberated, and

* The friend of the nurse, who slept with her, it is seen is not
suspected. There are reasons for this.

the mystery remains, and has remained, as unaccountable as it was on the first morning after the murder."

\*        \*        \*        \*        \*

Here Hardal, who by this time had a wild look in his eyes, rested for a moment, and then continued : " Now, Roddy, hear *my* version of the business, and then help me to prove it if you like. There are three questions to be answered :—

" 1. Was the murder committed by a non-occupant ?

" 2. Was the murder committed by an occupant ?

" 3. By whom, and wherefore, was the murder committed ?"

" 1. Was the murder committed by a non-occupant ?

" If so, he would act either with the connivance of some one within the house, or by himself. Now I think that the awful investigation to which the household has been submitted, pretty clearly proves the absence of an accomplice in the shape of one of its members. Yet there are no signs of a burglarious entry into the house, and therefore if a stranger did enter it, the entry was made by extraordinary means. The only probable one was by a first or upper floor window. Now could this have been done ? There is no vine or other creeper about the house by which a window could be reached, say by a revengeful gipsy whom Mr. Cumberland may have threatened, while if a ladder were used it seems impossible to suppose the dog, much less the whole household, could have slept through the noise of fixing it to a window. Again, a gipsy, the most likely man to take such a kind of revenge as the abstraction or killing of a child, would have silenced the dog—an art in which gipsies are known to be proficients.

"The health of the dog next morning, and his silence during the night, prove, first that he was not tampered with ; secondly, that he was disturbed by no stranger. Then did any one, not being an inmate of the house, and yet known to the dog, commit the crime? A means of entry to the house is totally absent. Again, did any one conceal himself in the house? This suggestion is the only one holding good in favour of the theory that the murder was committed by a non-occupant. But in the face of this argument stands the peculiarity that in such a case there was evident mystification of the household by leaving the premises, not by a door, but a window, and then partially closing that window.

"2. Was the murder committed by an occupant?

"If it has been shown that it is highly improbable that the crime was committed by a non-occupant, it results that the probability of its having been committed by an occupant is just in inverse proportion with that improbability.

"3. By whom, and wherefore was the murder committed?"

Here Hardal drew a long breath, drank off a large glass of water, and wiping his hot forehead, he continued—"I am going to commit myself to an extraordinary series of—of statements, and if you are like the majority of fools about one, you will pshaw me, and prove by naught that there's nothing in what I say.

"In the first place, let me back my statements with these extraordinary lines taken from a *Times* leader on the whole of this case.

"'As a painful result, therefore, we are left with the circle of suspicion as narrow as ever, and with the additional embarrassment ensuing on the successive failures of justice . . . It really seems almost a case for the art of clairvoyance, or the old machinery of the divining rod. Ordinary agencies are completely at fault.'

"This is the *Times!* You see a complete admission that the whole inquiry is a BALK; and yet a clinging to the belief that it is cunning and not ignorance which has foiled the inquirer, for the *Times* continues: 'But we trust that in one respect the views of the magistrate will be carried out. There should not be a remission, even for a single moment, of vigilance or observation.'

"Nor has there been—and nothing has been discovered.

"Now in the first place," continued Hardal, "let us see who were sleeping in the house on the night in question.

"The inmates on the night of the murder were thirteen in number, ten being adults, and of these some six were able in a measure to exonerate each other. Three slept in one apartment, three in a second, and two in a third, and two more in a fourth; so that, apart from the inmates of the nursery itself, there were but two persons in the house who could not call a certain kind of evidence to their behaviour throughout the night. The cook and the housemaid slept together, the two eldest sisters slept together, and Mr. and Mrs. Cumberland had a young child sleeping in their bed-room.  Mr. William Cumberland and Miss Constance Cumberland had each a room a-piece, whilst the two youngest children—the little boy who was murdered and an infant of two years old, were in the nursery with the nurse, as was also a visitor of the nurse, a kind of relation well known in the house and to the children, and who had frequently expressed extreme love for the little murdered child.

" Now," continued Hardal, " I venture to state at once that there is no evidence of ordinary murder in this case—that its whole facts exhibit an extraordi-nary amount of eccentricity ; and that the murder was eccentrically committed by an inmate of the house. And as most eccentricity is an evidence of mental weakness, I come to the conclusion that if the mur-derer (as I will call him or her) were aware of his crime, he being eccentric, and therefore weak, would not be able to resist such an extreme investigation as that which has been made.  Thus I deduce that the act was committed while the murderer was asleep, and while under the influence of murderous mono-mania.

" It now remains to be ascertained who was, by the facts of the case, the person most likely to have been under this influence.  As to the supposition that murder can be done in the sleep, and that a mania to destroy or act abnormally, may torment a human being for years without a second soul knowing anything

about the matter, there are too many well evidenced
cases to permit much doubt on these points.

" As regards somnambulism, we find the cases of
acts in a somnambulistic state are not frequent; yet,
at the same time, not so extremely rare as to be valueless in urging my argument.   In Rees' 'Cyclopædia'
we find Dr. Stewart saying :—'There are many cases
in which sleep seems to be partial; that is, when the
mind loses its influence over some powers and retains
it over others.'   Dr. Darwin considers somnambulism
not so much sleep as a state approximating to epilepsy.
Some cases of sleep-walking, where a series of acts
have been carried out, are on record.  *They all agree
with the waking thoughts in some measure.*   One case
we have of a boy who, being very fond of grapes,
starts off in the middle of the night for a vineyard,
and gathers the fruit.   In another case, a boy rising
in his sleep in the dark, calls for a light to find his
clothes by, and this being brought, he dresses with
ease, and a cuckoo-bell clock striking, he says, ' There be
cuckoos here.'   As a proof that the predominating
idea submerges all others, this same boy would be sen-
sible of pinches or slight blows, unless 'he was at the
time strongly impressed with some other thing.'   The
watcher of this lad bid him 'write a theme.'   They
say, 'We saw him light a candle, take pen, ink, and
paper from the drawer of his table, and begin to write
while one of those about him began to dictate.'   Here
is a series of events, and yet this case thoroughly illustrates my argument that the acts are imperfect, or
rather exhibit imperfection, for the inkstand, which

he had opened his eyes to find, being removed, 'his hand returned as usual to the place where he thought it was.' It must be observed that the motion of his hand was rapid till it reached the height of the inkstand, and then he moved it slowly till the pen gently touched the table as he was seeking for the ink.'*

"Of homicidal monomania, Dr. Copeland ('Dic. Medicine,' vol. ii., article Insanity) says :—'Murder, or attempts to murder, are made by insane persons, 1. When impelled by an involuntary impulse, or instinctive desire, which they are unable to resist; 2. When actuated by motives on which they are capable of reasoning, and whilst conscious of the evil they have committed ; 3. When influenced by delusions, hallucinations, or false perceptions ; 4. When excited by passion or opposition ; 5. When they believe they are opposing an enemy ; and 6. When the intelligence is so prostrate as to be incapable of distinguishing right from wrong, and when they act from imitation. The first of these cases is the most frequent, and to which I will draw attention. Persons will appear to enjoy reason ; they are irresistibly impelled, with a full consciousness of their state, to commit the crime they most hate. The question is, Is there really a form of insanity in which a person may enjoy reason unimpaired and yet commit the greatest crimes? I say, yes. One person suddenly becomes red in the face, imagines he hears a voice ad-

* For further information *see* Hoffman's "Dissertatio do Somnambulismo."

dressing him, and acts according to its injunction. Another, a husband, is persuaded his wife is unfaithful to him, although he has considered all the circumstances, and finds them in her favour—and an act of murder is committed. A third, a mother of a family, believes herself in distress, and in a fit of despair she attempts to kill them, when maternal tenderness, speaking louder than despair, exclaims? ' Protect my children from me.' Another well-authenticated instance is that of a maid, who, on each occasion of her dressing the infant committed to her care, was seized with an uncontrollable desire to kill it. All these instances may be referred to as *momentary* delusions or hallucinations, under the influence of which crimes or insane actions may be committed, after which a lucid period occurs.

"Now child-murder, as a rule, is always maniacal, for the simple reason that the child cannot excite motive. Those cases of infanticide in which no insanity is present, are those in which the mother kills from shame or want. Such a motive in this case is absent; while the majority of child-murders being committed by women, the inference perhaps stands, that in the absence of motive it is a female murderer who destroyed this child.

"The circumstantial evidence of the case goes to prove that the nurse or nurse's visitor, (present on the night of the murder,) committed the act in a state of unconsciousness (or sleep), because there is no waking evidence of guilt, and in a state of monomania, because there is no evidence of motive. There is one indirect evidence of 'unconscious thought' about the murdered child in the following statement :—

"'It has been stated by a young woman who lived as nursemaid in the family about twelve months since, that on one occasion when there were only two members of the family at home, the little boy who has been murdered was found in his cot with the bed-clothes turned back carefully, and some woollen socks and some flannels, in which he was put to bed, he being unwell on the previous night, were taken off. One of the socks was found in the morning on the table in the bedroom, and the other in the course of the following day on Mrs. Cumberland's bed, but Mrs. Cumberland was wholly unable to account for its appearance in that place.' 'These statements,' says the ignorant writer from whom we quote the last sentences, 'have, however, no immediate bearing upon this mysterious case.'

"They have much bearing, for they show in this house somewhere an abnormal unhealthy state in some one. They prove the work of one who can act in sleep; and supposing this person to be cursed with murderous monomania, and accepting the fact that a series of acts can be done in sleep, we come to the conclusion that the incident of the socks shadows out the possibility of the house being the scene of a series of unconscious deeds.

"I say," continued Hardal, "that the incomprehensible acts of this murder prove that they were done in unconsciousness, in insanity, and by a woman.

"In the first place, take the wrapping of the blanket about the child. Would a conscious, sane murderer do this? Whereas, would it not be the daily habit of a nurse of little children? Again, the quilt and sheet are straightened; this is the work of a nurse. But they are straightened over an unmade bed, which suggests an imperfect consciousness of action. Now, it has been urged that there must have been two persons engaged in this murder, because of these straightened bed-clothes; for it is asked, had a single murderer only been present, where was the child placed while this work was done? This question does not seem to have suggested itself—why was this uncalled-for, needless, and irrational act performed?

"I believe that the child was dead before taken from the bed—that he was suffocated with the pillow; and the whole of the doctor's evidence goes to prove that death took place before the victim was carried to the closet.

"The next act was to remove the body from the house, and, as you know, it was carried past the boundary of the house at that point farthest of all parts of the house from the spot where it was found—I mean one of the drawing-room windows, which was discovered open a foot wide the next morning. It has been argued, that as the window could not be opened higher than a foot without making a noise, which would have alarmed house and dog, and that as a foot was not width enough to allow of the passage of a human creature carrying a child, that therefore the opening of this window was a 'blind.' No such thing; a foot in width would be quite enough for a young person to press through, while the dead child may have been passed out first, laid upon the grass, and afterwards picked up.

"Now follows the most irrational fact of the case: the bearer of the child, in preference to carrying away the child, and flinging it in a pond, a well, or even hedge, as a sentient murderer would have done, prefers to pass in front of the house, before the road, past the gates below which the dog frequently growls at passers-by, and so to the closet, which a conscious member of the household must know is provided with a splash-board, which will at once arrest anything cast down the closet.

"The dog does not give the alarm, an evidence either that he is awake, and, knowing the person, does not bark, or that the person walks so lightly—as is the case with sleep-walkers—that the animal is not awakened by the footsteps.

"There is only one discrepancy in this part of the affair. It stands thus: if the murderer was a sleep-walker, and, being a servant of the house, therefore better acquainted with the kitchen (the nearest way across the yard, in which is the dog, to the servants' closet, where the body is found) than the drawing-room, how is it she avoided the kitchen and the kitchen-yard? I answer, that it is impossible to bound the limits either of instinct, reason, or insanity in sleep-walking. These qualities cross and recross each other in an unending tangle.

"I now approach a fact in the case which proves

monomaniac tendency and unconsciousness of act. The child is dead; and therefore if *sentient motive* only is present, the work now alone to be performed is the disposal of the body. Yet instead of this, we find the next act is the mutilation of the body in the most savage manner. The doctor tells us that the head was nearly severed from the body, and that great force must have been exerted to drive the weapon used into the breast. Now, where was the need to use the knife at all? The child was dead, or if not dead, to all appearance so, and yet it was mutilated, and blood spilt. The body is then wrapt in the blanket, which is another evidence of care; and the whole just thrown below the seat of the closet, so that it is found the moment after the blood is seen on the floor.

"The window is then left open, and so found in the morning.

"Upon the discovery of the murder nobody in the house betrays the least guilt, although all inferences but one point to the supposition that the murder has been committed in the house : that exception lying in the fact that a piece of bloody paper is found near the closet upon which a bloody knife has been wiped, and which paper has not been torn apparently from any paper in the house.

"The child's life has been taken away; it seems clear some one in the house has done it in the most slovenly manner, for the murder is found out in ten minutes after the alarm is given, and yet all appear innocent—all give exactly the same tale of a peaceful night and no disturbance. There is no apparent motive to kill the child, no evidence against anybody as the murderer, except an absent nightgown and a wretched piece of flannel, and after masses of investigation the fact remains where it was.

"Now see how beautifully my theory of sleeping monomania fits the difficulties of the case. The girl has a tendency to kill the child, such a tendency as many human beings experience, but have sufficient self-restraint to overcome. She is also a sleep-walker. The monomaniacal desire present in her sleep, she rises, and then commences an entanglement between her every-day and her monomaniacal acts. First she suffocates the child as a monomaniac, then as a nurse she envelopes it in the blanket, and smooths the unmade bed. Then she goes downstairs, no one hearing her, for the simple reason that sleep-walkers move and act without noise. Her half-sense warns her of the dog and of the creaking window. She stops raising it with its first signal of creaking—it is a foot wide, and she can press through the opening, dragging the dead child with her. Then, the half-mind bent on the dog, she forgets the roadway and the front of the house, and so reaches the closet, after either being recognised by the dog if awake, or walking so lightly as not to awake him if asleep. Then the monomaniacal desire is alight again, and hidden in the closet, the knife, whence taken I cannot tell, is used. There is no tell-tale blood on the girl's linen, because, as the doctor informs us, the dead blood did not spurt, but merely flowed. Then that most wild cut at the breast is

made, the ungaping wound also proving that the knife
entered dead flesh; and then the body is cast into the
closet, little attempt being made to conceal it. The
knife is then wiped on the unknown paper and hidden,
the reason of it not found being that, in all probability, it was not, in the true sense of the word, concealed, but just thrown where no one would think of
finding it. The girl then returns to the house,
forgetting in her half-consciousness that the window
remains open. She ascends quite noiselessly to her
room, goes to bed, sleeps, and awaking, knows nothing
of her dream or acts—a frequent case with sleep-
walkers. What is to warn her of the truth when the
murder is found out? No blood on her linen, no
marks of gravel on her feet—for, as a sleep-walker,
she may have rubbed them on the door-mat—nothing
to tell her she is guilty. In fact, she *is* innocent, and
so the mystery remains, and must remain, while the
belief exists that the murder of this boy was a sentient
act. Sentient—had it motive? Was it rationally
done? If knowingly by any person in the house, why?
If knowingly by any person not of the household,
why? I urge, those who are accursed with monomania
are many, and that in this case to monomania was
superadded somnambulism. You say," continued
Hardal, "you know the father of the boy; introduce
me to him, and let me try, for the sake of the many,
to fix this act upon the one."

"I will," said I to Hardal, as he stopped suddenly;
"let us at once start for the north."

He took my hand, and that evening set out.

Hear the result.   .   .   .   .

[At this point the MS. breaks off. Should I obtain its sequel, I will, if I find it advisable to do so, publish the paper immediately.   I never learnt my informant doctor's address.]

# THE UNKNOWN WEAPON.

I AM about to set out here one of the most remarkable cases which have come under my actual observation.

I will give the particulars, as far as I can, in the form of a narrative.

The scene of the affair lay in a midland county, and on the outskirts of a very rustic and retired village, which has at no time come before the attention of the world.

Here are the exact preliminary facts of the case. Of course I alter names, for as this case is now to become public, and as the inquiries which took place at the time not only ended in disappointment, but by some inexplicable means did not arrest the public curiosity, there can be no wisdom in covering the names and places with such a thin veil of fiction as will allow of the truth being seen below that literary gauze. The names and places here used are wholly fictitious, and in no degree represent or shadow out the actual personages or localities.

The mansion at which the mystery which I am about to analyse took place was the manor-house. while its occupant, the squire of the district, was also the lord of the manor. I will call him Petleigh.

I may at once state here, though the fact did not come to my knowledge till after the catastrophe, that the squire was a thoroughly mean man, with but one other passion than the love of money, and that was a greed for plate.

Every man who has lived with his eyes open has come across human beings who concentrate within themselves the most wonderful contradictions. Here is a man who lives so scampishly that it is a question if ever he earnt an honest shilling, and yet he would firmly believe his moral character would be lost did he enter a theatre; there is an individual who never sent away a creditor or took more than a just commercial discount, while any day in the week he may be arrested upon a charge which would make him a scandal to his family.

So with Squire Petleigh. That he was extremely avaricious there can be no doubt, while his desire for the possession and display of plate was almost a mania.

His silver was quite a tradition in the county. At every meal—and I have heard the meals at Petleigh-cote were neither abundant nor succulent—enough plate stood upon the table to pay for the feeding of the poor of the whole county for a month. He would eat a mutton chop off silver.

Mr. Petleigh was in parliament, and in the season came up to town, where he had the smallest and most miserable house ever rented by a wealthy county member.

Avaricious, and therefore illiberal, Petleigh would

not keep up two establishments; and so, when he came to town for the parliamentary season, he brought with him his country establishment, all the servants composing which were paid but third-class fares up to town.

The domestics I am quite sure, from what I learnt, were far from satisfactory people; a condition of things which was quite natural, seeing that they were not treated well, and were taken on at the lowest possible rate of wages.

The only servitor who remained permanently on the establishment was the housekeeper at the manor-house, Mrs. Quinion.

It was whispered in the neighbourhood that she had been the foster-sister ("and perhaps more") of the late Mrs. Petleigh; and it was stated with sufficient openness, and I am afraid also with some general amount of chuckling satisfaction, that the squire had been bitten with his lady.

The truth stood that Petleigh had married the daughter of a Liverpool merchant in the great hope of an alliance with her fortune, which at the date of her marriage promised to be large. But cotton commerce, even twenty-five years ago, was a risky business, and to curtail here particulars which are only remotely essential to the absolute comprehension of this narrative, he never had a penny with her, and his wife's father, who had led a deplorably irregular life, started for America and died there.

Mrs. Petleigh had but one child, Graham Petleigh, and she died when he was about twelve years of age.

During Mrs. Petleigh's life, the housekeeper at Petleighcote was the foster-sister to whom reference has been made. I myself believe that it would have been more truthful to call Mrs. Quinion the natural sister of the squire's wife.

Be that as it may, after the lady's death Mrs. Quinion, in a half-conceded, and after an uncomfortable fashion, became in a measure the actual mistress of Petleighcote.

Possibly the squire was aware of a relationship to his wife at which I have hinted, and was therefore not unready in recognising that it was better she should be in the house than any other woman. For, apart from his avariciousness and his mania for the display of plate, I found beyond all dispute that he was a man of very estimable judgment.

Again, Mrs. Quinion fell in with his avaricious humour. She shaved down his household expenses, and was herself contented with a very moderate remuneration.

From all I learnt, I came to the conclusion that Petleighcote had long been the most uncomfortable house in the county, the display of plate only tending to intensify the general barrenness.

Very few visitors came to the house, and hospitality was unknown; yet, notwithstanding these drawbacks, Petleigh stood very well in the county, and indeed, on the occasion of one or two charitable collections, he had appeared in print with sufficient success.

Those of my readers who live in the country will comprehend the style of the squire's household when

I say that he grudged permission to shoot rabbits on his ground. Whenever possible, all the year round, specimens of that rather tiring food were to be found in Squire Petleigh's larder. In fact, I learnt that a young curate who remained a short time at Tram (the village), in gentle satire of this cheap system of rations, called Petleighcote the " Warren."

The son, Graham Petleigh, was brought up in a deplorable style, the father being willing to persuade himself, perhaps, that as he had been disappointed in his hopes of a fortune with the mother, the son did not call for that consideration to which he would have been entitled had the mother brought her husband increased riches. It is certain that the boy roughed life. All the schooling he got was that which could be afforded by a foundation grammar school, which happened fortunately to exist at Tram.

To this establishment he went sometimes, while at others he was off with lads miserably below him in station, upon some expedition which was not perhaps, as a rule, so respectable an employment as studying the humanities.

Evidently the boy was shamefully ill-used ; for he was neglected.

By the time he was nineteen or twenty (all these particulars I learnt readily after the catastrophe, for the townsfolk were only too eager to talk of the unfortunate young man)—by the time he was nineteen or twenty, a score of years of neglect bore their fruit. He was ready, beyond any question, for any mad performance. Poaching especially was his delight, perhaps in a great measure because he found it profitable; because, to state the truth, he was kept totally without money, and to this disadvantage he added a second, that of being unable to spread what money he did obtain over any expanse of time.

I have no doubt myself that the depredations on his father's estate might have with justice been put to his account, and, from the inquiries I made, I am equally free to believe that when any small article of the mass of plate about the premises was missing, that the son knew a good deal more than was satisfactory of the lost valuables.

That Mrs. Quinion, the housekeeper, was extremely devoted to the young man is certain; but the money she received as wages, and whatever private or other means she had, could not cover the demands made upon them by young Graham Petleigh, who certainly spent money, though where it came from was a matter of very great uncertainty.

From the portrait I saw of him, he must have been of a daring, roving, jovial disposition—a youngster not inclined to let duty come between him and his inclinations; one, in short, who would get more out of the world than he would give it.

The plate was carried up to town each year with the establishment, the boxes being under the special guardianship of the butler, who never let them out of his sight between the country and town houses. The man, I have heard, looked forward to those journeys with absolute fear.

From what I learnt, I suppose the convoy of plate boxes numbered well on towards a score.

Graham Petleigh sometimes accompanied his father to town, and at other times was sent to a relative in Cornwall. I believe it suited father and son better that the latter should be packed off to Cornwall in the parliamentary season, for in town the lad necessarily became comparatively expensive—an objection in the eyes of the father, while the son found himself in a world to which, thanks to the education he had received, he was totally unfitted.

Young Petleigh's passion was horses, and there was not a farmer on the father's estate, or in the neighbourhood of Tram, who was not plagued for the loan of this or that horse—for the young man had none of his own.

On my part, I believe if the youth had no self-respect, the want was in a great measure owing to the father having had not any for his son.

I know I need scarcely add, that when a man is passionately fond of horses generally he bets on those quadrupeds.

It did not call for many inquiries to ascertain that young Petleigh had "put" a good deal of money upon horses, and that, as a rule, he had been lucky with them. The young man wanted some excitement, some occupation, and he found it in betting. Have I said that after the young heir was taken from the school he was allowed to run loose? This was the case. I presume the father could not bring his mind to incurring the expense of entering his son at some profession.

Things then at Petleighcote were in this condition; the father neglectful and avaricious; the son careless, neglected, and daily slipping down the ladder of life; and the housekeeper, Mrs. Quinion, saying nothing, doing nothing, but existing, and perhaps showing that she was attached to her foster-sister's son. She was a woman of much sound and discriminating sense, and it is certain that she expressed herself to the effect that she foresaw the young man was being silently, steadfastly, unceasingly ruined.

All these preliminaries comprehended, I may proceed to the action of this narrative.

It was the 19th of May (the year is unimportant), and early in the morning when the discovery was made, by the gardener to Squire Petleigh—one Tom Brown.

Outside the great hall-door, and huddled together in an extraordinary fashion, the gardener, at half-past five in the morning (a Tuesday), found lying a human form. And when he came to make an examination, he discovered that it was the dead body of the young squire.

Seizing the handle of the great bell, he quickly sounded an alarm, and within a minute the housekeeper herself and the one servant, who together numbered the household which slept at Petleighcote when the squire was in town, stood on the threshold of the open door.

The housekeeper was half-dressed, the servant wench was huddled up in a petticoat and a blanket.

The news spread very rapidly, by means of the

gardener's boy, who, wondering where his master was stopping, came loafing about the house, quickly to find the use of his legs.

"He must have had a fit," said the housekeeper; and it was a flying message to that effect carried by the boy into the village, which brought the village doctor to the spot in the quickest possible time.

It was then found that the catastrophe was due to no *fit*.

A very slight examination showed that the young squire had died from a stab caused by a rough iron barb, the metal shaft of which was six inches long, and which still remained in the body.

At the inquest, the medical man deposed that very great force must have been used in thrusting the barb into the body, for one of the ribs had been half severed by the act. The stab given, the barb had evidently been drawn back with the view of extracting it—a purpose which had failed, the flanges of the barb having fixed themselves firmly in the cartilage and tissue about it. It was impossible the deceased could have turned the barb against himself in the manner in which it had been used.

Asked what this barb appeared like, the surgeon was unable to reply. He had never seen such a weapon before. He supposed it had been fixed in a shaft of wood, from which it had been wrenched by the strength with which the barb, after the thrust, had been held by the parts surrounding the wound.

The barb was handed round to the jury, and every man cordially agreed with his neighbour that he had never seen anything of the kind before ; it was equally strange to all of them.

The squire, who took the catastrophe with great coolness, gave evidence to the effect that he had seen his son on the morning previous to the discovery of the murder, and about noon—seventeen and a half hours before the catastrophe was discovered. He did not know his son was about to leave town, where he had been staying. He added that he had not missed the young man ; his son was in the habit of being his own master, and going where he liked. He could offer no explanation as to why his son had returned to the country, or why the materials found upon him were there. He could offer no explanation in any way about anything connected with the matter.

It was said, as a scandal in Tram, that the squire exhibited no emotion upon giving his evidence, and that when he sat down after his examination he appeared relieved.

Furthermore, it was intimated that upon being called upon to submit to a kind of cross-examination, he appeared to be anxious, and answered the few questions guardedly.

These questions were put by one of the jurymen—a solicitor's clerk (of some acuteness it was evident), who was the Tram oracle.

It is perhaps necessary for the right understanding of this case, that these questions should be here reported, and their answers also.

They ran as follows :—

" Do you think your son died where he was found ?"

" I have formed no opinion."

" Do you think he had been in your house ?"

" Certainly not."

" Why are you so certain ?"

" Because had he entered the house, my housekeeper would have known of his coming."

" Is your housekeeper here ?"

" Yes."

" Has it been intended that she should be called as a witness ?"

" Yes."

" Do you think your son attempted to break into your house ?"

[The reason for this question I will make apparent shortly. By the way, I should, perhaps, here at once explain that I obtained all these particulars of the evidence from the county paper.]

" Do you think your son attempted to break into your house ?"

" Why should he ?"

" That is not my question. Do you think he attempted to break into your house ?"

" No, I do not."

" You swear that, Mr. Petleigh ?"

[By the way, there was no love lost between the squire and the Tram oracle, for the simple reason that not any existed that could be spilt.]

" I do swear it."

" Do you think there was anybody in the house he wished to visit clandestinely ?"

" No."

"Who were in the house?"

"Mrs. Quinion, my housekeeper, and one servant woman."

"Is the servant here?"

"Yes."

"What kind of a woman is she?"

"Really Mr. Mortoun you can see her and judge for yourself."

"So we can. I am only going to ask one question more."

"I reserve to myself the decision whether I shall or shall not answer it."

"I think you will answer it, Mr. Petleigh."

"It remains, sir, to be seen. Put your question."

"It is very simple—do you intend to offer a reward for the discovery of the murderer of your son?"

The squire made no reply.

"You have heard my question, Mr. Petleigh."

"I have."

"And what is your answer?"

The squire paused for some moments. I should state that I am adding the particulars of the inquest I picked up, or detected if you like better, to the information afforded by the county paper to which I have already referred.

"I refuse to reply," said the squire.

Mortoun thereupon applied to the coroner for his ruling.

Now it appears evident to me that this juryman had some hidden motive in thus questioning the squire. If this were so, I am free to confess I never discovered it beyond any question of doubt. I may or I may not have hit on his motive. I believe I did.

It is clear that the question Mr. Mortoun urged was badly put, for how could the father decide whether he would offer a reward for the discovery of a murderer who did not legally exist till after the finding of the jury? And indeed it may furthermore be added that this question had no bearing upon the elucidation of the mystery, or at all events it had no apparent bearing upon the facts of the catastrophe.

It is evident that Mr. Mortoun was actuated in all probability by one of two motives, both of which were obscure. One might have been an attempt really to obtain a clue to the murder, the other might have been the endeavour to bring the squire, with whom it has been said he lived bad friends, into disrespect with the county.

The oracle-juryman immediately applied to the coroner, who at once admitted that the question was not pertinent, but nevertheless urged the squire as the question had been put to answer it.

It is evident that the coroner saw the awkward position in which the squire was placed, and spoke as he did in order to enable the squire to come out of the difficulty in the least objectionable manner.

But as I have said, Mr. Petleigh, all his incongruities and faults apart, was a clear-seeing man of a good and clear mind. As I saw the want of consistency in the question, as I read it, so he must have remarked the same failure when it was addressed to him.

For after patiently hearing the coroner to the end
of his remarks, Petleigh said, quietly,—

"How can I say I will offer a reward for the discovery of certain murderers when the jury have not
yet returned a verdict of murder?"

"But supposing the jury do return such a verdict?"
asked Mortoun.

"Why then it will be time for you to ask your
question."

I learnt that the juryman smiled as he bowed and
said he was satisfied.

It appears to me that at that point Mr. Mortoun
must have either gained that information which fitted
in with his theory, or, accepting the lower motive for his
question, that he felt he had now sufficiently damaged
the squire in the opinion of the county.   For the re-
porters were at work, and every soul present knew
that not a word said would escape publication in the
county paper.

Mr. Mortoun however was to be worsted within the
space of a minute.

"Have you ceased questioning me, gentlemen?"
asked the squire.

The coroner bowed, it appeared.

"Then," continued the squire, "before I sit down—
and you will allow me to remain in the room until the
inquiry is terminated—I will state that of my own
free will which I would not submit to make public
upon an illegal and a totally uncalled-for attempt at
compulsion.   Should the jury bring in a verdict of
murder against unknown persons, I shall *not* offer a

reward for the discovery of those alleged murderers."

"Why not?" asked the coroner, who I learnt afterwards admitted that the question was utterly unpardonable.

"Because," said Squire Petleigh, "it is quite my opinion that no *murder* has been committed."

According to the newspaper report these words were followed by "sensation."

"No murder?" said the coroner.

"No ; the death of the deceased was, I am sure, an accident."

"What makes you think that, Mr. Petleigh?"

"The nature of the death. Murders are not committed, I should think, in any such extraordinary manner as that by which my son came to his end. I have no more to say."

"Here," says the report, "the squire took his seat."

The next witness called—the gardener who had discovered the body had already been heard, and simply testified to the finding of the body—was Margaret Quinion, the housekeeper.

Her depositions were totally valueless from my point of view, that of the death of the young squire. She stated simply that she had gone to bed at the usual time (about ten) on the previous night, and that Dinah Yarton retired just previously, and to the same room. She heard no noise during the night, was disturbed in no way whatever until the alarm was given by the gardener.

In her turn Mrs. Quinion was now questioned by the solicitor's clerk, Mr. Mortoun.

"Do you and this—what is her name?—Dinah Yarton; do you and she sleep alone at Petleighcote?"

"Yes—when the family is away."

"Are you not afraid to do so?"

"No."

"Why?"

"Why should I be?"

"Well—most women are afraid to sleep in large lonely houses by themselves. Are you not afraid of burglars?"

"No."

"Why not?"

"Simply because burglars would find so little at Petleighcote to steal that they would be very foolish to break into the house."

"But there is a good deal of plate in the house—isn't there?"

"It all goes up to town with Mr. Petleigh."

"All, ma'am?"

"Every ounce—as a rule."

"You say the girl sleeps in your room?"

"In my room."

"Is she an attractive girl?"

"No."

"Is she unattractive?"

"You will have an opportunity of judging, for she will be called as a witness, sir."

"Oh; you don't think, do you, that there was anything between this young person and your young master ?"

" Between Dinah and young Mr. Petleigh ?"

" Yes."

" I think there could hardly be any affair between them, for [here she smiled] they have never seen each other—the girl having come to Petleighcote from the next county only three weeks since, and three months after the family had gone to town."

" Oh ; pray have you not expected your master's son home recently ?"

" I have not expected young Mr. Petleigh home ·recently—he never comes home when the family is away."

" Was he not in the habit of coming to Petleighcote unexpectedly ?"

" No."

" You know that for a fact ?"

" I know that for a fact."

" Was the deceased kept without money ?"

" I know nothing of the money arrangements between the father and son."

" Well—do you know that often he wanted money ?"

" Really—I decline to answer that question."

" Well—did he borrow money habitually from you ?"

" I decline also to answer that question."

" You say you heard nothing in the night ?"

" Not anything."

" What did you do when you were alarmed by the gardener in the morning ?"

" I am at a loss to understand your question."

"It is very plain, nevertheless. What was your first act after hearing the catastrophe ?"

[After some consideration.] "It is really almost impossible, I should say, upon such terrible occasions as was that, to be able distinctly to say what is one's first act or words, but I believe the first thing I did, or the first I remember, was to look after Dinah."

"And why could she not look after herself ?"

"Simply because she had fallen into a sort of epileptic fit—to which she is subject—upon seeing the body."

" Then you can throw no light upon this mysterious affair ?"

" No light : all I know of it was the recognition of the body of Mr. Petleigh, junior, in the morning."

The girl Dinah Yarton was now called, but no sooner did the unfortunate young woman, waiting in the hall of the publichouse at which the inquest was held, hear her name, than she swooped into a fit which totally precluded her from giving any evidence " except," as the county paper facetiously remarked, " the proof by her screams that her lungs were in a very enviable condition."

" She will soon recover," said Mrs. Quinion, "and will be able to give what evidence she can."

" And what will that be, Mrs. Quinion ?" asked the solicitor's clerk.

" I am not able to say, Mr. Mortoun," she replied.

The next witness called (and here as an old police-constable I may remark upon the unbusiness-like way

in which the witnesses were arranged)—the next
witness called was the doctor.

His evidence was as follows, omitting the purely
professional points. "I was called to the deceased on
Tuesday morning, at near upon six in the morning.
I recognized the body as that of Mr. Petleigh junior.
Life was quite extinct. He had been dead about
seven or eight hours, as well as I could judge. That
would bring his death about ten or eleven on the
previous night. Death had been caused by a stab,
which had penetrated the left lung. The deceased
had bled inwardly. The instrument which had caused
death had remained in the wound, and stopped what
little effusion of blood there would otherwise have been.
Deceased literally died from suffocation, the blood
leaking into the lungs and filling them. All the
other organs of the body were in a healthy condition.
The instrument by which death was produced is one
with which I have no acquaintance. It is a kind
of iron arrow, very roughly made, and with a shaft.
It must have been fixed in some kind of handle when
it was used, and which must have yielded and loosed
the barb when an attempt was made to withdraw it—
an attempt which had been made, because I found
that one of the flanges of the arrow had caught behind
a rib. I repeat that I am totally unacquainted with
the instrument with which death was effected. It is
remarkably coarse and rough. The deceased might have
lived a quarter of a minute after the wound had been
inflicted. He would not in all probability have called
out. There is no evidence of the least struggle having

taken place—not a particle of evidence can I find to show that the deceased had exhibited even any knowledge of danger. And yet, nevertheless, supposing the deceased not to have been asleep at the time of the murder, for murder it undoubtedly was, or manslaughter, he must have seen his assailant, who, from the position of the weapon, must have been more before than behind him. Assuredly the death was the result of either murder or accident, and not the result of suicide, because I will stake my professional reputation that it would be quite impossible for any man to thrust such an instrument into his body with such a force as in this case has been used, as is proved by the cutting of a true bone-formed rib. Nor could a suicide, under such circumstances as those of the present catastrophe, have thrust the dart in the direction which this took. To sum up, it is my opinion that the deceased was murdered without, on his part, any knowledge of the murderer."

Mr. Mortoun cross-examined the doctor :

To this gentleman's inquiries he answered willingly.

"Do you think, Dr. Pitcherley, that no blood flowed externally ?"

"Of that I am quite sure."

"How ?"

"There were no marks of blood on the clothes."

"Then the inference stands that no blood stained the place of the murder ?"

"Certainly."

"Then the body may have been brought an im-

mense way, and no spots of blood would form a clue
to the road ?"

" Not one."

" Is it your impression that the murder was committed far away from the spot, or near the place where
the body was found ?"

" This question is one which it is quite out of my
power to answer, Mr. Mortoun, my duty here being to
give evidence as to my being called to the deceased,
and as to the cause of death. But I need not tell you
that I have formed my own theory of the catastrophe,
and if the jury desire to have it, I am ready to offer
it for their consideration."

Here there was a consultation, from which it resulted
that the jury expressed themselves very desirous of
obtaining the doctor's impression.

[I have no doubt the following words led the jury
to their decision.]

The medical gentleman said :—

" It is my impression that this death resulted out of
a poaching—I will not say affray—but accident. It
is thoroughly well-known in these districts, and at such
a juncture as the present I need feel no false delicacy,
Mr. Petleigh, in making this statement, that young
Petleigh was much given to poaching. I believe that
he and his companions were out poaching—I myself
on two separate occasions, being called out to night-
cases, saw the young gentleman under very suspicious
circumstances—and that one of the party was armed
with the weapon which caused the death, and which

may have been carried at the end of such a heavy stick as is frequently used for flinging at rabbits. I suppose that by some frightful accident—we all know how dreadful are the surgical accidents which frequently arise when weapons are in use—the young man was wounded mortally, and so died, after the frightened companion had hurriedly attempted to withdraw the arrow, only to leave the barb sticking in the body and hooked behind a rib, while the force used in the resistance of the bone caused the weapon to part company from the haft. The discovery of the body outside the father's house can then readily be accounted for. His companions knowing who he was, and dreading their identification with an act which could but result in their own condemnation of character, carried the body to the threshold of his father's house, and there left it. This," the doctor concluded, "appears to me the most rational mode I can find of accounting for the circumstances of this remarkable and deplorable case. I apologize to Mr. Petleigh for the slur to which I may have committed myself in referring to the character of that gentleman's son, the deceased, but my excuse must rest in this fact, that where a crime or catastrophe is so obscure that the criminal, or guilty person, may be in one of many directions, it is but just to narrow the circle of inquiry as much as possible, in order to avoid the resting of suspicion upon the greater number of individuals. If, however, any one can suggest a more lucid explanation of the catastrophe than mine, I shall indeed be glad to admit I was wrong."

[There can be little question, I repeat, that Dr. Pitcherley's analysis fitted in very satisfactorily and plausibly with the facts of the case.]

Mr. Mortoun asked Dr. Pitcherley no more questions.

The next witness called was the police-constable of Tram, a stupid, hopeless dolt, as I found to my cost, who was good at a rustic public-house row, but who as a detective was not worth my dog Dart.

It appeared that he gave his flat evidence with a stupidity which called even for the rebuke of the coroner.

All he could say was, that he was called, and that he went, and that he saw whose body it "be'd." That was "arl" he could say.

Mr. Mortoun took him in hand, but even he could do nothing with the man.

"Had many persons been on the spot where the body was found before he arrived?"

"Noa."

"How was that?"

"Whoy, 'cos Toom Broown, the gard'ner, coomed t'him at wuncet, and 'cos Toom Broown coomed t'him furst, 'cas he's cot wur furst coomed too."

This was so, as I found when I went down to Tram. The gardener, Brown, panic-stricken, after calling to, and obtaining the attention of the housekeeper, had rushed off to the village for that needless help which all panic-stricken people will seek, and the constable's cottage happening to be the first dwelling he reached the constable obtained the first alarm. Now, had the case been conducted properly, the constable being the first man to get the alarm, would have obtained such evidence as would at once have put the detectives on the right scent.

The first two questions put by the lawyerlike jury-man showed that he saw how important the evidence might have been which this witness, Joseph Higgins by name, should have given had he but known his business.

The first question was—

"It had rained, hadn't it, on the Monday night?"

[That previous to the catastrophe.]

"Ye-es t'had rained," Higgins replied.

Then followed this important question :

"You were on the spot one of the very first. Did you notice if there were any footsteps about?"

It appears to me very clear that Mr. Mortoun was here following up the theory of the catastrophe offered by the doctor. It would be clear that if several poaching companions had carried the young squire, after death, to the hall-door, that, as rain had fallen during the night, there would inevitably be many boot-marks on the soft ground.

This question put, the witness asked, "Wh-a-at?"

The question was repeated.

"Noa," he replied ; "ah didn't see noa foot ma-arks."

"Did you look for any?"

"Noa ; ah didn't look for any."

"Then you don't know your business," said Mr. Mortoun.

And the juryman was right; for I may tell the reader that boot-marks have sent more men to the gallows, as parts of circumstantial evidence, than any other proof whatever; indeed, the evidence of the boot-mark is terrible. A nail fallen out, or two or three put very close together, a broken nail, or all the nails perfect, have, times out of number, identified the boot of the suspected man with the boot-mark near the murdered, and has been the first link of the chain of evidence which has dragged a murderer to the gallows, or a minor felon to the hulks.

Indeed, if I were advising evildoers on the best means of avoiding detection, I would say by all means take a second pair of boots in your pocket, and when you near the scene of your work change those you have on for those you have in your pocket, and do your wickedness in these latter; flee from the scene in these latter, and when you have " made" some distance, why return to your other boots, and carefully hide the tell-tale pair. Then the boots you wear will rather be a proof of your innocence than presumable evidence of your guilt.

Nor let any one be shocked at this public advice to rascals; for I flatter myself I have a counter-mode of foiling such a felonious arrangement as this one of two pairs of boots. And as I have disseminated the mode amongst the police, any attempt to put the suggestions I have offered actually into action, would be attended with greater chances of detection than would be incurred by running the ordinary risk.

To return to the subject in hand.

The constable of Tram, the only human being in the town, Mortoun apart perhaps, who should have known, in the ordinary course of his duty, the value of every footmark near the dead body, had totally neglected a precaution which, had he observed it, must have led to a discovery (and an immediate one), which in consequence of his dullness was never publicly made.

Nothing could be more certain than this, that what is called foot-mark evidence was totally wanting.

The constable taking no observations, not the cutest detective in existence could have obtained any evidence of this character, for the news of the catastrophe spreading, as news only spreads in villages, the rustics tramped up in scores, and so obliterated what foot-marks might have existed.

To be brief, Mr. Josh. Higgins could give no evidence worth hearing.

And now the only depositions which remained to be given were those of Dinah Yarton.

She came into court "much reduced," said the paper from which I gain these particulars, "from the effects of the succession of fits which she had fallen into and struggled out of."

She was so stupid that every question had to be repeated in half-a-dozen shapes before she could offer a single reply. It took four inquiries to get at her name, three to know where she lived, five to know what she was; while the coroner and the jury, after a score of questions, gave over trying to ascertain whether she knew the nature of an oath. However,

as she stated that she was quite sure she would go to
a " bad place" if she did not speak the truth, she was
declared to be a perfectly competent witness, and I
have no doubt she was badgered accordingly.

And as Mr. Mortoun got more particulars out of
her than all the rest of the questioners put together,
perhaps it will not be amiss, as upon her evidence
turned the whole of my actions so far as I was concerned, to give that gentleman's questions and her
answers in full, precisely as they were quoted in the
greedy county paper, which doubtless looked upon the
whole case as a publishing godsend, the proprietors
heartily wishing that the inquest might be adjourned
a score of times for further evidence.

"Well now, Dinah," said Mr. Mortoun, " what
time did you go to bed on Monday ?"

[The answers were generally got after much ham-
mering in on the part of the inquirist. I will simply
return them at once as ultimately given.]

" 'Ten."

" Did you go to sleep ?"

" Noa—Ise didunt goa to sleep."

" Why not ?"

" Caize Ise couldn't."

" But why ?"

" Ise wur thinkin'."

" What of ?"

" Arl manner o' thing'."

" Tell us one of them ?"

[No answer—except symptoms of another fit.]

" Tut—tut !   Well, did you go to sleep at last ?"

"Ise did."

"Well, when did you wake?"

"Ise woke when missus ca'd I."

" What time ?"

" Doant know clock."

"Was it daylight ?"

" E-es, it wur day."

" Did you wake during the night ?"

"E-es, wuncet."

" How did that happen ?"

" Doant knaw."

"Did you hear anything ?"

" Noa."

" Did you think you heard anything ?"

" E-es."

" What ?"

" Whoy, it movin'."

"What was moving ?"

" Whoy, the box."

"Box—tut, tut," said the lawyer, "answer me properly."

Now here he raised his voice, and I have no doubt Dinah had to thank the juryman for the return of her fits.

" Do you hear ?—answer me properly."

" E-es."

" When you woke up did you hear any noise ?"

" Noa."

" But you thought you heard a noise ?"

" E-es, in the ——"

" Tut, tut. Never mind the box—where was it ?"

" Ter box ? In t' hall !"

" No—no, the noise."

" In t' hall, zur !"

" What—the noise was ?"

" Noa, zur, ter box."

" There, my good girl," says the Tram oracle, " never mind the box, I want you to think of this—did you hear any noise *outside the house ?*"

" Noa."

" But you said you heard a noise ?"

" No, zur, I didunt."

" Well, but you said you thought you heard a noise ?"

" E-es."

" Well—where ?"

" In ter box ——"

Here, said the county paper, the lawyer, striking his hand on the table before him, continued—

" Speak of the box once more, my girl, and to prison you go."

" Prizun !" says the luckless witness.

" Yes, jail and bread and water !"

And thereupon the unhappy witness without any further remarks plunged into a fit, and had to be carried out, battling with that strength which convulsions appear to bring with them, and in the arms of three men, who had quite their work to do to keep her moderately quiet.

" I don't think, gentlemen," said the coroner, " that this witness is material. In the first place, it seems doubtful to me whether she is capable of giving evidence ; and, in the second, I believe she has little evidence to give—so little that I doubt the policy of adjourning the inquest till her recovery. It appears to me that it would be cruelty to force this poor young woman again into the position she has just endured, unless you are satisfied that she is a material witness. I think she has said enough to show that she is not. It appears certain, from her own statement, that she retired to rest with Mrs. Quinion, and knows nothing more of what occurred till the housekeeper awoke her in the morning, after she herself had received the alarm. I suggest, therefore, that what evidence she could give is included in that already before the jury, and given by the housekeeper."

The jury coincided in the remarks made by the coroner, Mr. Mortoun, however, adding that he was at a loss to comprehend the girl's frequent reference to the box. Perhaps Mrs. Quinion could help to elucidate the mystery.

The housekeeper immediately rose.

" Mrs. Quinion," said Mr. Mortoun, " can you give any explanation as to what the young person meant by referring to a box ?"

" No."

" There are of course boxes at Petleighcote ?"

" Beyond all question."

" Any box in particular ?"

" No box in particular."

" No box which is spoken of as *the* box ?"

" Not any."

"The girl said it was in the hall. Is there a box in the hall?"

"Yes, several."

"What are they?"

"There is a clog and boot box, a box on the table in which letters for the post are placed when the family is at home, and from which they are removed every day at four; and also a box fixed to the wall, the use of which I have never been able to discover, and of the removal of which I have several times spoken to Mr. Petleigh."

"How large is it?"

"About a foot-and-a-half square and three feet deep."

"Locked?"

"No, the flap is always open."

"Has the young woman ever betrayed any fear of this box?"

"Never

"You have no idea to what box in the hall she referred in her evidence?"

"Not the least idea."

"Do you consider the young woman weak in her head?"

"She is decidedly not of strong intellect."

"And you suppose this box idea a mere fancy?"

"Of course."

"And a recent one?"

"I never heard her refer to a box before."

"That will do."

The paper whence I take my evidence describes Mrs. Quinion as a woman of very great self-possession, who gave what she had to say with perfect calmness and slowness of speech.

This being all the evidence, the coroner was about to sum up, when the Constable Higgins remembered that he had forgotten something, and came forward in a great hurry to repair his error.

He had not produced the articles found on the deceased.

These articles were a key and a *black crape mask.*

The squire being recalled, and the key shown to him, he identified the key as (he believed) one of his " household keys." It was of no particular value, and it did not matter if it remained in the hands of the police.

The report continued : " The key is now in the custody of the constable."

With regard to the crape mask the squire could offer no explanation concerning it.

The coroner then proceeded to sum up, and in doing so he paid many well-termed compliments to the doctor for that gentleman's view of the matter (which I have no doubt threw off all interest in the matter on the part of the public, and slackened the watchfulness of the detective force, many of whom, though very clever, are equally simple, and accept a plain and straightforward statement with extreme willingness)—and urged that the discovery of the black crape mask appeared to be very much like corroborative proof of the doctor's suggestion. " The young man," said the

coroner, " would, if poaching, be exceedingly desirous
of hiding his face, considering his position in the
county, and then the finding of this black crape
mask upon the body would, if the poaching explanation were accepted, be a very natural discovery
But——"

And then the coroner proceeded to explain to the
jury that they had to decide not upon suppositions but
facts. They might all be convinced that Dr. Pitcherley's explanation was the true one, but in law it could
not be accepted. Their verdict must be in accordance
with facts, and the simple facts of the case were these :
—A man was found dead, and the causes of his death
were such that it was impossible to believe that the deceased had been guilty of suicide. They would therefore under the circumstances feel it was their duty to
return an open verdict of murder.

The jury did not retire, but at the expiration of a
consultation of three minutes, in which (I learnt) the
foreman, Mr. Mortoun, had all the talking to himself,
the jury gave in a verdict of wilful murder against
some person or persons unknown.

Thus ended the inquest.

And I have little hesitation in saying it was one of
the weakest inquiries of that kind which had ever taken
place. It was characterized by no order, no comprehension, no common sense.

The facts of the case made some little stir, but the
plausible explanations offered by the doctor, and the
several coinciding circumstances, deprived the affair of
much of its interest, both to the public and the detec-

tive force ; to the former, because they had little room for ordinary conjecture ; to the latter, because I need not say the general, the chief motive power in the detective is gain, and here the probabilities of profit were almost annihilated by the possibility that a true explanation of the facts of this affair had been offered, while it was such as promised little hope of substantial reward.

But the mere fact of my here writing this narrative will be sufficient to show that *I* did not coincide with the general view taken of the business.

That I was right the following pages will I think prove.

Of course the Government offered the usual reward, £100, of which proclamation is published in all cases of death where presumably foul play has taken place.

But it was not the ordinary reward which tempted me to choose this case for investigation. It was several peculiar circumstances which attracted me.

They were as follows :—

(1.) Why did the father refuse to offer a reward ?

(2.) Why did the deceased have one of the household keys with him at the time of his death, and how came he to have it at all ?

(3.) What did the box mean ?

(1.) It seemed to me that the refusal by the father to offer a reward must arise from one of three sources. Either he did not believe a murder had been committed, and therefore felt the offer was needless ; or he knew murder was committed, and did not wish to accelerate the action of the police ; or, thirdly, whether he believed or disbelieved in the murder, knew or did not know it to be a murder, that he was too sordid to offer a reward by the payment of which he would lose without gaining any corresponding benefit.

(2.) How came the deceased to have one of the keys of his father's establishment in his pocket? Such a possession was extremely unusual, and more inexplicable. How came he to possess it? Why did he possess it? What was he going to do with it?

(3.) What did the box mean? Did the unhappy girl Dinah Yarton refer to any ordinary or extraordinary box? It appeared to me that if she referred to any ordinary box it must be an ordinary box under extraordinary circumstances. But fools have very rarely any imagination, and knowing this I was not disposed to accredit Dinah with any ability to invest the box ordinary with any extraordinary attributes. And then remembering that there was nobody in the house to play tricks with her but a grave housekeeper who would not be given to that kind of thing, I came to the conclusion that the box in question was an extraordinary box. "*It was in the hall.*" Now if the box were no familiar box, and it was in the hall, the inference stood that it had just arrived there. Did I at this time associate the box intimately with the case? I think not.

At all events I determined to go down to Tram and investigate the case, and as with us detectives action is as nearly simultaneous with determination to act as it can be, I need not say that, making up my mind to visit Tram, I was soon nearing that station by the first train which started after I had so determined.

Going down I arranged mentally the process with which I was to go through.

Firstly, I must see the constable.

Secondly, I must talk to the girl Dinah.

Thirdly, I must examine the place of the murder.

All this would be easy work.

But what followed would be more difficult.

This was to apply what I should discover to any persons whom my discoveries might implicate, and see what I could make of it all.

Arrived at Tram at once I found out the constable, and I am constrained to say—a greater fool I never indeed did meet.

He was too stupid to be anything else than utterly, though idiotically, honest.

Under my corkscrew-like qualities as a detective he had no more chance than a tender young cork with a corkscrew proper. I believe that to the end of the chapter he never comprehended that I was a detective. His mind could not grasp the idea of a police officer in petticoats.

I questioned him as the shortest way of managing him, smoothing his suspicions and his English with shillings of the coin of this realm.

Directly I came face to face with him I knew what I had to do. I had simply to question him. And here I set out my questions and his answers as closely as I can recollect them, together with a narrative of the actions which resulted out of both.

I told him at once I was curious to know all I could about the affair; and as I illustrated this statement with the exhibition of the first shilling, in a moment I had the opportunity of seeing every tooth he had in his head—thirty-two. Not one was missing.

"There was found on the body a key and a mask—where are they?"

"War be they—why, in my box, sin' I be coonstubble!"

"Will you show them me?"

"Oh, Ise show they ye!"

And thereupon he went to a box in the corner of the room, and unlocked it solemnly.

As the constable of Tram it was perfectly natural that he should keep possession of these objects, since a verdict of wilful murder had been given, and at any time, therefore, inquiries might have to be made.

From this box he took out a bundle; this opened, a suit of clothes came to view, and from the middle of these he produced a key and a mask.

I examined the key first. It was a well-made—a beautifully-made key, and very complicated. We constables learn in the course of our experience a good deal about keys, and therefore I saw at a glance that it was the key to a complicated and more than ordinarily valuable lock.

On the highly-polished loop of the key a carefully-cut number was engraved—No. 13.

Beyond all question this key was no ordinary key to an ordinary lock.

Now, extraordinary locks and keys guard extraordinary treasures.

The first inference I arrived at, therefore, from my interview with the Tram constable was this—that the key found upon the body opened a lock put upon something valuable.

Then I examined the mask.

It was of black crape, stretched upon silver wire. I had never seen anything like it before, although as a detective I had been much mixed up with people who wore masks, both at masquerades and on other occasions even less satisfactory.

I therefore inferred that the mask was of foreign manufacture.

[I learnt ultimately that I was right, and no great credit to me either, for that which is not white may fairly be guessed to be of some other colour. The mask was what is called abroad a *masque de luxe*, a mask which, while it changes the countenance sufficiently to prevent recognition, is made so delicately that the material, crape, admits of free perspiration— a condition which inferior masks will not admit.]

"Anything else found on the body ?"

"Noa."

"No skeleton keys ?"

"Noa ; on'y wan key."

So, if the constable were right, and *if the body had remained as it fell*, when found by the gardener, Brown, the only materials found were a key and mask.

But, surely, there was something else in the pockets.

"Was there no purse found?" I asked.

"Noa; noa poorse."

"No handkerchief?"

"Ooh, 'ees; thar war a kerchiefer."

"Where is it?"

He went immediately to the bundle.

"Are these the clothes in which he was found?"

"Ees, they be."

So far, so good, I felt.

The constable, stupid and honest as he appeared, and as he existed, was very suspicious, and therefore I felt that he had to be managed most carefully.

Having hooked the handkerchief out from some recess in the bundle with the flattest forefinger I think I ever remarked, he handed it to me.

It was a woman's handkerchief.

It was new; had apparently never been used; there was no crease nor dirt upon it, as there would have been had it been carried long in the pocket; and it was marked in the corner "Freddy"—undoubtedly the diminution for Frederica.

"Was the 'kerchiefer,'" I asked, using the word the constable had used—"was it wrapped in anything?"

"Noa."

"What pocket was it in?"

"Noa poockut."

"Where was it, then?"

"In's weskit, agin 's hart, an' joost aboove th' ole made in 'um."

Now, what was the inference of the handkerchief.

It was a woman's; it was not soiled; it had not been worn long; it was thrust in his breast; it was marked.

The inference stood thus:

This handkerchief belonged to a woman, in all probability young, whose Christian name was Frederica; as it was not soiled, and as it was not blackened by wear, it had recently been given to, or taken, by him; and as the handkerchief was found in the breast of his shirt, it appeared to have been looked upon with favour. Suppose then we say that it was a gift by a young woman to the deceased about the time when he was setting out on his expedition?

Now, the deceased had left London within eighteen hours of his death; had the handkerchief been given him in London or after he left town?

Again, had the mask anything to do with this woman?

Taking it up again and re-examining it, the delicacy of the fabric struck me more than before, and raising it close to my eyes to make a still narrower examination I found that it was scented.

The inference stood, upon the whole, that this mask had belonged to a woman.

Again I began to question Joseph Higgins, constable.

"I should be glad to look at the clothes," I said.

"Lard, thee may look," said the constable.

They were an ordinary suit of clothes, such as a middle-class man would wear of a morning, but not so good or fashionable as one might have expected to find in wear by the son of a wealthy squire.

[This apparent incongruity was soon explained away by my learning, as I did in the evening of my arrival, that the squire was mean and even parsimonious.]

There was nothing in the pockets, but my attention was called to the *fluffy* state of the cloth, which was a dark grey, and which therefore in a great measure hid this fluffiness.

" You have not been taking care of these clothes, I am afraid."

" They be joost as they coomed arf him !"

" What, was all this fluff about the cloth ?"

" Yoa."

[Yoa was a new version of "e-es," and both meant " yes."]

"They look as though they had been rolled about a bed."

"Noa."

The clothes in question were stained on their under side with gravel-marks, and they were still damp on these parts

The remarking of this fact, recalled to my mind something which came out at the inquest, and which now I remembered and kept in mind while examining the state of the clothes.

On the Monday night, as the body was discovered on the Tuesday morning, it had rained.

Now the clothes were not damp all over, for the fluff was quite wavy, and flew about in the air. It was necessary to know what time it left off raining on the Monday night, or Tuesday morning.

It was very evident that the clothes had not been

exposed to rain between the time of their obtaining
the fluffiness and the discovery of the body.   Therefore ascertain at what hour the rain ceased, and I had
the space of time (the hour at which the body was
discovered being half-past five) within which the body
had been deposited.

The constable knew nothing about the rain, and I
believe it was at this point, in spite of the shillings,
that the officer began to show rustic signs of impa-
tience.

I may add here that I found the rain had only ceased
at three o'clock on the Tuesday morning.   It was
therefore clear that the body had been deposited
between three and half-past five—*two hours and a-half*.

This discovery I made that same evening of my landlady, a most useful person.

Now, does it not strike the reader that three o'clock
on a May morning, and when the morning had almost
come, was an extraordinarily late hour at which to be
poaching ?

This indisputable fact, taken into consideration with
the needlessness of the mask (for poachers do not
wear masks), and the state of the clothes, to say
nothing of the kind of clothes found on the deceased,
led me to throw over Mr. Martoun's theory that the
young squire had met his death in a poaching affray,
or rather while out on a poaching expedition.

I took a little of the fluff from the clothes and carefully put it away in my pocket-book.

The last thing I examined was the barb which had
caused the death.

And here I admit I was utterly foiled—completely, positively foiled. I had never seen anything of the kind before—never.

It was a very coarse iron barb, shaped something like a queen's broad arrow, only that the flanges widened from their point, so that each appeared in shape like the blade of a much-worn penknife. The shaft was irregular and perhaps even coarser than the rest of the work. The weapon was made of very poor iron, for I turned its point by driving it, not by any means heavily, against the frame of the window—to the intense disgust of the constable, whose exclamation, I remember thoroughly well, was "Woa."

Now what did I gain by my visit to the constable? This series of suppositions :—

That the deceased was placed where he was found between three and half-past five a.m. on the Tuesday; that he was not killed from any result of a poaching expedition; and that he had visited a youngish woman named Frederica a few hours before death, and of whom he had received a handkerchief and possibly a mask.

The only troublesome point was the key, which, by the way, had been found in a small fob-pocket in the waist of the coat.

While taking my tea at the inn at which I had set down, I need not say I asked plenty of questions, and hearing a Mrs. Green frequently referred to, I surmised she was a busybody, and getting her address, as that of a pleasant body who let lodgings, I may at once add that that night I slept in the best room of the pleasant body's house.

She was the most incorrigible talker ever I encountered. Nor was she devoid of sharpness; indeed, with more circumspection than she possessed, or let me say, with ordinary circumspection, she would have made a good ordinary police-officer, and had she possessed that qualification I might have done something for her. As it was the idea could not be entertained for any part of a moment.

She was wonderful, this Mrs. Green.

You only had to put a question on any point, and she abandoned the subject in which she had been indulging, and sped away on a totally new tack.

She was ravenous to talk of the murder; for it was her foregone conclusion that murder had been committed.

In a few words, all the information afforded to this point, which has not arisen out of my own seeking, or came by copy from the county newspaper (and much of that information which is to follow) all proceeded from the same gushing source—Mrs. Green.

All I had to do was to put another question when I thought we had exhausted the previous one, and away she went again at score, and so we continued from seven to eleven. It was half-past eight for nine before she cleared away the long-since cold and sloppy tea-things.

"And what has become of Mrs. Quinion?" I asked, in the course of this to me valuable entertainment on the part of Mrs. Green, throughout the whole of which she never asked me my business in these parts (though I felt quite sure so perfect a busybody was dying to know my affairs), because any inquiry would have called for a reply, and this was what she could not endure while I was willing to listen to her. Hence she chose the less of two evils.

"And what became of the girl?"

"What gal?"

"Dinah."

"Dinah Yarton?"

"Yes. I believe that *was* her name."

"Lor' bless 'ee! it's as good and as long as a blessed big book to tell 'ee all about Dinah Yarton. She left two days after, and they not having a bed for she at the Lamb and Flag, and I having a bed, her came here—the Lamb and Flag people always sending me their over beds, bless 'em, bless 'ee! and that's how I comes to know arl about it, bless 'ee, and the big box!"

[The box—now this was certainly what I did want Mrs. Green to come to. The reader will remember that I laid some stress upon the girl's frequent reference to the trunk.]

"Bless 'ee! the big box caused arl the row, because Mrs. Quinion said she were a fool to have been frightened by a big box; but so Dinah would be, and so her did, being probable in the nex' county at this time, at Little Pocklington, where her mother lives making lace, and her father a farmer, and where her was born —Dinah, and not her mother—on the 1st o' April, 1835, being now twenty years old. What art thee doing? bless 'ee!"

[I was making a note of Little Pocklington.]

Nor will I here make any further verbatim notes of Mrs. Green's remarks, but use them as they are required in my own way, and as in actuality really I did turn them to account.

I determined to see the girl at once; that is, after I had had a night's rest. And therefore next morning, after carefully seeing my box and bag were locked, I made a quick breakfast, and sallied out. Reaching the station, there was Mrs. Green. She had obviously got the start of me by crossing Goose Green fields, as in fact she told me.

She said she thought I must have dropped that, and had come to see.

"That" was a purse so old that it was a curiosity.

"Bless 'ee!" she says, "isn't yourn? Odd, beant it? But, bless 'ee! ye'll have to wait an hour for a train. There beant a train to anywhere for arl an hour."

"Then I'll take a walk," said I.

"Shall I come, and tark pleasant to 'ee?" asked Mrs. Green.

"No," I replied; "I've some business to transact."

I had an hour to spare, and remembering that I had seen the things at Higgins's by a failing evening light, I thought I would again visit that worthy, and make a second inspection.

It was perhaps well I did so.

Not that I discovered anything of further importance, but the atom of novelty of which I made myself master, helped to confirm me in my belief that the deceased had visited a young woman, probably a lady, a very short time before his death.

Higgins, a saddler by trade, was not at all delighted at my re-appearance, and really I was afraid I should have to state what I was in order to get my way, and then civilly bully him into secrecy. But happily his belief in me as a mild mad woman overcame his surliness, and so with the help of a few more shillings I examined once more the clothes found on the unfortunate young squire.

And now, in the full blazing spring morning sunlight, I saw what had missed my view on the previous evening. This was nothing less than a bright crimson scrap of silk braid, such as ladies use in prosecuting their embroidery studies.

This bit of braid had been wound round and round a breast button, and then tied in a natty bow at the top.

"She is a lady," I thought; "and she was resting her head against his breast when she tied that bit of braid there. She is innocent, I should think, or she never would have done such a childish action as that."

Higgins put away the dead youth's clothes with a discontented air.

"Look ye yere—do'ee think ye'l want 'em wuncet more ?"

"No."

"Wull, if ee do, 'ee wunt have 'un."

"Oh, very well," I said, and went back to the station.

Of course there was Mrs. Green on the watch, though in the morning I had seen about the house symptoms of the day being devoted to what I have heard comic Londoners describe as "a water party"—in other words, a grand wash.

That wash Mrs. Green had deserted.

"Bless 'ee, I'm waitin' for a dear fren'!"

"Oh, indeed, Mrs. Green."

"Shall I take ticket for 'ee, dear?"

"Yes, if you like. Take it for Stokeley," said I.

"Four mile away," says Mrs. Green. "*I've* got a fren' at Stokeley. I wounds if your fren' be *my* fren'! Who *be* your fren', bless 'ee?"

"Mrs. Blotchley."

"What, her as lives near th' peump?" (pump)

"Yes."

"Oh, I don't know *she*."

It seemed to me Mrs. Green was awed—I never learnt by what, because as I never knew Mrs. Blotchley, and dropped upon her name by chance, and indeed never visited Stokeley, why Green had all the benefit of the discovery.

"And, Mrs. Green, if I am not home by nine, do not sit up for me."

"*Oh!*—goin' maybe to sleep at *her* hoose?"

"Very likely."

"*Oh!*"

And as Mrs. Green here dropped me a curtsey I have remained under the impression that Mrs. B. was a lady of consequence whose grandeur Mrs. Green saw reflected upon me.

I have no doubt the information she put at once in

circulation helped to screen the actual purpose for which I had arrived at Tram from leaking out.

When the train reached Stokeley I procured another ticket on to Little Pocklington, and reached that town about two in the afternoon. It was not more than sixty miles from Tram.

The father of this Dinah Yarton was one of those small few-acre farmers who throughout the country are gradually but as certainly vanishing.

I may perhaps at once say that the poor girl Dinah had no less than three fits over the cross-examination to which I submitted her, and here (to the honour of rustic human nature) let it be recorded that actually I had to use my last resource, and show myself to be a police-officer, by the production of my warrant in the presence of the Little Pocklington constable, who was brought into the affair, before I could overcome the objections of the girl's father. He with much justifiable reason urged that the "darned" business had already half-killed his wench, and he would be "darned" if I should altogether send her out of the "warld."

As I have said, the unhappy girl had three fits, and I have no doubt the family were heartily glad when I had turned my back upon the premises.

The unhappy young woman had to make twenty struggles before she could find one reply.

Here I need not repeat her evidence to that point past which it was not carried when she stood before the coroner and jury, but I will commence from that point.

"Dinah," I inquired in a quiet tone, and I believe the fussiness betrayed by the girl's mother tended as much to the fits as the girl's own nervousness— "Dinah, what was all that about the big box?"

"Darn the box," said the mother.

And here it was that the unfortunate girl took her second fit.

"There, she's killed my Dinah now," said the old woman, and it must be confessed Dinah was horribly convulsed, and indeed looked frightful in the extreme. The poor creature was quite an hour fighting with the fit, and when she came to and opened her eyes, the first object they met made her shut them again, for that object was myself.

However, I had my duty to perform, and therein lies the excuse for my torture.

"What—oh—o-o-oh wha-at did thee say?"

"What about the big box?"

"Doa noa." [This was the mode in those parts of saying "I do not know."]

"Where was it?"

"In th' hall."

"Where did it come from?"

"Doa noa."

"How long had it been there?"

"Sin' the day afore."

"Who brought it?"

"Doa noa."

"Was it a man?"

"Noa."

"What then?"

" Two men."

" How did they come ?"

" They coomed in a great big waggoon."

"And did they bring the box in the waggon !"

" Yoa." [This already I knew meant " Yes."]

" And they left the box at the hall ?"

" Yoa."

" What then ?"

" Whoa ?" [This I guessed meant " What."]

" What did they say ?"

" Zed box wur for squoire."

" Did they both carry it ?"

" Yoa."

" How ?"

" Carefool loike." [Here there were symptoms of another convulsion.]

" What became of the big box ?"

"Doa noa."

" Did they come for it again ?"

"Doa noa."

" Is it there now ?"

" Noa."

" Then it went away again ?"

" Yoa."

" You did not see it taken away ?"

"Noa."

" Then how do you know it is not there now ?"

" Doa noa.

" But you say it is not at the hall—how do you know that ?"

" Mrs. Quanyan (Quinion) told I men had been for it."

" When was that ?"

" After I'd been garne to bed."

" Was it there the next morning ?"

" Whoa ?"

" Was it there the morning when they found the young squire dead outside the door ?"

And now " Diney," as her mother called her, plunged into the third fit, and in the early throes of that convulsion I was forced to leave her, for her father, an honest fellow, told me to leave his house, " arficer or no arficer," and that if I did not do so he would give me what he called a " sta-a-art."

Under the circumstances I thought that perhaps it was wise to go, and did depart accordingly.

That night I remained in Little Pocklington in the hope, in which I was so grievously disappointed, of discovering further particulars which the girl might have divulged to her companions. But in the first place Diney had no companions, and in the second all attempts to draw people out, for the case had been copied into that county paper which held sway at Little Pocklington, all attempts signally failed.

Upon my return to Tram, Mrs. Green received me with all the honours, clearly as a person who had visited Mrs. Blotchley, and I noticed that the parlour fire-place was decorated with a new stove-ornament in paper of a fiery and flaring description.

I thanked Mrs. Green, and in answer to that lady's inquiries I was happy to say Mrs. Blotchley was well— except a slight cold. Yes, I had slept there. What did I have for dinner at Mrs. Blotchley's ? Well, really I had forgotten. "Dear heart," said Mrs. Green, "'ow unfortnet."

After seeing " Diney," and in coming home by the train (and indeed I can always think well while travelling), I turned over all that I had pinched out of Dinah Yarton in reference to the big box.

Did that box, or did it not, in any way relate to the death ?

It was large ; it had been carried by two men ; and according to Dinah's information it had been removed again from the hall.

At all events I must find out what the box meant.

The whole affair was still so warm—not much more than a fortnight had passed since the occurrence—that I still felt sure all particulars about that date which had been noticed would be remembered.

I set Mrs. Green to work, for nobody could better suit my purpose.

"Mrs. Green, can you find out whether any strange carrier's cart or waggon, containing a very big box, was seen in Tram on the Monday, and the day before young Mr. Petleigh's body was found ?"

I saw happiness in Mrs. Green's face ; and having thus set her to work, I put myself in the best order, and went up to Petleighcote Hall.

The door was opened (with suspicious slowness) by a servant-woman, who closed it again before she took my message and a card to Mrs. Quinion. The message consisted of a statement that I had come after the character of a servant.

A few moments passed, and I was introduced into the housekeeper's presence.

I found her a calm-looking, fine, portly woman, with much quiet determination in her countenance. She was by no means badly featured.

She was quite self-possessed.

The following conversation took place between us. The reader will see that not the least reference was made by me to the real object of my visit—the prosecution of an inquiry as to the mode by which young Mr. Petleigh had met his death. And if the reader complains that there is much falsity in what I state, I would urge that as evil-doing is a kind of lie levelled at society, if it is to be conquered it must be met on the side of society, through its employés, by similar false action.

Here is the conversation.

"Mrs. Quinion, I believe ?"

"Yes, as I am usually termed—but let that pass. You wish to see me ?"

"Yes ; I have called about the character of a servant."

"Indeed—who ?"

"I was passing through Tram, where I shall remain some days, on my way from town to York, and I thought it would be wise to make a personal inquiry, which I find much the best plan in all affairs relating to my servants."

"A capital plan ; but as you came from town, why did you not apply to the town housekeeper, since I have no doubt you take the young person from the town house?"

"There is the difficulty. I should take the young person, if her character were to answer, from a sort of charity. She has never been in town, and here's my doubt. However, if you give me any hope of the young person——"

"What is her name?"

"Dinah—Dinah—you will allow me to refer to my pocket-book."

"Don't take that trouble," said she, and I thought she looked pale; but her pallor might have been owing, I thought at the time, to the deep mourning she was wearing; "you mean Dinah Yarton."

"Yarton—that is the name. Do you think she will suit?"

"Much depends upon what she is wanted for."

"An under nurserymaid."

"Your own family?"

"Oh, dear no—a sister's."

"In town?"

[She asked this question most calmly.]

"No—abroad."

"Abroad?" and I remarked that she uttered the word with an energy which, though faint in itself, spoke volumes when compared with her previous serenity.

"Yes," I said, "my sister's family are about leaving England for Italy, where they will remain for years. Do you think this girl would do?"

"Well—yes. She is not very bright, it is true, but she is wonderfully clean, honest, and extremely fond of children."

Now, it struck me then and there that the experience of the housekeeper at childless Petleighcote as to Dinah's love of children must have been extremely limited.

"What I most liked in Dinah," continued Mrs. Quinion, "was her frankness and trustworthiness. There can be no doubt of her gentleness with children."

"May I ask why you parted with her?"

"She left me of her own free will. We had, two or three weeks since, a very sad affair here. It operated much upon her; she wished to get away from the place; and indeed I was glad she determined to go."

"Has she good health?"

"Very fair health."

Not a word about the fits.

It struck me Mrs. Quinion relished the idea of Dinah Yarton's going abroad.

"I think I will recommend her to my sister. She tells me she would have no objection to go abroad."

"Oh! you have seen her?"

"Yes—the day before yesterday, and before leaving for town, whence I came here. I will recommend the girl. Good morning."

"Good morning, ma'am; but before you go, will you allow me to take the liberty of asking you, since you are from London, if you can recommend me a town servant, or at all events a young person who comes from a distance. When the family is away I require only one servant here, and I am not able to obtain this one now that the hall has got amongst the scandal-mongers, owing to the catastrophe to which I have already referred. The young person I have with me is intolerable; she has only been here four days, and I am quite sure she must not remain fourteen."

"Well, I think I can recommend you a young person, strong and willing to please, and who only left my sister's household on the score of followers. Shall I write to my sister's housekeeper and see what is to be done?"

"I should be most obliged," said Mrs. Quinion; "but where may I address a letter to you in event of my having to write?"

"Oh!" I replied, "I shall remain at Tram quite a week. I have received a telegraphic message which makes my journey to the north needless; and as I have met here in Tram with a person who is a friend of an humble friend of mine, I am in no hurry to quit the place.

"Indeed! may I ask who?"

"Old Mrs. Green, at the corner of the Market Place, and her friend is Mrs. Blotchley of Stokeley."

"Oh, thank you. I know neither party."

"I may possibly see you again," I continued.

"Most obliged," continued Mrs. Quinion; "shall be most happy."

"Good morning,"

She returned the salute, and there was an end of the visit.

And then it came about that upon returning to the house of old Mrs. Green, I said in the most innocent manner in the world, and in order to make all my acts and words in the place as consistent as possible, for in a small country town if you do not do your falsehood deftly you will very quickly be discovered—I said to that willing gossip—

"Why, Mrs. Green, I find you are a friend of Mrs. Blotchley of Stokeley!"

"E-es," she said in a startled manner, "Ise her fren', bless 'ee."

"And I'm gratified to hear it, for as her friend you are mine, Mrs. Green."

And here I took her hand.

No wonder after our interview was over that she went out in her best bonnet, though it was only Wednesday. I felt sure it was quite out of honour to Mrs. Blotchley and her friend, who had claimed her friendship, and the history of which she was taking out to tea with her.

Of the interview with Mrs. Green I must say a few words, and in her own expressions.

"Well, Mrs. Green, have you heard of any unusual cart having been seen in Tram on the day before Mr. Petleigh was found dead?"

"Lardy, lardy, e-es," said Mrs. Green; "but bless 'ee, whaty want to know for?"

"I want to know if it was Mrs. Blotchley's brother's cart, that's all."

"Des say it war. I've been arl over toon speering aboot that waggoon. I went to Jones the baker, and Willmott, who married Mary Sprinters—which wur on'y fair; the grocer, an' him knowed nought about it; an' the bootcher in froont street, and bootcher in back street; and Mrs. Macnab, her as mangles, and no noos, bless 'ee, not even of Tom Hatt the milkman, but, lardy, lardy! when Ise tarking for a fren' o' my fren's Ise tark till never. 'Twur draper told I arl aboot the ca-art."

"What?" I said, I am afraid too eagerly for a detective who knew her business thoroughly.

"Why, draper White wur oot for stroll loike, an' looking about past turning to the harl (hall), and then he sees coming aloong a cart him guessed wur coming to him's shop; but, bless 'ee, 'twarnt comin' to his shop at ARL!"

"Where was it going?"

"Why the cart turned roight arf to harl, and that moost ha' been wher they cart went to; and, bless 'ee, that's arl."

Then Mrs. Green, talking like machinery to the very threshold, went, and I guess put on her new bonnet instanter, for she wore it before she went out, and when she brought in my chop and potatoes.

Meanwhile I was ruminating the news of the box, if I may be allowed the figure, and piecing it together.

It was pretty clear to me that a box had been taken to the hall, for the evidence of the girl Dinah and that which Mrs. Green brought together coincided in supporting a supposition to that effect.

The girl said a big box (which must have been large, seeing it took two men to carry it) had been brought to the hall in a large cart on the day previous to the finding of the body.

It was on that day the draper, presumably, had seen a large cart turn out of the main road towards Petleighcote.

Did that cart contain the box the girl Dinah referred to ?

If so, had it anything to do with the death ?

If so, where was it ?

If hidden, who had hidden it ?

These were the questions which flooded my mind, and which the reader will see were sufficiently important and equally embarrassing.

The first question to be decided was this,—

Had the big box anything to do with the matter ?

I first wrote my letter to head quarters putting things in train to plant one of our people as serving woman at Petleighcote, and then I sallied out to visit Mr. White, the draper.

He was what men would call a "jolly" man, one who took a good deal of gin-and-water, and the world as it came. He was a man to be hail met with the world, but to find it rather a thirsty sphere, and diligently to spirit-and-water that portion of it contained within his own suit of clothes.

He was a man to be rushed at and tilted over with confidence.

" Mr. White," said I, " I want an umbrella, and also a few words with you."

"Both, mum," said he; and I would have bet, for though a woman I am fond of a little wager now and then,—yes, I would have bet that before his fourth sentence he would drop the "mum."

"Here are what we have in umberellers, mum."

"Thank you. Do you remember meeting a strange cart on the day, a Monday, before Mr. Petleigh—Petleigh—what was his name?—was found dead outside the hall? I mention that horrid circumstance to recall the day to your mind."

"Well, yes, I do, mum. I've been hearing of this from Mary Green."

"What kind of cart was it?"

"Well, mum, it was a wholesale fancy article manufacturer's van."

"Ah, such as travel from drapers to drapers with samples, and sometimes things for sale."

"Yes; that were it."

[He dropped the mum at the fourth sentence.]

"A very large van, in which a man could almost stand upright?"

"A man, my dear!" He was just the kind of man to "my dear" a customer, though by so doing he should offend her for life. "Half-a-dozen of 'em, and filled with boxes of samples, in each of which you might stow away a long—what's the matter, eh? What do you want to find out about the van for, eh?"

"Oh, pray don't ask me, White," said I, knowing the way to such a man's confidence is the road of familiarity. "Don't, don't inquire what. But tell me, how many men were there on the van?"

" Two, my dear."

" What were they like ?"

" Well, I didn't notice."

" Did you know them, or either of them ?"

" Ha ! *I* see," said White ; and I am afraid I allowed him to infer that he had surprised a personal secret. " No ; I knew neither of 'em, if *I* know it. Strangers to me. Of course *I* thought they were coming with samples to *my* shop ; for I am the only one in the village. But they DIDN'T."

" No ; they went to the hall, I believe ?"

" Yes. *I* thought they had turned wrong, and I hollered after them, but it was no use. I wish I could describe them for you, my dear, but I can't. However, I believe they looked like gentlemen. Do you think *that* description will answer ?"

" Did they afterwards come into the town, Mr. White ?"

" Well, my dear, they did, and baited at the White Horse, and then it was I was so surprised they did not call. And then—in fact, my dear, if you would like to know all——"

" Oh, don't keep anything from me, White."

" Well, then, my dear, I went over as they were making ready to go, and I asked them if they were looking for a party of the name of White ? And then——"

" Oh, pray, pray continue."

" Well, then, one of them told me to go to a place, to repeat which before you, my dear, I would not ;

from which it seemed to me that they did *not* want a person of the name of White."

"And, Mr. White, did they quit Tram by the same road as that by which they entered it ?"

"No, they did *not*; they drove out at the other end of the town."

"Is it possible ? And tell me, Mr. White, if they wanted to get back to the hall, could they have done so by any other means than by returning through the village ?"

"No, not without—let me see, my dear—not without going thirty miles round by the heath, which," added Mr. White, "and no offence, my dear, I am bound to submit they were not men who seemed likely to take any unnecessary trouble ; or why—why in fact did they tell me to go to where in fact they told me to go to ?"

"True ; but they may have returned, and you not know anything about it, Mr. White."

"There you have it, my dear. You go to the gate-man, and as it's only three weeks since, you take his word, for Tom remembers every vehicle that passes his 'pike—there are not many of them, for business is woundily slack. Tom remembers 'em all for a good quarter."

"Oh, thank you, Mr. White. I think I'll take the green umbrella. How much is it ?"

"Now look here, my dear," the draper continued, leaning over the counter, and dropping his voice ; "I know the umbereller is the excuse, and though business *is* bad. I'm sure I don't want you to take it ; unless, indeed, you want it," he added, the commercial spirit struggling with the spirit proper of the man.

"Thank you," said I. "I'll take the green—you will kindly let me call upon you again ?"

"With pleasure, my dear ; as often as you like ; the more the better. And look here, you need not buy any more umberellers or things. You just drop in in a friendly way, you know. *I* see it all."

"Thank you," I said ; and making an escape I was rather desirous of obtaining, I left the shop, which, I regret to say, I was ungrateful enough not to revisit. But, on the other hand, I met White several and at most inconvenient times.

Tom the 'pikeman's memory for vehicles was, I found, a proverb in the place ; and when I went to him, he remembered the vehicle almost before I could explain its appearance to him.

As for the question—"Did the van return ?"—he treated the " Are you sure of it ?" with which I met his shake of the head—he treated my doubt with such violent decision that I became confident he was right.

Unless he was bribed to secrecy ?

But the doubt was ridiculous ; for could all the town be bribed to secrecy ?

I determined that doubt at once. And indeed it is the great gain and drawback to our profession that we have to doubt so imperiously. To believe every man to be honest till he is found out to be a thief, is a motto most self-respecting men cling to ; but we detectives on the contrary would not gain salt to our bread, much less the bread itself, if we adopted such a belief. We have to believe every man a rogue till, after turning all sorts of evidence inside out, we can only discover that he is an honest man. And even then I am much afraid we are not quite sure of him.

I am aware this is a very dismal way of looking upon society, but the more thinking amongst my profession console themselves with the knowledge that our system is a necessary one (under the present condition of society), and that therefore in conforming to the melancholy rules of this system, however repulsive we may feel them, we are really doing good to our brother men.

Returning home after I left the 'pikeman—from whom I ascertained that the van had passed his gate at half-past eight in the evening, I turned over all my new information in my mind.

The girl Dinah must have seen the box in the hall as she went to bed. Say this was half-past nine; at half-past five, at the time the alarm was given, the box was gone.

This made eight hours.

Now, the van had left Tram at half-past eight, and to get round to the hall it had to go thirty miles by night over a heath. (By a reference to my almanack I found there was no moon that night.) Now, take it that a heavy van travelling by night-time could not go more than five miles an hour, and allowing the horse an hour's rest when half the journey was accomplished, we find that seven hours would be required to accomplish that distance.

This would bring the earliest time at which the van could arrive at the hall at half-past three, assuming no impediments to arise.

There would be then just two hours before the body was discovered, and actually as the dawn was breaking.

Such a venture was preposterous even in the contemplation.

In the first place, why should the box be left if it were to be called for again ?

In the second, why should it be called for so early in the morning as half-past three ?

And yet at half-past five it had vanished, and Mrs. Quinion had said to the girl (I assumed the girl's evidence to be true) that the box had been taken away again.

From my investigation of these facts I inferred— firstly:

That the van which brought the box had not taken it away.

Secondly: That Mrs. Quinion, for some as yet unexplained purpose, had wished the girl to suppose the box had been removed.

Thirdly: That the box was still in the house.

Fourthly: That as Mrs. Quinion had stated the box was gone, while it was still on the premises, she had some purpose (surely important) in stating that it had been taken away.

It was late, but I wanted to complete my day's work as far as it lay in my power.

I had two things to do.

Firstly, to send the "fluff" which I had gathered from the clothes to a microscopic chemist ; and secondly, to make some inquiry at the inn where the van attendants had baited, and ascertain what they were.

Therefore I put the "fluff" in a tin box, and directed it to the gentleman who is good enough to control these kind of investigations for me, and going out I posted my communication. Then I made for the tavern, with the name of which Mrs. Green had readily furnished me, and asked for the landlady.

The interest she exhibited showed me in a moment that Mrs. Green's little remarks and Mr. White's frank observations had got round to that quarter.

And here let me break off for a moment to show how nicely people will gull themselves. I had plainly made no admission which personally identified me with the van, and yet people had already got up a very sentimental feeling in my favour in reference to that vehicle.

For this arrangement I was unfeignedly glad. It furnished a motive for my remaining in Tram, which was just what I wanted.

And furthermore, the tale I told Mrs. Quinion about my remaining in Tram because I had found a friend of my own friend, would, if it spread (which it did not, from which I inferred that Mrs. Quinion had no confidences with the Tram maiden at that hour with her, and that this latter did not habitually listen) do me no harm, as I might ostensibly be supposed to invent a fib which might cover my supposed tribulation.

Here is a condensation of the conversation I had with the landlady.

"Ah! I know; I'm glad to see you. Pray sit down. Take that chair—it's the easiest. And how are you, my poor dear?"

"Not strong," I had to say.

"Ah! and well you may not be."

"I came to ask, did two persons, driving a van—a large black van, picked out with pale blue (this description I had got from the 'pikeman)—stop here on the day before Mr.——I've forgotten his name—the young squire's death?"

"Yes, my poor dear, an' a tall gentleman with auburn whiskers, and the other shorter, without whiskers."

"Dear me; did you notice anything peculiar in the tall gentleman?"

"Well, my poor dear, I noticed that every now and then his upper lip flitched a bit, like a dog's asleep will sometimes go."

Here I sighed.

"And the other?" I continued.

"Oh! all that seemed odd in him was that he broke out into bits of song, something like birds more nor English Christian singing; which the words, if words there were, I could not understand."

"Italian scraps," I thought; and immediately I associated this evidence of the man with the foreign mask.

If they were commercial travellers, one of them was certainly an unusual one, operatic accomplishments not being usually one of the tendencies of commercial men.

" Were they nice people ?"

" Oh !" says the landlady, concessively and hurriedly; " they were every inch gentlemen ; and I said to mine, said I—'they aint like most o' the commercial travellers that stop here ;' and mine answers me back, ' No,' says he, ' for commercials prefers beers to sherries, and whiskies after dinner to both !' "

" Oh ! did they only drink wine ?"

" Nothing but sherry, my dear ; and says they to mine—'Very good wine,'—those were their very words—' whatever you do, bring it dry ;' and said mine—I saying his very words—' Gents, I will.' "

Some more conversation ensued, with which I need not trouble the reader, though I elicited several points which were of minor importance.

I was not permitted to leave the hotel without " partaking,"—I use the landlady's own verb—without partaking of a warmer and stronger comfort than is to be found in mere words.

And the last inference I drew, before satisfactorily I went to bed that night, was to the effect that the apparent commercial travellers were not commercial travellers, but men leading the lives of gentlemen.

And now as I have set out a dozen inferences which rest upon very good evidence, before I go to the history of the work of the following days, I must recapitulate these inferences—if I may use so pompous a word.

They are as follow :—

1. That the key found on the body opened a receptacle containing treasure.

2. That the mask found on the body was of foreign manufacture.

3. That the handkerchief found on the body had very recently belonged to a young lady named Frederica, and to whom the deceased was probably deeply attached.

4. That the circumstances surrounding the deceased showed that he had been engaged in no poaching expedition, nor in any house-breaking attempt, notwithstanding the presence of the mask, because no house-breaking implements were found upon him.

6. That the young lady was innocent of participation in whatever evil work the deceased may have been engaged upon. [This inference, however, was solely based upon the discovery of the embroidery braid round the button of the deceased's coat. This inference is the least supported by evidence of the whole dozen.]

7. That a big box had been taken to the hall on the day previous to that on which the deceased was found dead outside the hall.

8. That the box was not removed again in the van in which it had been brought to the house.

9. That whatever the box contained that something was heavy, as it took the two men to carry it into the house.

10. That Mrs. Quinion, for some so far unexplainable reason, had endeavoured to make the witness Dinah

Yarton believe that the box had been removed; while, in fact, the box was still in the house.

11. That as Mrs. Quinion had stated the box was gone while it was still on the premises, she had some important motive for saying it had been taken away.

12. That the van-attendants, who were apparent commercial travellers, were not commercial travellers, and were in the habit of living the lives of gentlemen.

And what was the condensed inference of all these inferences?

Why—THAT THE FIRST PROBABLE MEANS BY WHICH THE SOLUTION OF THE MYSTERY WAS TO BE ARRIVED AT WAS THE FINDING OF THE BOX.

To hunt for this box it was necessary that I should obtain free admission to Petleighcote, and by the most extraordinary chance Mrs. Quinion had herself thrown the opportunity in my way by asking me to recommend her a town servant.

Of course, beyond any question, she had made this request with the idea of obtaining a servant who, being a stranger to the district, would have little or not any of that interest in the catastrophe of the young squire's death which all felt who, by belonging to the neighbourhood, had more or less known him.

I had now to wait two days before I could move in the matter—those two days being consumed in the arrival of the woman police-officer who was to play the part of servant up at the hall, and in her being accepted and installed at that place.

On the morning of that second day the report came from my microscopic chemist.

He stated that the fluff forwarded him for inspection consisted of two different substances ; one, fragments of feathers, the other, atoms of nap from some linen material, made of black and white stuff, and which, from its connexion with the atoms of feather, he should take to be the fluff of a bed-tick.

For a time this report convinced me that the clothes had been covered with this substance, in consequence of the deceased having lain down in his clothes to sleep at a very recent time before he was found dead.

And now came the time to consider the question—"What was my own impression regarding the conduct of the deceased immediately preceding the death ?"

My impression was this—that he was about to commit some illegal action, but that he had met with his death before he could put his intention into execution.

This impression arose from the fact that the mask showed a secret intention, while the sound state of the clothes suggested that no struggle had preceded the bloody death—struggle, however brief, generally resulting in clothes more or less damaged, as any soldier who has been in action will tell you (and perhaps tell you wonderingly), to the effect that though he himself may have come out of the fight without a scratch, his clothes were one vast rip.

The question that chiefly referred to the body was, who placed it where it was found between three o'clock (the time when the rain ceased, before which hour the body could not have been deposited, since the clothes, where they did not touch the ground, were dry) and half-past five ?

Had it been brought from a distance ?.

Had it been brought from a vicinity ?

The argument against distance was this one, which bears in all cases of the removal of dead bodies—that if it is dangerous to move them a yard, it is a hun dred times more dangerous to move them a hundred yards.

Granted the removal of young Petleigh's body, in a state which would at once excite suspicion, and it is clear that a great risk was run by those who carried that burden.

But was there any apparent advantage to compen-sate that risk ?

No, there was not.

The only rational way of accounting for the deposi-tion of the body where it was found, lay in the sup-position that those who were mixed up with his death were just enough to carry the body to a spot where it would at once be recognised and cared for.

But against this argument it might be held, the risk was so great that the ordinary instinct of self-preservation natural to man would prevent such a risk being encountered. And this impression becomes all the deeper when it is remembered that the identi-fication of the body could have been secured by the slipping of a piece of paper in the pocket bearing his address.

Then, when it is remembered that it must have been quite dawn at the time of the assumed conveyance, the improbability becomes the greater that the body was brought any great distance.

Then this probability became the greater, that the young man had died in the vicinity of the spot where he was found.

Then followed the question, how close?

And in considering this point, it must not be forgotten that if it were dangerous to bring the body to the hall, it would be equally dangerous to remove the body *from the hall; supposing* the murder (if murder it were) had been committed within the hall.

Could this be the case?

Beyond all question, the only people known to be at the hall on the night of the death were Mrs. Quinion and Dinah.

Now we have closed in the space within which the murder (as we will call it) had been done, as narrowly circumscribing the hall. Now was the place any other than the hall, and yet near it?

The only buildings near the hall, within a quarter of a mile, were the gardener's cottage, and the cottage of the keeper.

The keeper was ill at the time, and it was the gardener who had discovered the body. To consider the keeper as implicated in the affair, was quite out of the question; while as to the gardener, an old man, and older servant of the family (for he had entered the service of the family as a boy), it must be remembered that he was the discoverer of the dead body.

Now is it likely that if he was implicated in the

affair that he would have identified himself with the discovery? Such a supposition is hardly holdable.

Very well; then, as the doctor at six A.M. declared death had taken place from six to eight hours; and as the body, from the dry state of the clothes, had *not* been exposed during the night's rain, which ceased at three, it was clear either that the murder had been committed within doors, or that the body had been sheltered for some hours after death beneath a roof of some kind.

Where was that roof?

Apart from the gardener's cottage and the keeper's, there was no building nearer than a quarter of a mile; and if therefore the body had been carried after three to where it was found, it was evident that those cognizant of the affair had carried it a furlong at or after dawn.

To suppose such an amount of moral courage in evil-doers was to suppose an improbability, against which a detective, man or woman, cannot too thoroughly be on his or her guard.

But what of the supposition that the body had been removed from the hall, and placed where it was found?

So far, all the external evidences of the case leant in favour of this theory.

But the theory was at total variance with the ordinary experience of life.

In the first place, what apparent motive could Mrs. Quinion have for taking the young heir's life? Not any apparently.

What motive had the girl ?

She had not sufficient strength of mind to hold a fierce motive.  I doubt if the poor creature could ever have imagined active evil.

I may here add I depended very much upon what that girl said, because it was consistent, was told under great distress of mind, and was in many particulars borne out by other evidence.

I left Dinah Yarton quite out of my list of suspects.

But in accepting her evidence I committed myself to the belief that no one had been at Petleighcote on the night of the catastrophe beyond the girl and the housekeeper.

Then how could I support the supposition that the young man had passed the night and met his death at the hall ?

Very easily.

Because a weak-headed woman like Dinah did not know of the presence of the heir at Petleighcote, it did not follow he could not be there—his presence being known only to the housekeeper.

But was there any need for such secrecy ?

Yes.

I found out that fact before the town servant arrived.

Mrs. Quinion's express orders were not to allow the heir to remain at the hall while the family were in town.

Then here was a good reason why the housekeeper

should maintain his presence a secret from a stupid blurting servant maid.

But I have said motive for murder on the part of the housekeeper could scarcely be present.

Then suppose the death was accidental (though certainly no circumstance of the catastrophe justified such a supposition), and suppose Mrs. Quinion the perpetratress, what was the object in exposing the body outside the house ?

Such an action was most unwomanly, especially where an accident had happened.

I confess that at this point of the case (and up to the time when my confederate arrived) I was completely foiled. All the material evidence was in favour of the murder or manslaughter having been committed under the roof of Petleighcote Hall, while the mass of the evidence of probability opposed any such belief.

Up to this time I had in no way identified the death with the "big box," although I identified that box with the clearing up of the mystery. This identification was the result of an ordinary detective law.

The law in question is as follows :—

In all cases which are being followed up by the profession, a lie is a suspicious act, whether it has relation or no relation, apparent or beyond question, with the matter in hand. As a lie it must be followed to its source, its meaning cleared up, and its value or want of value decided upon. The probability stands good always that a lie is part of a plot.

So as Mrs. Quinion had in all probability lied in reference to the removal of the box, it became necessary to find out all about it, and hence my first directions to Martha—as she was always called (she is now in Australia and doing well) at our office, and I doubt if her surname was known to any of us—hence my first instruction to Martha was to look about for a big box.

" What kind of box ?"

" That I don't know," said I.

" Well there will be plenty of boxes in a big house —is it a new box ?"

" I can't tell ; but keep an eye upon boxes, and tell me if you find one that is more like a new one than the rest."

Martha nodded.

But by the date of our first interview after her induction at Petleighcote, and when Quinion sent her down upon a message to a tradesman, I had learnt from the polished Mr. White that boxes such as drapers' travellers travelled with were invariably painted black.

This information I gave her. Martha had not any for me in return—that is of any importance. I heard, what I had already inferred, that Quinion was a very calm, self-possessed woman, " whom it would take," said Martha, " one or two good collisions to drive off the rails."

" You mark my words," said Matty, " she'd face a judge as cool as she faces herself in a looking-glass, and that I can tell you she does face cool, for I've seen her do it twice."

Martha's opinion was, that the housekeeper was all right, and I am bound to say that I was unable to suppose that she was all wrong, for the suspicion against her was of the faintest character.

She visited me the day after Martha's arrival, thanked me coolly enough for what I had done, said she believed the young person would do, and respectfully asked me up to the hall.

Three days passed, and in that time I had heard nothing of value from my aide-de-camp, who used to put her written reports twice a day in a hollow tree upon which we had decided.

It was on the fourth day that I got a fresh clue to feel my way by.

Mrs. Lamb, the publican's wife, who had shown such a tender interest in my welfare on the night when I had inquired as to the appearance of the two persons who baited the van-horses at their stables on the night of the death—Mrs. Lamb in reluctantly letting me leave her (she was a most sentimental woman, who I much fear increased her tendencies by a too ready patronage of her own liquors) intreated me to return, "like a poor dear as I was"—for I had said I should remain at Tram—"and come and take a nice cup of tea" with her.

In all probability I never should have taken that nice cup of tea, had I not learnt from my Mrs. Green that young Petleigh had been in the habit of smoking and drinking at Lamb's house.

That information decided me.

I "dropped in" at Mrs. Lamb's that same afternoon, and I am bound to say it was a nice cup of tea.

During that refreshment I brought the conversation round to young Petleigh, and thus I heard much of him told to his credit from a publican's point of view, but which did not say much for him from a social standing-place.

" And this, my poor dear, is the very book he would sit in this very parlour and read from for an hour together, and—coming !"

For here there was a tap-tap on the metal counter with a couple of halfpence.

Not thinking much of the book, for it was a volume of a very ordinary publication, which has been in vogue for many years amongst cheap literature devotees, I let it fall open, rather than opened it, and I have no doubt that I did not once cast my eyes upon the page during the spirting of the beer-engine and the return of Mrs. Lamb.

"Bless me !" said she, in a moved voice, for she was one of the most sentimental persons ever I encountered. " Now that's very odd !—poor dear."

" What's odd, Mrs. Lamb ?" I asked.

" Why if you haven't got the book open at his fav'rite tale !"

" Whose, Mrs. Lamb ?"

" Why that poor dear young Graham Petleigh."

I need not say I became interested directly.

" Oh ! did he read this tale ?"

" Often ; and very odd it is, my own dear, as you

should be about to read it too ; though true it is that that there book do always open at that same place, which I take to be his reading it so often the place is worn and—coming !"

Here Mrs. Lamb shot away once more, while I, it need not be said, looked upon the pages before me.

And if I say that, before Mrs. Lamb had done smacking at the beer-engine, and ending her long gossip with the customer, I had got the case by the throat —I suppose I should astonish most of my readers.

And yet there is nothing extraordinary in the matter.

Examine most of the great detected cases on record, and you will find a little accident has generally been the clue to success.

So with great discoveries. One of the greatest improvements in the grinding of flour, and by which the patentee has made many thousands of pounds, was discovered by seeing a miller blow some flour out of a nook ; and all the world knows that the cause which led the great Newton to discover the great laws of the universe was the fall of an apple.

So it frequently happens in these days of numberless newspapers that a chance view of a man will identify him with the description of a murderer.

Chance !

In the history of crime and its detection chance plays the chief character.

Why, as I am writing a newspaper is near me, in which there is the report of a trial for attempt to murder, where the woman who was shot at was only saved by the intervention of a piece of a ploughshare, which was under her shawl, and which she had *stolen* only a few minutes before the bullet struck the iron !

Why, compared with that instance of chance, what was mine when; by reading a tale which had been pointed out to me as one frequently read by the dead young man, I discovered the mystery which was puzzling me?

The tale told of how, in the north of England, a pedlar had left a pack at a house, and how a boy saw the top of it rise up and down ; how they supposed a man must be *in* it who intended to rob the house; and how the boy shot at the pack, and killed a man.

I say, before Mrs. Lamb returned to her "poor dear" I had the mystery by heart.

The young man had been attracted by the tale, remembered it, and put it in form for some purpose· What?

In a moment I recalled the mania of the squire for plate, and, remembering how niggardly he was to the boy, it flashed upon me that the youth had in all probability formed a plan for robbing his father of a portion of his plate.

It stood true that it was understood the plate went up to town with the family.   But was this so ?

Now see how well the probabilities of the case would tell in with such a theory.

The youth was venturesome and daring, as his poaching affrays proved.

He was kept poor.

He knew his father to possess plate.

He was not allowed to be at Petleighcote when the father was away.

He had read a tale which coincided with my theory.

A large box had been left by strangers at the hall.

The young squire's body had been found under such circumstances, that the most probable way of accounting for its presence where it was found was by supposing that it had been removed there from the hall itself.

Such a plot explained the presence of the mask.

Finally, there was the key, a key opening, beyond all question, an important receptacle—a supposition very clear, seeing the character of the key.

Indeed, by this key might be traced the belief of treasure in the house.

Could this treasure really exist?

Before Mrs. Lamb had said "Good night, dear," to a female customer who had come for a pint of small beer and a gallon of more strongly brewed scandal, I had come to the conclusion that plate might be in the house.

For miserly men are notoriously suspicious and greedy. What if there were some of the family plate which was not required at the town house then at Petleighcote, and which the squire, relying for its security upon the habitual report of his taking all his plate to town, had not lodged at the county bank, because of that natural suspiciousness which might lead him to believe more in his own strong room than a banker's?

Accept this supposition, and the youth's motive was evident.

Accept young Petleigh's presence in the house under these circumstances, and then we have to account for the death.

Here, of course, I was still at fault.

If Mrs. Quinion and the girl only were in the house, and the girl was innocent, then the housekeeper alone was guilty.

Guilty—what of? Murder or manslaughter?

Had the tale young Petleigh used to read been carried out to the end?

Had he been killed without any knowledge of who he was?

That I should have discovered the real state of the case without Mrs. Lamb's aid I have little doubt, for even that very evening, after leaving Mrs. Lamb, and promising to bear in mind the entreaty to "come again, you *dear* dear," my confederate brought me a piece of information which must have put me on the track.

It appeared that morning Mrs. Quinion had received a letter which much discomposed her. She went out directly after breakfast, came down to the village, and returned in about an hour. My confederate had picked the pocket (for, alas! we police officers have sometimes to turn thieves—for the good of society of course) of the housekeeper while she slept that afternoon, and while the new maid was supposed to be putting Mrs. Quinion's stockings in wearable order. and she had made a mental copy of that communica-

tion. It was from a Joseph Spencer, and ran as follows :—

"My dear Margaret,—For God's sake look all
over the place for key 13. There's such a lot of 'em
I never missed it; and if the governor finds it out
I'm as good as ruined. It must be somewhere about.
I can't tell how it ever come orf the ring. So no
more at present. It's post time. With dear love,
from your own

"Joseph Spencer."

Key 13!

Why, it was the same number as that on the key
found on the dead man.

A letter was despatched that night to town, direct-
ing the police to find out who Joseph Spencer was,
and giving the address heading the letter—a printed
one.

Mrs. Green then came into operation.

No, she could not tell who lived at the address I
mentioned. Thank the blessed stars *she* knowed
nought o' Lunnon. What! Where had Mrs. Quinion
been that morning? Why, to Joe Higgins's. What
for? Why, to look at the young squire's clothes and
things. What did she want with them? Why, she
"actially" wanted to take 'em "arl oop" to the Hall.
No, Joe Higgins wouldn't.

Of course I now surmised that Joseph Spencer was
the butler.

And my information from town showed I was
right.

Now, certain as to my preliminaries, I knew that my work lay within the walls of the Hall.

But how was I to reach that place?

Alas! the tricks of detective police officers are infinite. I am afraid many a kindly-disposed advertisement hides the hoof of detection. At all events I know mine did.

It appeared in the second column of the *Times*, and here is an exact copy of it. By the way, I had received the *Times* daily, as do most detectives, during the time I had been in Tram :—

"Wanted, to hear of Margaret Quinion, or her heirs-at-law. She was known to have left the South of England (that she was a Southener I had learnt by her accent) about the year 1830 to become house-keeper to a married foster-sister, who settled in a midland county (this information, and especially the date, Mrs. Green had to answer for). Address, ——" Here followed that of my own solicitors, who had their instructions to keep the lady hanging about the office several days, and until they heard from me.

I am very much afraid I intended that should the case appear as black against her as I feared it would, she was to be arrested at the offices of the gentlemen to whom she was to apply in order to hear of something to her advantage. And furthermore, I am quite sure that many an unfortunate has been arrested who has been enticed to an office under the promise of something to his or her special benefit.

For of such misrepresentations is this deplorable world.

When this advertisement came out, the least acute reader is already aware of the use I made of it.

I pointed out the news to Mrs. Green, and I have no doubt she digited the intelligence to every soul she met, or rather overtook, in the course of the day. And indeed before evening (when I was honoured with a visit from Mrs. Quinion herself), it was stated with absolute assurance that Mrs. Quinion had come in for a good twenty-two thousand pounds, and a house in Dyot Street, Bloomsbury Square, Lunnun.

It was odd, and yet natural, that Mrs. Quinion should seek me out. I was the only stranger with whom she was possibly acquainted in the district, and my strangeness to the neighbourhood she had already, from her point of view, turned to account. Therefore (human nature considered) I did not wonder that she tried to turn me to account again. My space is getting contracted, but as the following is the last conversation I had with Mrs. Quinion, I may perhaps be pardoned for here quoting it. Of course I abridge it very considerably. After the usual salutations, and an assurance that Martha suited very fairly, she said,—

" I have a favour to ask you."

" Indeed ; pray what is it ?"

" I have received some news which necessarily takes me from home."

" I think," said I, smiling, " I know what that news is," and I related how I had myself seen the advertisement in the morning.

I am afraid I adopted this course the more readily to attract her confidence.

I succeeded.

"Indeed," said she, "then since you have identified yourself with that news, I can the more readily ask you the favour I am about to——"

"And what is that?"

"I am desirous of going up to town—to London —for a few hours, to see what this affair of the advertisement means, but I hesitate to leave Martha alone in the house. You have started, and perhaps you feel offended that I should ask a stranger such a favour, but the fact is, I do not care to let anyone belonging to the neighbourhood know that I have left the Hall—it will be for only twenty-four hours. The news might reach Mr. Petleigh's ears, and I desire that he should hear nothing about it. You see the position in which I am placed. If, my dear lady, you can oblige me I shall be most grateful; and, as you are staying here, it seemed—to—me——"

Here she trailed off into silence.

The cunning creature! How well she hid her real motive—the desire to keep those who knew of the catastrophe out of the Hall, because she feared their curiosity.

Started! Yes, indeed I had started. At best I had expected that I should have to divulge who I was to the person whom she would leave in the place did the advertisement take, and here by the act of what she thought was her forethought, she was actually placing herself at my mercy, while I still remained screened in all my actions referring to her. For I need not say that had I had to declare who I was, and had

I failed, all further slow-trapping in this affair would have been at an end—the "game" would have taken the alarm, and there would have been an end to the business.

To curtail here needless particulars, that same evening at nine I was installed in the housekeeper's parlour, and she had set out for the first station past Tram, to which she was going to walk across the fields in order to avoid all suspicion.

She had not got a hundred yards away from the house, before I had turned up my cuffs, and I and Martha, (a couple of detectives,) were hard at work, trying to find that box.

Her keys we soon found, in a work-basket, and lightly covered with a handkerchief.

Now, this mode of hiding should have given me a clue.

But it did not.

For three hours—from nine till midnight, we hunted for that box, and unsuccessfully.

In every room that, from the absence of certain dusty evidences, we knew must have been recently opened—in every passage, cellar, corridor, and hall we hunted.

No box.

I am afraid that we even looked in places where it could not have gone—such as under beds.

But we found it at last, and then the turret-clock had gone twelve about a quarter of an hour.

It was in her bedroom ; and what is more, it formed her dressing-table.

And I have no doubt I should have missed it had it not been that she had been imperfect in her concealment.

Apparently she comprehended the value of what I may call " audacity hiding"—that is, such concealment that an ordinary person searching would never dream of looking for the object where it was to be found.

For instance, the safest hiding-place in a drawing-r⸺ ı for a bank note, would be the bottom of a loosely-filled card-basket. Nobody would dream of looking for it in such a place.

The great enigma-novelist, Edgar Poe, illustrates this style of concealment where he makes the holder of a letter place it in a card-rack over the mantelpiece, when he knows his house will be ransacked, and every inch of it gone over to find the document.

Mrs. Quinion was evidently acquainted with this mode of concealment.

Indeed, I believe I should not have found the box had it not been that she had overdone her unconcealed-concealment. For she had used a bright pink slip with a white flounce over it to complete the appearance of a dressing-table, having set the box up on one side.

And therefore the table attracted my notice each time I passed and saw it. As it was Martha, in passing between me and the box, swept the drapery away with her petticoats, and showed a *black corner.*

The next moment the box was discovered.

I have no doubt that being a strong-minded woman she could not endure to have the box out of her sight while waiting for an opportunity to get rid of it.

It was now evident that my explanation of the case, to the effect that young Petleigh had been imitating the action of the tale, was correct.

The box was quite large enough to contain a man lying with his legs somewhat up ; there was room to turn in the box ; and, finally, there were about two dozen holes round the box, about the size of a crown piece, and which were hidden by the coarse black canvas with which the box was covered.

Furthermore, the box was closeable from within by means of a bolt, and therefore openable from within by the same means.

Furthermore, if any further evidence were wanting, there was a pillow at the bottom of the box (obviously for the head to rest on), and from a hole the feathers had escaped over the bottom of the box, which was lined with black and white striped linen bed-tick, this material being cut away from the holes.

I was now at no loss to comprehend the fluff upon the unhappy young man's coat.

And, finally, there was the most damnifying evidence of all.

For in the black canvas over one of the holes *there was a jagged cut.*

" Lie down, Martha," said I, " in the box, with your head at this end."

" Why, whatever——"

"Tut—tut,—girl ; do as I tell you."

She did ; and using the stick of a parasol which lay on the dressing-table, I found that by passing it through the hole its end reached the officer in exactly the region by a wound in which young Mr. Petleigh had been killed.

Of course the case was now clear.

After the young woman, Dinah, had gone to bed, the housekeeper must have had her doubts about the chest, and have inspected it.

Beyond all question, the young man knew the hour at which the housekeeper retired, and was waiting perhaps for eleven o'clock to strike by the old turret clock before he ventured out—to commit what?

It appeared to me clear, bearing in mind the butler's letter, to rob the plate-chest No. 13, which I inferred had been left behind, a fact of which the young fellow might naturally be aware.

The plan doubtless was to secure the plate without any alarm, to let himself out of the Hall by some mode long-since well-known to him, and then to meet his confederates, and share with them the plunder, leaving the chest to tell the tale of the robbery, and to exculpate the housekeeper.

It struck me as a well-executed scheme, and one far beyond the ordinary run of robbery plots.

What had caused that scheme to fail?

I could readily comprehend that a strong-minded woman like Quinion would rely rather upon her own than any other assistance.

I could comprehend her discovery; perhaps a low-muttered blasphemy on the part of the young man; or maybe she may have heard his breathing.

Then, following out her action, I could readily suppose that once aware of the danger near her she would prepare to meet it.

I could follow her, silent and self-possessed, in the hall, asking herself what she should do.

I could mark her coming to the conclusion that there must be holes in the box through which the evildoer could breathe, and I apprehended readily enough that she had little need to persuade herself that she had a right to kill one who might be there to kill her.

Then in my mind's eye I could follow her seeking the weapon, and feeling all about the box for a hole.

She finds it.

She fixes the point for a thrust.

A movement—and the manslaughter is committed.

That the unhappy wretch had time to open the box is certain, and doubtless it was at that moment the fierce woman, still clutching the shaft of the arrow, or barb—call it what you will—leant back, and so withdrew the shaft from the rankling iron.

Did the youth recognise her? Had he tried to do so?

From the peacefulness of the face, as described at the inquest, I imagined that he had, after naturally unbolting the lid, fallen back, and in a few moments died.

Then must have followed her awful discovery, succeeded by her equally awful determination to hide the fault of her master's, and perhaps of her own sister's son.

And so it came to pass that she dragged the youth's dead body out into the cold morning atmosphere, as the bleak dawn was filling the air, and the birds were fretfully awaking.

No doubt, had a sharp detective been at once employed, she would not have escaped detection.

As it was she had so far avoided discovery.

And I could easily comprehend that a powerfully-brained woman like herself would feel no compunction and little grief for what she had done—no compunction, because the act was an accident; little grief, because she must have felt she had saved the youth from a life of misery—for a son who at twenty robs a father, however bad, is rarely at forty, if he lives so long, an honest man.

But though I had made this discovery I could do nothing so far against the housekeeper, whom of course it was my duty to arrest, if I could convince myself she had committed manslaughter. I was not to be ruled by any feeling of screening the family—the motive indirectly which had actuated Quinion, for, strong-minded as she was, it appeared to me that she would not have hesitated to admit the commission of the act which she had completed had the burglar, as I may call the young man, been an ordinary felon, and unknown to her.

No, the box had no identification with the death, because it exhibited no unanswerable signs of its connexion with that catastrophe.

So far, how was it identifiable (beyond my own

circumstantial evidence, known only to myself,) with the murder ?

The only particle of evidence was that given by the girl, who could or could not swear to the box having been brought on the previous day, and to the house-keeper saying that it had been taken away again—a suspicious circumstance certainly, but one which, without corroborative evidence, was of little or indeed no value.

As to the jagged cut in the air-hole, in the absence of all blood-stain it was not mentionable.

Corroborative evidence I must have, and that cor-roborative evidence would best take the shape of the discovery of the shaft of the weapon which had caused death, or a weapon of similar character.

This, the box being found, was now my work.

" Is there any armoury in the house, Martha ?"

" No ; but there's lots of arms in the library."

We had not searched in the library for the box, because I had taken Martha's assurance that no boxes were there.

When we reached the place, I remarked imme-diately—" What a damp place."

As I said so I observed that there were windows on each side of the room, and that the end of the chamber was circular.

" Well it may be," said Martha, "for there's water all round it—a kind of fountain-pond, with gold fish in it. The library," continued Martha, who was more sharp than educated, " butts out of the house.'

Between each couple of book-cases there was fixed a handsome stand of arms, very picturesque and taking to the eyes.

There were modern arms, antique armour, and foreign arms of many kinds ; but I saw no arrows, though in the eagerness of my search I had the chandelier, which still held some old yellow wax-candles, lighted up.

No arrow.

But my guardian angel, if there be such good creatures, held tight on to my shoulder that night, and by a strange chance, yet not a tithe so wonderful as that accident by which the woman was saved from a bullet by a piece of just stolen iron, the origin of the weapon used by Quinion came to light.

We had been searching amongst the stands of arms for some minutes, when I had occasion suddenly to cry—

"Hu-u-sh ! what are you about ?"

For my confederate had knocked off its hook a large drum, which I had noticed very coquettishly finished off a group of flags, and cymbals, and pikes.

"I'm very sorry," she said, as I ran to pick up the still reverberating drum with that caution which, even when useless, generally stands by the detective, when——

There, sticking through the drum, and hooked by its barbs, was the point of such a weapon—the exact counterpart—as had been used to kill young Petleigh.

Had a ghost, were there such a thing, appeared I had not been more astounded.

The drum was ripped open in a moment, and there

came to light an iron arrow with a wooden shaft about eighteen inches long, this shaft being gaily covered with bits of tinsel and coloured paper.

[I may here at once state, what I ultimately found out—for in spite of our danger I kept hold of my prize and brought it out of battle with me—that this barb was one of such as are used by picadors in Spanish bull-fights for exciting the bull. The barbs cause the darts to stick in the flesh and skin. The cause of the decoration of the haft can now readily be comprehended. Beyond all doubt the arrow used by Quinion and the one found by me were a couple placed as curiosities amongst the other arms. The remaining one the determined housekeeper had used as suiting best her purpose, the other (which I found) had doubtless at some past time been used by an amateur picador, perhaps the poor dead youth himself, with the drum for an imaginary bull, and within it the dart had remained till it was to reappear as a witness against the guilty and yet guiltless housekeeper.

I had barely grasped my prize when Martha said— "What a smell of burning!"

"Good God!" I cried, "we have set the house on fire!"

The house was on fire, but we were not to blame.

We ran to the door.

We were locked in!

What brought her back I never learnt, for I never saw or heard of her again. I guess that the motion of the train quickened her thought (it does mine), that she suspected—that she got out at the station some distance from Tram, and that she took a post-chaise back to Petleighcote.

All this, however, is conjecture.

But if not she, who locked us in? We could not have done it ourselves.

We were locked in, and I attribute the act to her—though how she entered the house I never learnt.

The house was on fire, and we were surrounded by water.

This tale is the story of the "Unknown Weapon," and therefore I cannot logically here go into any full explanation of our escape. Suffice it to our honour as detectives to say, that we did not lose our presence of mind, and that by the aid of the library tables, chairs, big books, &c., we made a point of support on one side the narrow pond for the library ladder to rest on, while the other end reached shallow water.

Having made known the history of the "Unknown Weapon," my tale is done; but my reader might fancy my work incomplete did I not add a few more words.

I have no doubt that Quinion returning, her quick mind in but a few moments came to the conclusion that the only way to save her master's honour was the burning of the box by the incendiarism of the Hall.

The Petleighs were an old family, I learnt, with almost Spanish notions of family honour.

Effectually did she complete her work.

I acknowledge she conquered me. She might have burnt the same person to a cinder into the bargain;

and, upon my word, I think she would have grieved little had she achieved that purpose.

For my part in the matter — I carried it no further.

At the inquiry, I appeared as the lady who had taken care of the house while Mrs. Quinion went to look after her good fortune ; and I have no doubt her disappearance was unendingly connected with my advertisement in the *Times*.

I need not say that had I found Quinion I would have done my best to make her tremble.

I have only one more fact to relate—and it is an important one. It is this—

The squire had the ruins carefully examined, and two thousand ounces of gold and silver plate, melted into shapelessness of course, were taken out of the rubbish.

From this fact it is pretty evident that the key No. 13, found upon the poor, unhappy, ill-bred, and neglected boy, was the " Open Sesamè" to the treasure which was afterwards taken from the ruins—perhaps worth £4000, gold and silver together.

Beyond question he had stolen the key from the butler, gone into a plot with his confederates—and the whole had resulted in his death and the conflagration of Petleighcote, one of the oldest, most picturesque, and it must be admitted dampest seats in the midland counties.

And, indeed, I may add that I found out who was the " tall gentleman with the auburn whiskers and the twitching of the face ;" I discovered who was the short gentleman with no whiskers at all; and finally I have seen the young lady (she was very beautiful) called Frederica, and for whose innocent sake I have no doubt the unhappy young man acted as he did.

As for me, I carried the case no further.

I had no desire to do so—had I had, I doubt if I possessed any further evidence than would have sufficed to bring me into ridicule.

I left the case where it stood.

# THE MYSTERY.

[It often happens that the police are egregiously foiled, but in all my experience such a compact case as the following never came under my observation. The incident being grotesque, I have put it into a grotesque, perhaps even an extravagant, form. It will be readily seen that it was a case in which the police could easily be thrown completely out—as they were. The sergeant employed to clear up the mystery was, and is, a clever, shrewd' man. He has admitted, in his most friendly moments, that no case so thoroughly mystified him as this, which I now proceed to tell, in the admissible shape of a tale.]

"Nelly," said Old Bang (he was a very perverse, red-headed old gentleman, whose belief in the same personage was quite as perfect as the chorus at Covent Garden), "Nelly, I've got a present for you."

"Have you?" said Nelly. "What?" She was one of those bright, clear-headed girls, who, somehow, you feel would never come down to breakfast in curl-papers and the sulks. You felt that as your wife she never would assail you the moment you entered the house with the complaint that she had seen in a looking-glass, Mary Jane insolently squinting at her behind her back, or, that she had distinctly remarked the baker blow the cook a kiss down the area steps. One of those women, in fact, who take the hands which are working for them, smile in the husband's face, and even sometimes go before, and still with a cheerful face drag the helpmate after them.

"Nelly," said Old Bang, "I've got a present for you."

"Have you?" said Nelly. "What?"

'A husband."

Mademoiselle Nelly flung herself at the personage who, upon her advent into this blessed world, had immediately grown an inch in the opinion of his friends, and several cubits in his own estimation, and said, "Oh, papa, has Jack spoken?"

"Jack? his name's Hezekiah."

"Hezekiah What?" asked Nelly.

"No," returned matter-of-fact Bang; "Hezekiah Trunk."

If she had been a proper young lady, she would have fainted. As it happened she was only thunderstruck.

"He hasn't a hair on his head, papa!"

"But he's got 7000*l.* in the three per cent. Consols, and——"

"But what are they to do with me?"

"And," said Old Bang, his voice rising, "seventeen preference shares in the Great Northern."

"But I've got no preference for him."

"That's nothing to do with it," remarked Old Bang. "He's got 7000*l.* in the three per cent. Consols, and seventeen——"

"Fiddlesticks, papa. I wont hear anything about it—*him* I mean."

" Do you know who I am ?" asked Old Bang.

" Yes, I do know you; you're my father, papa."

" Do you want to be shut up, Nelly ?"

" No, papa, I don't."

" I'm your father."

" And I'm eighteen. I'm a patient girl; but I can't stand Mr. Hezekiah Trunk."

" Seven thousand pounds in the three per cent. Consols," repeated Old Bang; " and seventeen——"

" Preference shares in the Great Northern. I think I know it," said Nelly. " I shall tell Jack——"

" Jack Who ?" said Old Bang, ready to explode.

" No : Jack Wilson. I shall tell Jack all about it, and then I pity Mr. Trunk and his preference shares too."

" You wont accept my present ?"

" No."

" Then I'll lock you up."

" Then I'll make you a present instead, papa."

" What do you mean ?"

" Papa, I refuse to state."

" Then come along," said Old Bang; and he jerked her upstairs till they reached the young lady's own room, the little second floor front, and there he locked her in.

" Don't forget my supper, papa."

" Will you have my present ?"

" No."

" Then there you stop."

" Very well, then you shall have mine."

Perhaps it will hardly be believed that *Mrs.* Bang

had assisted at this interview; but she had, up in a corner, and smacking to her hands like the claws of a cray-fish, or rather, perhaps, like damp and very lively flounders. She had said nothing, if we except the mild statement, "Bang's Bang, and mussy deliver us." Not that Mrs. B. desired to see her good man carried upwards prematurely. But we all have our little ways, and such was Mrs. B.'s, poor dear.

Mr. B. did not forget Nelly's supper. As a father, he could not give way; but there was mercy in the mass of pudding he sent her up.

"Jenny," said Nelly to the official, "would you like your wages raised?"

Up went the young person's eyebrows.

"Because, if so, you *shall*—in *my* house."

The young person's eyebrows couldn't go higher, or they would have done it.

"Take this letter to its address at once, and wait for an answer."

The eyebrows *did* go higher. "Lor, miss, its 'arf past nine o'clock, an' I should lose me krakter an' me place if I stepped houtside the door."

"Have the toothache, and say you are going to get it out."

"O lor, no, miss."

But every young person has her price—to do good. She was not moved by the presentation of Nelly's little turquoise ring, nor the offer of that cameo brooch, but she could *not* resist the magenta ribbon. Jenny at once had an attack of that ache said to be imaginary by all people unknown to dentists, and satirical.

Down went Jenny to Mrs. B., who, seeing the young person with an apparently swelled face, and certainly a handkerchief round her artful jaw, immediately exclaimed—" Mussy deliver us, go and have it out."

Away the young person went. At half-past ten she returned ; at twenty-five minutes to eleven Miss Nelly had the letter ; at twenty minutes to eleven Miss Nelly began packing up ; at twenty-five to twelve she had corded all her boxes, hidden them under the bed, and was prepared to fly. How could it be managed ? She was locked in her room, and Old Bang had actually dragged a heavy chest against the door. Fly—that was it. She left the wings to Jack's providing. She was quite sure that he knew. The letter said—

" Dear Nell,—Keep a bright look-out at two in the morning. We'll use the license to-morrow at ten. Pack up. There will be no difficulty about the tubs now. Try and forget them. Yours everlastingly,

" JACK WILSON."

Perhaps the intelligent reader has remarked how fond small householders are of bolting the doors, and allowing the windows to look after themselves, as though burglars looked on them as walls. Good. Bolt at top of stout door—bolt at bottom of stout door— chain put up, and key double turned. And there, a little way off, is a tiny window, with no shutter, and a feeble little bolt. But the door is fast, and so let's go to bed comfortable. It is true that old Bang's place was not a very small household, but he locked up all the doors, and bolted, and barred, and chained, like a respectable British tenant as he was. Bang slept in the second floor front big, by the side of Nelly in the second floor front little, and it need hardly be said Mrs. Bang slept with him. It is very important, however, that this should be remembered. The last thing B. did before turning in was to knock at the wall that divided him from Nelly and say—" Will you have my present ?"

" No," said Nelly.

" Then there you stop."

" Then, papa, you must have mine."

The first thing B. did in the morning was to thwack at the wall again, and once more ask——well, repetition is tedious. There was no answer. Old Bang hit at the wall, and once more roared like a bull " Will you have ?" &c. &c. No answer.

" Bang's Bang, an' mussy deliver us," said the good lady, smacking her hands as though the flounders had grown both in circumference and liveliness.

" You'd much better get out o' bed, ma'am," said Bang, " and pass a petticoat, and shake that girl up."

Then he rushed to the wall again, " Will you have," &c.

Mrs. Bang got up, passed two petticoats—one about her dear head to save her from the tic-doloureux, to which the poor love was subject. She took the key, and left the room. An anxious minute passed. Good, he heard the key turn—the door opened. The next moment he heard a cry : " Mussy deliver us—oh !" The last word seemed smothered. Bang rushed into the little second-floor front. He saw only a mass of petticoats on the floor. But he could nowhere discover his daughter. In fact, to be very plain, she was gone. Where? How?

Old Bang had locked the door, and kept the key under his pillow. Ha! was she under the bed? Old Bang and Mrs. B. simultaneously whisked up the valance on opposite sides, and stared at each other under those novel circumstances with the air of not having seen each other for a full quarter of a century. Well, she must be somewhere, musn't she? Well, was she between the mattress and the bed? Mr. and Mrs. B. immediately touzled each other in their efforts in this direction. No; there was nothing but a faint smell of feathers between the bed and the mattress. Mrs. B. was gradually growing cold upwards from the toes. Old B. was boiling. Hang it! she *must* be somewhere! Ha! horror! Had she jumped into the area? They rushed madly to the window. They both went to raise it. Ha! it was fast.

And now it is necessary to show how it was fast. There is a little fastening which is acted on by the sash; when the sash is brought down the little fastening is in operation. This is an exceedingly delicate portion of the mystery. Such was the fastening to Nelly's window. It was fast; yet old B. and Mrs. B. opened the lattice, and with eyes of horror peered into the area. No; she was not in the area. Ha! the cupboard. No; she was *not* in the cupboard. Well, drowning men will catch at a straw, so it is not wonderful that an anxious father, as a last resort, should investigate the chimney. If Mrs. B. had been in a laughing humour she must have indulged as she saw her Bang gradually vanish up the orifice, and leave only his shanks to swear by. Suddenly these shanks were convulsed, and B. came down quicker than he had gone up. His face was covered with soot, but it did not hide his consternation. He had come crash up against some iron bars, placed there possibly when it was the burglarious fashion to bribe chimney-sweeping lads to creep down these arrangements and open hall doors.

Suddenly old B. had an idea—had Jenny a duplicate key? Upstairs he tore and summoned Jenny in thunderous style.

"Oh, sir, is it fire?" asked that maiden.

"Have you helped in this business?"

"Oh, sir, help *me*, pray, if it's danger!"

"Where's Miss Nelly?"

"Oh, sir, hadn't you better ask her?"

Downstairs came Bang; not a sign of getting out of the house in a legitimate way. He had taken the street-door key to bed, as usual. He had possessed himself of the area door-key, as usual. Query, had Nelly got out at the front kitchen window, and clambered over the area railings? Query, how could she have first got out of her room? Query, had Jenny unlocked the door? Query, how could she?

All this time Mrs. B. was smacking her hands dolefully, and sitting in her flannel on the floor, ejaculating,—"Oh my pore, pore daughter!"

Query, had Mrs. B. heard anything in the night? No; yes; that is, perhaps; she woke because she

thought she was going to have the tic-doloureux. She
thought she heard a rumbling; then she fell asleep
again; then she woke again because she felt sure she
was going to have the tic-doloureux. It was at this
period she thought she heard some one utter a peculiar
cry. What was it like? Why like "*lullietie.*" Then
she heard a rumbling again, that was all; and then
she fell asleep again.

By this time Jenny was shivering in her clothes,
and the other young person, Mary, was trembling in
her garments, and neither could light the kitchen fire.

Mary had staggers (to which she was subject) directly Jenny was sent for a detective policeman.

Sergeant Gimlet, oh, such a man; but he *was* foiled.

"You see," says the sergeant, "a rope ladder were
not it, for why? It were have been fastened to this
here windy-cell, and no fastening *is*—and, besides, she'd
a come down on the hairy spikes. It were a ladder—
though were it, I'm doubters."

"Try every ladder in the neighbourhood," says old
B., and up to one o'clock, to which time Mrs. B. had
never once left off clapping her hands, or the young
persons trembling (Mary, poor soul, had had seven
staggers) up to one o'clock they had found as many
ladders. This one ladder B. had had brought to the
house, and as after ten minutes' contention with the
area railings, the only result achieved was driving it
clean through the drawing-room window, the experiment was not felicitous, especially as its owner swore
all the time, and wanted to know whether Sergeant
Gimlet thought him "a 'complice o' burglars?" The

ladder would not reach the second floor within six feet, and it was impossible to believe that Nelly could have taken such a step down in life as that. The mystery was marvellous.

"Yer see," said Sergeant Gimlet, it were not a ladder which—why? Builders wont lend ladders o' night-time, 'cos why? it looks burglarious. Again, it took all a quarter o' an hour to bring that ladder yere, and ten minutes to fix it with half-a-dozen fellers, and *then* it went through the windy. Now *do* you think as a party could be with a ladder in the street in the night for a quarter to the place, a quarter at the house without smashing glass, and a quarter back again without being seen by one of the force? No, it warn't a ladder."

"Then, what was it?"

Sergeant Gimlet never had said, "I *don't know*," so he inquired—"Are you quite sure she were there?"

This was too much; indignation was in the very rattle of the five-pound Bank of England note Old B. held out to the officer. Whereon "No," said Gimlet; "no, I never takes no money as I don't yarn. Though fivers is more scarce with me than they mabbey with some folk, I'd blessed be if I wouldn't pay one in instalments to tell how your gal's hooked."

Mrs. B. had not yet done clapping her hands; Jenny still had the creeps; and Mary was recovering her eighth stagger on the kitchen sofa.

It was five o'clock. Tat—tat!

The shock was so great that Mary nearly had her

ninth. Upstairs Jenny tore. A letter—yoop, she had caught her breath—Miss Nelly's handwriting.

"You see, papa, I'm quite safe. When shall I come home with my present? Advertise in the second column of the *Times*. Good-bye; love to all.

" NELLY."

Quite safe—then Old B. was in a rage again. Mrs. B., who was quite sure she had got the tic-douloureux by this time, all owing to staring at the broken drawing-room window, per the experimental ladder, beat her hands in such an agony that she looked quite low.

"No; she should never darken his doors again—never. No; he would never own her again. Yet she must have got away somehow! No; not once more."

But Old Bang was soft-hearted, and very curious. He would have come round sooner or later, but the agony of the mystery made short work of his indignation.

The next day but one, the following appeared in the second column of the *Times :*—" Dear Nelly—return home. All is forgiven. Bring your present."

That afternoon, a cab drove up to the door—in it Nelly and her present—Jack Wilson.

"I've a respect for Old Bang, so I shall not dilate upon how he tried to play Brutus and broke down, and performed the part of a clear-headed father.

"You know, sir," said Jack, "I shall have more than seven thousand pounds in the three per cent. Consols before I am Trunk's age."

"And the seventeen preference shares?" Old B. began.

"In the Great Northern? Well, I've got seven of them already, for Uncle Trunk gave 'em me this morning—oh, yes, Trunk's my maternal uncle—for the clever way in which I won Nelly here."

"And how the devil did you do it, sir?"

"Why," remarked Jack Wilson, a dashing, clearheaded young man, "I just went round the corner, and bribed the FIRE-ESCAPE. Don't tell any one, or you may get the fireman into a row."

"No, I wont," said Old B., in a mild and an annihilated manner; "no; not at all."

But he did; or how should I come to know it?

Wasn't it odd?

THE END.